Leaning back in Sam's arms, Marina stared into his eyes— and what she saw there made her heart skip a beat.

It made no sense, but she wanted him to go on holding her. No, she wanted him to *kiss* her, more than she had ever wanted anything in her life.

She couldn't explain it, even to herself. The man with his arms around her was a stranger. Yet she felt she'd known him all her life—no, longer than that, forever....

Did he want to know the touch of her lips as badly as she wanted to know his?

She was playing with fire, she knew. She was falling in love with a man who wouldn't be born until centuries after her own death. And she could not exist in his world, because the things she wanted most—love, a home, a family—were denied him and his people....

Dear Reader,

Talk about starting the new year off with a bang! Look at the Intimate Moments lineup we have for you this month.

First up is Rachel Lee's newest entry in her top-selling Conard County miniseries, *A Question of Justice*. This tale of two hearts that seem too badly broken ever to mend (but of course are about to heal each other) will stay in your mind—and your heart—long after you've turned the last page.

Follow it up with Beverly Barton's *The Outcast*, a Romantic Traditions title featuring a bad-boy hero— and who doesn't love a hero who's so bad, he's just got to be good? This one comes personally recommended by #1-selling author Linda Howard, so don't miss it! In *Sam's World*, Ann Williams takes us forward into a future where love is unknown—until the heroine makes her appearance. Kathleen Creighton is a multiple winner of the Romance Writers of America's RITA Award. If you've never read her work before, start this month with *Eyewitness* and you'll know right away why she's so highly regarded by her peers—and by readers around the world. Many of you have been reading Maura Seger's Belle Haven Saga in Harlequin Historicals. Now read *The Surrender of Nora* to see what Belle Haven—and the lovers who live there—is like today. Finally there's Leann Harris's *Angel at Risk,* a story about small-town secrets and the lengths to which people will go to protect them. It's a fittingly emotional—and suspenseful—close to a month of nonstop fabulous reading.

Enjoy!

Leslie Wainger
Senior Editor and Editorial Coordinator

Please address questions and book requests to:
Silhouette Reader Service
U.S.: 3010 Walden Ave., P.O. Box 1325, Buffalo, NY 14269
Canadian: P.O. Box 609, Fort Erie, Ont. L2A 5X3

SAM'S WORLD

ANN WILLIAMS

Silhouette®
INTIMATE™ MOMENTS®
Published by Silhouette Books
America's Publisher of Contemporary Romance

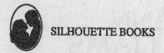 SILHOUETTE BOOKS

ISBN 0-373-07615-0

SAM'S WORLD

Books by Ann Williams

Silhouette Intimate Moments

Devil in Disguise #302
Loving Lies #335
Haunted by the Past #358
What Lindsey Knew #384
Angel on My Shoulder #408
Without Warning #436
Shades of Wyoming #468
Cold, Cold Heart #487
Wild Horses, Wild Men #585
Sam's World #615

ANN WILLIAMS

gave up her career as a nurse, then as the owner and proprietor of a bookstore, in order to pursue her writing full-time. She was born and married in Indiana, and after a number of years in Texas, she now lives in Arizona with her husband and their children.

Reading, writing, crocheting, classical music and a good romantic movie are among her diverse loves. Her dream is to one day move to a cabin in the Carolina mountains with her husband and "write to my heart's content."

For Marina Marie Buckner,
my granddaughter

Prologue

In the year 2393 A.D. life on planet Earth had taken an unprecedented turn. The Earth was once more filled with life and beauty. Animals lived free without fear of extinction, because hunting had been outlawed.

The average life expectancy of a human being was one hundred years. Jobs, food, clothing, shelter and health care were all taken care of by the government without worry to any person. There was no hunger, no pollution and no war. There were no prisons, because there was no crime. Weapons were possessed only by law-enforcement agencies.

Man had finally been freed from worry and the need to make choices concerning everyday life. He lived within the iron bars of the society forged by that desire to be totally *free*.

And so he desperately sought a way to be freed from the shackles of that freedom—*before it spread like a plague throughout history*.

Chapter 1

Sammell placed the small pink vase in the center of the Recep and took his seat at the computer terminal. One last time he checked the equipment for signs of malfunction. Next he checked the electronic jamming device that would ensure against a government probe, seeking high levels of energy within the city sector. Everything looked good.

Turning back to the monitor, he stared at the blank screen and white blinking cursor. Once he keyed in the formula, the transference would begin and nothing could stop it until the process was complete.

His eyes swerved toward the chronometer. In two minutes it would be midnight. Flexing his fingers hovering over the keyboard, he felt a strange cold excitement begin to fill him. It was time. Taking a deep breath, he lowered his hands until the tips of his fingers touched the cold plastic keys and began to move with a will of their own.

Mathematical equations filled the screen and a low humming began to vibrate the air around him. The letters and numbers typed into the computer were being transformed into electrical impulses and sent to MDAT—Molecular

Displacement Activator and Transporter. Quicker than a fleeting thought, details of distance, time and space were being coordinated with energy and mass. And with this information, MDAT was able to adjust the level of power needed for this particular experiment.

Sammell's fingers flew and the screen became a rolling white blur. MDAT's steady hum grew and leveled to a low-pitched roar, filling Sammell's head with the sound of the ocean on a windy day.

His breathing quickened. The ends of his hair felt electrified. The exposed skin of his face and neck, hands and arms tingled as though a million tiny insects invaded each pore. The level of static energy in the room grew to a never-before-equaled proportion.

All at once a low-pitched beeping began as MDAT's lens slowly opened. An instant later, a laser-thin jet of deep blue light shot toward the Recep. Flamelike excitement licked along Sammell's veins. He swung eager eyes toward the grid and saw it begin to glow with a deep violet light.

The beeping escalated until it became a high-pitched whine, bouncing off the walls and echoing inside his head. His heart bumped in unison with it, and a vein began to throb at his temple.

The Recep's glow intensified. Sammell's breath became trapped in his chest as the metal frame began to waver like bands of heat over a hot pavement. There was a sudden flash of blue light. Sammell wrenched his head to one side—and the room was suddenly silent.

Opening his eyes, he turned slowly toward the Recep. It no longer glowed. *And the vase was gone!*

For a moment, he couldn't seem to move. He sat staring at the spot where the vase had rested within the Recep's confines only moments ago, half expecting to blink and find it had reappeared.

His head swiveled toward the monitor. *Transfer complete* flashed across the screen and MDAT's mechanical voice confirmed it.

Success! The word flowed over and through him like an electric current. Releasing a pent-up breath, he allowed his shoulders to sag. The first half of the experiment was complete.

Sitting back in his chair, Sammell turned once more to stare at the empty Recep, trying to envision the vase taking shape high atop a sharp mountain peak, or in some verdant sheltered valley miles from here. And then an uncomfortable thought gnawed at the edges of his mind. What would Lord Bartell, the director of the state lab where he worked, do if he knew what Sammell had just accomplished?

He frowned. There was no question about it. He'd have Sammell arrested. It was only because of his brilliance in the field of physics and related sciences that he was even working on project Deliverance. And even that wouldn't stop the inevitable if anyone learned about the information and equipment he'd been stealing from the government archives and lab over the past year.

In the past week, there had been plenty of indication that someone in the lab was being investigated. There was nothing unusual about having government people snooping into everything, but Sammell had noticed a heavier concentration of gun-toting guards at all the doors in the building. And by listening to conversations not meant for his ears, he knew Bartell was discussing each small bit of progress made with a government adviser.

Though Sammell had no tangible reason to think he was the one under investigation, he'd been especially careful to appear as mindlessly subservient as everyone else. He knew that given the government's paranoid perspective, a complaint lodged against him for any reason could spell disaster, not only for his unauthorized work at home, but on a personal level, as well.

It was a well-known fact that enemies of the state disappeared without a trace. His own parents had disappeared that way when he was a young boy. That's why Sammell didn't want the government to—

MDAT began to hum. The message on the screen now read *Inversion begun.* And again, the metallic voice echoed the words.

The vase was returning.

Sammell had set the chronometer for only a short span of time for this first attempt at matter transfer. All he wanted was to verify that his new formula worked.

In the state lab they'd had a problem with returning objects losing their uniformity. And until that problem was solved, only inanimate material could be transported, bringing the project to a virtual standstill.

Because he'd been working on the idea of matter transfer for most of his adult life, Sammell had a theory about what they were doing wrong. He'd been carefully directing the project scientists working with him away from the area he thought to be in error. Now, in a few moments, he'd know whether he'd been right.

MDAT's hum grew to a low-pitched roar and the warning beep began to sound as the lens started to open, but this time, there was no beam of light. Now the machine acted as a gigantic magnet, attracting the ionized particles into which it had earlier transformed the vase.

Sammell felt the hair stand up on the back of his neck as the warning beep grew louder. His eyes flew to the Recep's luminous frame.

The vase arrived without ceremony, simply materializing as he watched. *Transfer complete,* MDAT verbalized softly once again. With a nod of satisfaction, Sammell rose and started toward the Recep.

The machine at his back faltered. He hesitated, threw a puzzled glance over his shoulder, checked the monitor for signs of a problem and, finding none, swung back toward the Recep.

Though there was no indication of a malfunction, he hesitated. MDAT leveled out and he relaxed and continued across the floor. He was reaching for the vase when it exploded.

Diving to the floor, he held his hands up over his head just as a blast of hot wind roared over him. The sound of breaking glass and tumbling equipment was all around him.

In moments it was over. Sammell raised his head warily and looked toward the Recep. The vase was gone. Not so much as a granule of it remained. It had completely vaporized.

He glanced around the room. Except for some broken glass, no doubt from shattered equipment, the unchanneled flow of energy had done little obvious damage. Getting stiffly to his feet, he stepped around the debris and stopped before the monitor. To his relief the screen was undamaged.

Hurrying to MDAT, he checked the lens. It, too, appeared to have come through the explosion without harm.

Seating himself at the console, Sammell asked the computer for an explanation. All at once the screen flashed *Overload! Overload!* and MDAT's metallic voice quickly echoed the words.

Sammell switched off voice communications and attempted to ask for more pertinent information. But the only response he received was *Overload!*

In growing disgust, he turned away from the computer. Failure. The word was as bitter on his tongue as some of the fruit he occasionally stole from the public gardens. After all the work he'd put into it, all the chances he'd taken by stealing the necessary components to build MDAT and the Recep, this was the result.

Getting wearily to his feet, he threw a regretful glance toward the Recep and—froze.

While he watched, a small creature with reddish brown fur along its back, grayish white fur along its underside and a long tail was taking shape where the vase had stood only moments before. Sammell moved closer. He recognized the creature as a mammal of the *Rodentia* order, family *Scuiridae*. Or what had been commonly known as a squirrel.

Squatting, he observed it for a long moment, moved around behind the Recep and observed it from the opposite side. It didn't appear to be a hologram.

Holding his breath, he reached toward it, still wondering if his fingers might pass right through it. They didn't. He was touching a three-dimensional animal. Pushing his fingers through the soft fur, he felt for a heartbeat. It was alive!

Once again excitement laced through him as he sat back on his heels and continued to visually examine the animal. On closer inspection, it appeared to be without deformity.

Did he dare to hope the experiment wasn't a complete failure, after all?

Taking his place before the computer, he studied the information he'd typed into it earlier. What had gone wrong? Why had the vase disintegrated?

Could it be because of the squirrel—something to do with both of them trying to occupy the same space at the same time? He'd tried to prevent this. He'd studied maps he'd taken from the Government Archives and chosen an unpopulated area on the North American continent called Arizona as the safest destination for the vase. But he hadn't counted on an animal wandering into the Recep's periphery and getting caught in its force field.

Or could the problem stem from their different molecular structures?

He was greatly concerned about the destruction of the vase, but the appearance of the animal intrigued him. If it survived until morning, he'd know if his new theory was correct. If not, then he had to start all over again, and time was growing short. He couldn't continue to sabotage MDAT's twin in the state lab without someone's eventually realizing what he was doing.

Long into the night Sammell tested his equipment, went over his figures and charts and periodically studied the small animal. No matter how many times he recalculated, his equations appeared to be sound. Therefore, he had to conclude that his theory was correct and unplanned forces outside his realm of control had interfered with the experiment, causing the vase's destruction.

As the night drifted into early morning, Sammell's eyelids grew heavy and his brain refused to function on a conscious level. He fell asleep at his workbench.

Sometime later, he was wakened by an unidentifiable sound. Sitting up, he rubbed his eyes with both hands and listened intently.

He'd turned off all but the lights in his work area, and the room outside its limited periphery lay in deep shadow. The sound that had wakened him came again, and Sammell stiffened, momentarily uncertain of its source. And then he realized it was coming from the Recep.

Jumping to his feet, he reached toward the light panel and illuminated the whole room. His little visitor was awake. Pleased at the prospect of being able to evaluate the animal's physical responses now instead of having to wait until the end of the next workday, Sammell took an eager step in the animal's direction, only to come to a dead stop.

He looked closer. Nothing had changed. Stepping carefully, he crossed the floor, halting a short distance from the chattering squirrel—and the reclining form of the animal's new companion.

This was a creature Sammell had never seen, and chills of an unknown origin slipped up and down his spine. The squirrel was one thing, but this . . .

Sammell's eyes were drawn to the creature's head. There was so much hair. It curled around its face and down across its shoulders, pooling on the floor in a fiery tangle.

Fascinated despite himself, Sammell knelt, studying the springy hair. It looked coarse.

One hand inched toward a curl lying near the toe of his boot. Taking it between finger and thumb, he rubbed it gently. To his surprise it had a soft resilience. It wasn't only the hair itself that fascinated him. Until now, he'd never seen hair that looked as though firelight danced along its strands.

His glance moved from the curl to the creature's face, but the hair obscured most of it from view. Using two fingers, he smoothed it back. Now he could see the faint spots of light brown color across the creature's nose, forehead and cheeks. He compared his own pale skin to that of his visitor's. Very curious.

He studied the wide-set eyes and thick curling lashes, a shade darker than the hair, lying against the rosy cheeks. Like the hair, the skin drew his touch. He wanted to see if it felt as smooth as it looked. Laying a tentative finger against one cheek, he trailed it slowly to the full red lips.

Sammell was well attuned to the aesthetic quality of his own environment—the government reminded them daily of how they were wholly responsible for it. But he'd never seen anything as breathtaking as the creature, genus Homo sapiens: female of the species, lying at his feet.

The woman stirred, stretching the garment covering her upper body tight across her chest. Sammell drew back, holding his breath, his eyes snared by the gentle swell of flesh visible at its open neck. With a soft sigh, the woman settled back into unconsciousness, and Sammell breathed again.

He knew about breasts. A thorough study of the human anatomy was part of every child's school curriculum. But he'd never seen any this size. He felt a sudden overwhelming desire to touch one.

With one finger, he gently probed the nearest mound, jerking back with a quickly smothered cry of alarm when she moved in protest. His heart raced and he felt a curious, tingling shock. He'd never felt anything so soft yet resilient. He was about to investigate the hard little bump he'd noticed, when the squirrel's sudden chatter drew his attention.

Unattended by Sammell, the animal had moved closer to the woman. It stood on its hind legs, studying him curiously. There was something almost protective about the smaller creature's attitude, and Sammell drew away from the woman.

Scooting back a few feet in a move to reassure the animal, Sammell resumed his study of the woman. Abandoning the allure of her upper body, he surveyed her narrow waist, flaring hips and rounded thighs. She was wearing short pants that stopped just below the curve of her hips.

With a sudden sense of confusion, he realized that he was seeing more of this woman than he'd ever seen of anyone—including himself—in all his twenty-nine years. Sammell continued his visual examination, noting the thin straps of material between her toes and across the top of her feet and fastened to a flat sole.

Her ankles were thin and shapely and—he leaned closer—her toenails were a deep bronze color. His glance swept up her frame to her hands, over the delicate wrists and long fingers to her fingernails. They matched her toenails. Did they grow that way?

His nostrils flared in bewilderment. He noted a light delicate scent in the air and sniffed the air curiously. He leaned toward the woman. The scent emanated from her body—and the longer he smelled it, the stranger he felt.

Surging to his feet a little unsteadily, he backed away, keeping his glance on her. What was he going to do about this unexpected turn of events?

Backing against the chair near the computer, he sat down abruptly, his mind overrun with strange impressions. If she created this much pandemonium in him while unconscious, what was likely to happen when she awakened?

And how was he to deal with her presence in his lab? He had no way of knowing what she required to exist in his world.

Sammell turned to the monitor. As though nothing extraordinary had occurred, the white cursor blinked steadily at him. What was he to do?

Life for the most part was simple as long as you obeyed the rules. If you obeyed them, you could live a hundred years in good health and reasonable comfort.

If you disobeyed—which he'd learned to do at an early age—you were likely to be arrested and never heard from again. *Unless you were very resourceful.* And he'd been very resourceful all his life. Especially since working in the lab at Government House. He'd had to be in order to remove documents from the archives and steal parts to advance MDAT beyond the limits of its twin at work.

Sammell didn't kid himself that he'd been particularly clever in what he'd done. It had been relatively easy to find a way into the locked rooms where all knowledge of the past was stored, because the armed guards never really expected anyone to try to get inside. And it had been no problem to hide folded plans and a book or two among similar items when he left work. Bartell was concerned about who and what came into the lab but showed very little concern about what went out of it.

Sammell studied the Recep and its contents. The squirrel would be no trouble. He knew about squirrels, because there were plenty of squirrels in the public gardens.

His gaze edged toward the woman. But there was nothing like *her* in his world. Hiding her was going to be a bit tricky.

Marina stirred, stretched, yawned and sat up. She hadn't meant to fall asleep. No, wait a minute, she hadn't fallen asleep....

"What in the world...?" she murmured aloud, looking around the room in confusion.

Where was she? Frowning, she tried to identify the place, but it was completely foreign to her. How had she gotten here? The last thing she remembered was the park.

She'd been in the park, the one she visited daily on her way home from work. Putting a hand to her head, she tried to think. What had she been doing in the park? Had she been alone?

The last thing she remembered—the *only* thing she could remember at the moment—was a kaleidoscope of color racing toward her as though down a long dark tunnel.

So how did she get here? Marina balanced herself with her hands against the floor and twisted to peer around the room.

It looked...*sterile* was the only word she could come up with. Like a lab—no, a hospital.

That's it, she thought in sudden relief, this must be the emergency room at County General. She had probably passed out and that couple had heard her and called an ambulance.

Her glance rested on the squirrel. Why would a squirrel be sitting on the floor of the emergency room watching her? Shouldn't it have gone to a veterinary hospital?

Her eyes slid to the floor. Why was she on the floor? It was too much of a stretch of the imagination for her to believe that a hospital would have placed a patient on the floor—even if the hospital was overflowing with patients—without the benefit of a mattress and blankets.

All at once she became aware of a splitting headache. Had she fallen and struck her head? Is that why she was here and why nothing seemed to make sense?

Concentrating, she finally got a picture of herself sitting down beneath her favorite tree in the park—that's it—now she remembered.

She'd sat down beneath her favorite tree and opened the sack of peanuts she always brought the gray squirrel she'd made friends with on her first visit to the park. All of a sudden she'd heard him chattering excitely and looked up to see him acting very strangely.

At first she'd thought he was ill. But the longer she'd watched his antics, the more she came to realize that he was struggling against something—something that allowed him to move so far in her direction and no farther.

Without really giving it much thought, she'd put the sack of nuts on the ground and stood up. She was going to find out what was wrong with her little friend and help him.

Moving across the springy grass, arms swinging at her sides, she'd felt the warmth of the sun on the top of her head and given a passing thought to the hat she'd left lying on the ground beside the nuts. The sun's rays brought out the freckles on her creamy skin and she already had her fair share of them.

With her next step, she'd felt as though she'd walked into an invisible curtain. It flowed back and around her just enough to let her pass through. But in sudden apprehension, she'd hesitated on its threshold and tried to withdraw. It wouldn't let her.

Eyes going wide, she'd wrenched at her arms and feet, trying desperately to disengage herself. She was stuck fast. Panic seized her in its powerful grip. She couldn't get loose! Nothing visible was holding her, yet she couldn't move.

Except for her head. She could move her head. She stared around her, seeing only grass and trees and the snow-capped peaks of the San Francisco mountains in the distance.

What was she going to do? It felt as though she'd stepped into a huge invisible spider's web. And the more she struggled, the more entangled she became.

And then she'd realized not only was she unable to withdraw, but she was being pulled inside it—whatever it was. Twisting her head, she looked back over her shoulder and spied a couple strolling among the trees.

Opening her mouth, she'd prepared to let out a blood-curdling scream. Suddenly the thing around her shifted—like a pair of powerful jaws suddenly opening wide—and she'd felt herself sucked inside.

Releasing her own breath in what should have been a terrified shout, she'd been shocked to realize that no sound at all came from between her lips. The couple in the trees had disappeared without ever having become aware of her existence, and Marina had quickly discovered there was no air to breathe in whatever this thing was that she'd gotten caught up in.

Her thoughts had become chaotic, her vision blurred. Dropping to her knees, she'd clawed at her own throat, struggling for air. Random pictures had flashed through her mind like scenes on a roll of film stuck on fast forward, making her feel dizzy.

Putting a hand to her head, she rubbed at her temple. In her dream—my God! That was it! She was dreaming! She'd read about a study conducted by the government on people who dreamed crazy things and knew all the time they were dreaming.

The pain in her head became worse and her mind became fuzzy. It must be the aftereffects of whatever they'd given her when they'd brought her to the emergency room— no, wait a minute—she'd already concluded that this couldn't have been a hospital.

The pictures returned in living color, but this time she viewed them as though down a long dark tunnel. Tunnel? What had she read about flashes of light and long dark tunnels?

A tremor of fear shook her. Oh...God...no...what if this was the morgue...?

Chapter 2

Sammell strode briskly down the wide granite walkway toward the angular, two-story building constructed of pure white yule marble. The first floor of the spare structure was without windows. It housed labs like the one where Sammell worked.

The top floor contained the offices of the Western Zone of the World State Government, headed by ancestors of the original Founding Fathers with Carson B. Wyndom at their head. The offices located there had a wraparound view of the countryside from large smoked-glass windows. From these offices every aspect of life in the Western Hemisphere was carefully scrutinized and manipulated, according to the Wyndom government standards.

Government House, as it was called, stood atop the highest peak of the Solvo Mountains. Sammell and the other scientists who worked there were transported from the small village located at the base of the mountain range by horse-drawn carriage.

He didn't like working at Government House, preferring the smaller lab closer to his cell. But every day he walked to a spot at the edge of the village and waited for the carriage that would take him up into the mountains.

There was one good thing about the transfer. It had given him access to data he'd never imagined to be still in existence. He'd always thought the government had destroyed all records of the world's history to prevent someone's finding them. It had also given him access to components he needed to work on his secret project in his home lab.

Taking his place in line, Sammell studied the neck of the man in front of him, wondering what project he was involved in. Discussion between labs was forbidden by law, but Sammell was well aware that there were projects in the building ranging from genetic restructuring to the creation of black holes for waste-disposal purposes.

He knew this because he made it a point to listen to everything. The state guards sometimes talked among themselves when he was within hearing distance. And since they were convinced he was under the influence of the Wyndom drug, they occasionally divulged information Sammell would otherwise never have learned.

When his turn finally came, Sammell stepped up onto the dais, stuck his head into the Ident Casque and waited for the all-clear signal. Every citizen had an identification code. It was laser-tattooed into the frontal bone of each newborn seconds after birth. It could only be read by a government Probe computer. And all those who worked at Government House were put through an ID check before being allowed to enter the building.

The all-clear sounded and the black energy curtain divided. Sammell always felt a slight tremor of uneasiness and walked a little faster as he passed through it. He'd never forget the first day of his reassignment to the new lab. The Probe computer had malfunctioned, trapping a man in the curtain. His screams had been instantaneous and terrible and then they'd abruptly stopped. No trace of him was ever found.

Quickening his step, Sammell entered the long corridor down which his lab was situated. Stepping into the empty room, he moved to his desk, where a pile of work from the day before awaited him.

At the end of each day, all members of the scientific team placed the work they'd done that day on Sammell's desk for analysis. Everyone on the project worked independently, each on a small area involving their own special field.

Sammell, as project head, had a working knowledge of all scientific fields involved in the work. Each morning he pieced together everyone's work from the previous day into one formula, adding his own notes before passing it along to Bartell, the project director.

Bartell wasn't a scientist, he was a government coordinator. But still, he made all decisions on the project, relying on Sammell to explain what he didn't understand.

Sammell understood, if no one else did, the reasoning behind this careful division of labor. It kept everyone, except Sammell and Bartell, from having a complete picture of the end formula. Bartell was a loyal subject to the House of Wyndom, and Sammell was supposedly under the influence of their carefully developed drug and that made him powerless to do anything on his own.

Still, because of Bartell's paranoia, Sammell was plagued with unannounced visits to his cell from Government Inspection Squads. It was because of those visits that he'd had to waste precious time, which he could have been using on further development of MDAT, to develop an EWS, or Early Warning System, that would alert him in advance and allow him enough time to prepare his lab for police inspection.

"Good day, Sammell."

Sammell glanced over his shoulder with a slight nod of recognition. Larkin, another scientist on the project, and a man with whom Sammell felt a growing kinship, stood directly behind him.

"Good day to you," Sammell replied.

"Yesterday's work?" Larkin asked, his glance resting on the pile of papers lying at Sammell's elbow.

Surprised by the question, Sammell responded with an automatic "Yes." Curiosity among employees was not encouraged in the lab, and Larkin had never evidenced any before now.

"I think I have found the solution!" the other man suddenly burst out, casting a furtive glance over his shoulder.

"The solution to what?" Sammell asked in surprise.

"To the problem that has been plaguing this project."

Sammell studied the man's overbright eyes, becoming uneasy. "Is it in your notes from yesterday?" he asked tautly.

"No," Larkin answered, without looking at Sammell.

"Why is that?"

Larkin inched closer. Dropping his voice, he murmured, "I would speak with you alone—if that is possible." He eyed Sammell sharply.

Excitement stirred Sammell's blood. If Larkin had stumbled upon the correct answer...

"I would speak with you, too," Sammell murmured in barely audible tones.

Larkin's work on gravity and its effects on a body traveling at the speed of light was astounding. His help with the problem that now faced Sammell, due to the unexpected results of his experiment with MDAT in his home lab, would be invaluable.

Many times in the past few months he had wished that he dared discuss his secret work with the man. Yet caution and the fear of betrayal at the man's hands that he couldn't quite cast aside had always held him back.

Sammell studied the keen look in the dark eyes above him. Were Larkin's body and mind free of the effects of the Wyndom drug? Had he, too, discovered it in his nutrient injections and taken steps to remove it? The clear look in his eyes almost convinced Sammell that he had.

"There is something—"

"Sammell!" Bartell bellowed from the doorway across the room. "I wish to speak to you."

Larkin froze, and for a moment Sammell thought he saw a look of anger enter the dark eyes before he turned away to head to his own desk.

"You, too, Larkin," Bartell added, stabbing a finger in the other man's direction. "Both of you, come to my office immediately."

Without looking at Sammell, Larkin changed course and walked toward the empty doorway. Sammell waited a beat before following. How he resented the peremptory command from Bartell, though there was little he could do about it at the moment.

Larkin was standing to one side of Bartell's desk, hands clasped behind a rigid back, when Sammell entered the room. Taking up a stance of pseudo respect at the other side of the desk, he waited with an outward show of calm for the project director to tell them why they had been summoned to his office. But underneath that calm exterior, he was very conscious of the armed guards standing outside the door. And considering what lay hidden in his lab at home, Sammell had to beat down a persistent voice that urged him to run from this office and from this building as quickly as possible.

"It has come to my attention," Bartell began in guttural tones, "that you are both approaching an unprecedented birthday.

"Is that not correct?" he asked, spearing each man in turn with a cold blue razor-sharp glance.

"Yes, Lord Bartell," Larkin answered respectfully.

Sammell gave a slight nod, silently heaving a sigh of relief. He had not been summoned for arrest.

"It is time to prepare yourselves for marriage," Bartell thundered as though they were standing in the next room instead of on the other side of the desk. Picking up a thin sheaf of papers, he thrust them at the two men. The thick gold-crested ring with a solitary ruby at its center glittered at them like a baleful red eye.

The ring was a symbol of Bartell's high rank. Only those who were direct descendants of the original pact-signing coalition responsible for the present government wore the ring.

Other government employees were recognizable by their triangular-shaped silver lapel pins with the dove of peace at the top, the lightning bolt of power on the left and the silhouette of the masses on the right with the motto Peaceful Power to the People below.

Sammell sneered inwardly at the thought of the motto, knowing it for the lie that it was.

"These papers must be filled out," the director continued, "and returned to me by the end of the day."

Sammell reached for the paper with his name at the top, noted the official government seal and turned to leave. He couldn't get out of there fast enough. He neither liked nor respected *Lord* Bartell.

"Sammell—stay!" Bartell ordered. "Larkin, go."

When they were alone, Bartell pointed to a chair. Sammell lowered himself onto it reluctantly, keeping his expression neutral and his eyes on the face of the man sitting behind the wide glass-topped desk.

"Why has another test not been scheduled?" the older man demanded abruptly, eyeing Sammell with shrewd blue eyes set beneath thick black brows. "It has been more than a week since the last one. What is the holdup?"

"We have made no progress, my lord, in solving the problem with the plasma jet," Sammell responded, nearly choking on the term of implied deference. "I can let you know by the end of the day if recent work indicates another test."

The director stared hard at Sammell, his thoughts carefully shielded from Sammell's own veiled scrutiny. Abruptly he nodded, making a peremptory gesture of dismissal.

Sammell was at the door, his hand on it, when Bartell's voice stopped him cold. "What was Larkin doing in your work space just now?"

He should have known the question was coming. The man missed little and what he missed his spies did not.

Sammell thought quickly and answered, "He wanted to go over some of the notes he made yesterday."

"I see." The silence lasted an eternity, but Sammell knew he had not been dismissed. "Have you noticed any-thing—" Bartell hesitated "—unusual in his manner of late?"

Sammell turned around. Was the question a trap?

"He works hard, my lord," Sammell responded, meet-ing the other man's narrow gaze with a bland expression. They all did—Bartell saw to that.

Bartell's sour expression said that wasn't an endorse-ment of the man's allegiance. "I want you to watch him carefully in the coming weeks. Report anything odd in his manner directly to me. Is that understood?"

"Yes, my lord," Sammell replied, once again turning away.

Here was the proof he'd been looking for. Obviously the government was gathering evidence against someone on the project. And despite Bartell's cunning pretense, Sammell didn't think it was Larkin they were after. His own time on the project might be shorter than he had previously thought. And there was research yet to be done, which he could only do as long as he had access to the Government Archives housed in this building.

Back in the lab Larkin gave Sammell a fleeting glance as he passed the man's desk. A few moments later Larkin ap-proached Sammell with a paper in his hand and bent down as though to point out some salient point he wanted to make.

"Is something wrong?" he asked in low tones.

"You are being watched," Sammell responded without guile.

Larkin gave a slight jerk and darted a swift glance of shock at Sammell's face, his glance returning almost im-mediately to the quivering paper in his own hand.

"Why do you say that?" His thin lips barely moved with the words.

"Bartell wants me to report on your behavior."

"Why are you telling me this?" Larkin asked stiffly.

Sammell wasn't certain about his reasons himself. "I wish we could meet outside work," he muttered almost to himself.

Larkin shot him another quick glance. "Why?"

"So we could discuss...things," he said, finishing lamely. "What things?"

Sammell picked up the marriage document, resisting an urge to crumble it in his hand and toss it into the waste holder. "Things like this," he muttered through clenched lips.

The information on this paper would be fed into a government computer, assimilated by it and result in his being genetically and intellectually matched with a mate.

"I do not want to get married," he said, "I prefer living alone."

How would he work on his own experiment with someone else living in his cell? Worse yet, if it turned out that he couldn't send his "guests" home, how would he hide them from his new mate?

Larkin eyed him searchingly. "Perhaps we can work out a way to speak alone," he began, suddenly breaking off when out of the corner of his eye he caught sight of two co-workers, male and female, who appeared to be taking an inordinate interest in Sammell and Larkin's whispered conversation, making their way slowly toward Sammell's work area.

"I think I know why the plasma jet is not working. I will try to speak with you later," he muttered out the side of his mouth before turning away.

The approaching couple cast a quick glance in Sammell's direction, then continued on their way. Sammell stared after them, pondering their obvious interest in his and Larkin's conversation.

Marina's eyes popped open. She stared at the ceiling. Taking a quick inventory, she realized two things right off the bat. Her body ached all over and she had to go to the bathroom.

"Well," she muttered aloud, "at least I know I'm not dead."

Elevating herself by her elbows to a sitting position, she twisted a hand behind her, shifted her weight to one hip and rubbed at a particularly tender spot at the base of her spine.

"What a nightmare," she said aloud. Raising her knees and cupping a hand to her forehead, she closed her eyes.

She'd had the strangest dream. In it she had been lost in a large house, rushing from one immense room to another and stumbling on people reenacting a series of short skits that appeared to be scenes from history. And then she'd found herself in some bizarre hospital...

She peered cautiously through her fingers. "Oh, no," she groaned in mounting horror, "what now?" It was impossible to see anything but a blank wall a few feet in either direction. Where was she now? Confined to a padded cell?

Maybe that's where she belonged. Ever since she'd arrived at the park it seemed she'd gone a little crazy.

A slight sound drew her attention. "Well, at least I'm not alone," she murmured softly, staring at the small gray squirrel. "I'm glad I didn't imagine you."

The squirrel, commonly known as a pine squirrel, stood on its hind legs and eyed her in silence. Suddenly it began to chatter excitedly, hopping up and down.

"I wish I knew what you were trying to tell me," Marina said sadly. "I'll bet you know more about what's happened to the two of us than I do."

The animal's chatter stopped abruptly, but the up-and-down motion continued. Marina watched until she began to feel dizzy, then stood up.

Apparently she hadn't been in an accident. At least not a very serious one, because her limbs all functioned normally and without pain. In fact everything seemed to function normally except for her mind—her thoughts were in a jumble.

She thought she remembered being in a hospital. But now she appeared to be in some kind of a cell. Her gaze traveled over the walls of her small prison. Was this real? Or was she dreaming?

She could see nothing but light-colored walls. On closer inspection, they looked insubstantial. Maybe...

She took two steps forward with her hands stretched out before her, palms up, and bounced three steps back. "What the—"

And then she suddenly remembered the "thing" she'd gotten trapped in at the park. Marina backed away from the wall. She'd only gone a few feet when the same resiliency at her back sent her scurrying to the center of her prison.

This was too much! She had never liked puzzles. She had no patience with them. She always read the last page of a book first, too.

Frowning, she reached out with one hand and hesitantly felt the pliable *wall*. Shades of Spock! It had to be some kind of an energy field.

To be enclosed in a wall of energy sounded unbelievable. But no more unbelievable than what she'd run across in the park. That's always providing that the "thing" she'd encountered there—along with this strange wall—really existed, and she wasn't at this very moment lying in the peaceful arms of Morpheus, beneath her favorite tree in said park.

Marina felt the wall give beneath her tentative touch and a tremor of fear ran through her. There was a distinct difference between the wall—or force field—she'd encountered in the park and this one. Nothing appeared able to pass through this one, no matter how hard she pushed. Using both hands, she began to measure it.

A few minutes later she again stood in the center of her prison with both hands on her hips, staring at her furry companion. They were confined in an area that extended from the floor to a couple of feet above her head, about six feet in length and four feet wide—or the approximate size of a grave. Her findings were not particularly reassuring.

How had she and the squirrel gotten here? Why were they here? And better still, how would they get out?

All at once Marina realized she was very thirsty and her stomach kept reminding her at ever-shortening intervals that she hadn't eaten in a while. But at the top of her list of immediate priorities was finding a bathroom.

She stared at the wall around her, the ceiling over her, and hysteria hovered near the surface. She was not a hysterical sort of person. Then again, she had never suffered from claustrophobia, either. And having measured the diameter of her prison, she was beginning to feel distinctly uneasy, rather as though the walls and ceiling were closing in on her, while the air was slowly being sucked out.

And then she wondered if she was being observed. Someone had to be responsible for her present predicament. And that someone could at this very minute be watching the results of his—or her—labors.

"If you're out there," she began in a small voice, "I don't know what this is all about, but I want you to let me out of here. Do you hear me?"

She revolved slowly, praying she was right and that whoever held her captive was out there somewhere listening. "Please—what's this all about? Why am I here?"

She paused, listening for an answer. When none was forthcoming, close to tears, she glanced down at the squirrel at her feet, telling herself it wouldn't do any good to get so upset.

Maybe no one was out there. Maybe they were at work, or at home, sleeping, or eating dinner. She wasn't wearing a watch and had no idea of the time or the day of the week.

She sat down cross-legged on the floor. "I suppose I should be grateful that I'm not alone," she said softly, holding out her hand to see if the squirrel would come to her. "But I can't help wishing that you were six feet tall with black bangs and pointed ears and carried a phaser, or whatever they called it, so you could blast a hole in this wall and get us out of here."

The animal hadn't responded to her overture of friendship. "I'm Marina," she said. "Don't you remember me? I'm the one who's been keeping you and your family in peanuts for the past couple of months."

The squirrel tilted its head to one side, watching her for a moment without moving, then edged close enough to sniff her hand. And Marina could almost believe that in this strange place where nothing appeared rational the animal was able to understand her.

Resting an elbow on one knee and her chin on her closed fist, she studied her companion, keeping her thoughts fixed on him and off their present situation. "I wonder if you have a name? I don't suppose I could pronounce it if I knew it, since I don't speak squirrel.

"I'll tell you what, how would it be if I gave you a name, so I won't have to keep calling you 'hey you,' or Mr. Squirrel? That's much too formal for friends. Don't you think?"

The squirrel turned and began to scamper around the floor as though trying to get away from her and her silly conversation. It bumped into the wall a couple of times, turned to look at her, then began running around in circles again.

Marina rolled her eyes, then laughed. "I don't blame you. Sometimes I bore myself. But I do like the idea of a name for you."

She thought quickly. "How about Monday? That's the day this bizarre adventure began. What do you say, Monday, do you like your new name?"

As though understanding and approving, Monday stopped his aimless running and sat near her crossed legs. They contemplated each other in silence.

Marina's head began to droop. "I don't know what it is about this place . . ." She yawned and put a hand over her mouth. "All I want to do is sleep . . ."

Sammell had been observing his guests for some time through a two-way mirror in the wall. Every word Marina spoke had come to him loud and clear over the lab's intercom. And the question he'd been asking himself since her arrival about whether he'd have difficulty communicating with her had been answered. They spoke the same language.

Her conversation with the squirrel had fascinated him. She spoke to the animal as though they were equals. The idea intrigued him. Did her people communicate with animals? She had mentioned being unable to speak squirrel. He would have to find out about that.

All at once the woman shook her head and climbed to her feet.

"This is ridiculous," she muttered angrily. "I'm tired of being cooped up in here." Staring directly at Sammell, though she didn't know it, Marina demanded, "Why are you doing this to me?"

Sammell gave a guilty start before realizing that she couldn't see him. She was voicing her question to the air.

"I know you're out there," she continued, "and I'll just bet you're watching and listening to me right now. What do you want with me? With us?" she demanded, glancing at her small companion. "Why have you brought us here?

"Damn it!" she shouted in frustration. "Answer me! Somebody answer me!"

Raising clenched fists, she shook them at her unseen host. "I want out of here! Let me out!

"What kind of a monster kidnaps a person and then lets them suffer from hunger and thirst?" A split second later she added, "I need a bathroom!"

Sammell listened in growing consternation. He hadn't considered their need for nourishment. Though he should have realized they'd need water and a... *bathroom?*

He saw her sit on the floor and remove a shoe. A moment later she was banging it against the floor and yelling. He couldn't let that continue. She would eventually draw attention from the other cells around him, and it would be impossible for him to explain why he, an unmated man, had a female in his cell. And especially one like her.

He hadn't planned on making contact with her, not until he was more prepared for it. But the woman had changed that now, with the clamor she was making. Placing his right hand flat against a small panel inset at the top of the door, he pressed lightly. The area around his hand glowed red, then green and the door sprang open.

Without entering the room, he called, "Silence! I will bring water."

Stunned into silence by the sound of his voice, Marina listened carefully before asking, "How do I get out of here? And what about a bathroom?"

"I do not understand... bathroom. Explain."

Marina got to her feet slowly. Was he joking? Explain bathroom?

"A bathroom is... it's where you go to bathe, among other, more personal, things. You know, things that might... soil your clothing?"

"Necessary," Sammell said abruptly, "you mean the necessary."

"Okay," she conceded. If that's what he wanted to call it, it was perfectly all right with her. As long as he showed her to it soon.

"How do I get beyond this wall?" Marina asked impatiently. "I can't walk through it—believe me," she added wryly, "I've tried."

Sammell had forgotten about the protective force field he'd placed around the Recep before leaving the lab that morning. He was wearing the special glasses he'd designed to see through it. Without them, all anyone would see was a holographic image of the empty Recep.

Crossing to the computer, he touched a button hidden below the console. "You may leave the Recep now," he said, removing the glasses and turning to face her.

Marina blinked and gave a slight shiver as the wall simply vanished. One moment it was there and the next it was gone. She now looked into the room she'd first thought to be a hospital emergency room.

"Who are you?" she asked warily. "Do I know you?"

A tall figure stepped out of the shadows at the far end of the room and started toward her. Marina took an involuntary step backward. She'd never seen anything like him.

He was wearing a one-piece jumpsuit in a shade of royal blue. It gave him a clean-cut look that impressed her. But less reassuring was the stunned expression in the dark eyes fastened on her face.

"Do I know you?" she asked again on a note of uncertainty as he paused within a yard of her.

His square jaw tensed and her eyes were irresistibly drawn to the cleft in his strong chin.

"You said you needed the...bathroom," he stumbled slightly over the unfamiliar word, his glance resting on her eyes—blue eyes, *the color of royalty.*

And now he was close enough to smell that elusive fragrance she exuded. Again it made him feel light-headed. Was it some kind of defense mechanism that kept would-be predators at bay?

"I will not harm you," he reassured her. "There is no need to defend yourself against me."

"Defend?"

"Yes, what you wear overpowers me."

"My clothing?" she asked in bewilderment, looking down at her shorts.

"No, the scent."

"Scent?" Marina looked puzzled. "Scent—oh, you mean my perfume?"

"Perfume?"

"Yes, fragrance—you know, *Gossamer.*" she mentioned the name of the cologne she was wearing. "It's my favorite scent."

"Why do you wear this...perfume?"

"To smell good."

"Your people smell bad?"

Marina drew herself up in affront. "I beg your pardon," she said angrily. "If I smell bad, it's your fault. I could hardly shower in that prison where you've kept me."

"The... perfume is not a defense mechanism against predators?"

At first she looked flabbergasted and then she began to laugh. "Not exactly," she answered between chuckles, going along with his act. "Just the opposite, in fact. It's supposed to attract the male, not chase him away."

"You wear it to attract males?" Sammell's eyebrows were nearly at his hairline.

Marina sobered. "I wear it because I want to. Is there something wrong with that?"

Though still puzzled, Sammell said, "No."

"Good. Now that we're through with that, can I please go to the bathroom?"

"There." He pointed toward an arched doorway at the back of the room.

Marina couldn't help but note the strength and beauty of the hand, or the swatch of wavy gold hair that fell across his forehead when he nodded in her direction. And even though he was a kidnapper and acted kind of weird, she had to admit that he was darned good-looking.

A moment later she poked her head through the arched doorway to complain, "There's no door." But she complained to an empty room. Her host—or captor—was nowhere in sight.

She shrugged, deciding it was probably the lack of privacy that had sent him temporarily out of the room. Turning back to the room, which was really little more than a small cubicle, she studied it critically, wondering if it came with instructions.

As she'd entered it a light had come on. She didn't actually see a light per se—not that she recognized, anyway—but light was coming from somewhere.

She'd seen some really bizarre decorating schemes in her time, but she'd never seen anything like this one. There were no handles or faucets in sight. The room's accoutrements consisted of a shiny black circular projection on one wall about knee-high. She assumed it was the toilet. A three-cornered object on the wall directly opposite could be the sink, and there was something slightly resembling a shower stall in one corner.

Apart from that, the room was bare. No window, no mirror, no shower curtain, no shelves, no towels, no soap— *no toilet paper!* She frowned and contemplated the arched doorway but decided against seeking her host.

A moment later, she understood the omission of the paper and towels. As she centered her hands over the sink, an opening appeared in the wall and a jet of warm water mixed with soap—she hoped—automatically sprayed them. After a short interval, it sprayed them again with clear water. And when the water shut off, a beam of light dried them in seconds.

She was still pondering the advancement of modern technology when she re-entered the lab.

"You found everything?"

Marina gave a slight start and spun to face the man. Straight and slender and somewhat shorter than he'd first appeared, her host stood near a work island a few feet away. At this distance she could fully see the startling contrast made by coffee brown eyes, dark eyebrows and eyelashes against pale skin and light hair.

"Yes," she murmured warily, "I found everything. But I have to admit I've never seen anything like your bathroom—what's wrong?" He was staring at her as though she had two heads.

"Nothing." Sammell tore his glance from her face and the sight of those startling blue eyes to indicate the glass sitting at his elbow. "I brought water."

Marina moved a little closer, her eyes narrowing on the delicately shaped blue glass. Now that she thought about it, she wasn't convinced it was smart to eat or drink anything he offered her. What if the water was drugged?

She had no idea where she was or why she'd been brought here. And she didn't know a single thing about this man, except that he was very handsome and very weird.

Sensing her hesitancy, Sammell picked up the glass and offered it to her.

"How do I know it's only water?" she asked suspiciously.

"Is that not what you wanted?" he asked with a puzzled air, keeping his glance directed on something other than her face.

Marina lifted an eyebrow and asked, "How do I know you didn't put something into it?"

"What?" He spared her a fleeting glance.

"I don't know." She shrugged. "But after all this..." She indicated the room around them. "Am I supposed to trust you?" The place looked like the set of a sci-fi movie from the 1960s.

Sammell's dark eyes locked with hers. Lifting the glass, he took a deliberate sip from it. Swallowing, he held it out to her.

Marina stared at the rim of the glass a long time before reaching for it. He gave it up hastily, withdrawing his hand before it could make contact with hers, as though her touch might somehow contaminate him.

Once the glass was in her hand, Marina lost little time tilting it to her lips. It tasted like ambrosia. The water at home tasted so bad that she bought bottled water for drinking and cooking, and even that sometimes left a bad taste in her mouth.

When she'd drunk the whole glass, she gave a guilty start and remembered her little companion. "Monday—"

Sammell held up a hand and pointed toward the other side of the room. Marina turned to see a basin of water on the floor near the small creature.

"Thank you," she murmured softly, giving him the first genuine smile.

Sammell reached for the empty glass without an answering smile. Being in this woman's presence made him very uncomfortable. She confused him.

Marina's stomach growled. Placing a hand against it in embarrassment, she murmured, "I'm sorry, but I haven't eaten in a while."

In fact, she should have been angry with him, because *he* was the reason she hadn't eaten. But something in his attitude made it almost impossible to be angry with him. She couldn't quite put her finger on what it was about him... He was so... what was the word ... *sterile?*

Actually, the word that came to mind was *virginal,* but that was a ridiculous idea. She doubted that any man in this day and age reached adulthood still in that chaste state, unless he lived a monastic life. And she just couldn't see a priest kidnapping her and keeping her a prisoner in a laboratory.

This man reminded her of one of those people who wouldn't say dirt if they had a mouth full of it. But she still didn't trust him. He hadn't given her an explanation for bringing her here. And besides, she was hungry and being hungry always made her feel cranky.

"Look, I don't want to seem ungrateful for the water, but I really need some nourishment."

Sammell picked up a small rectangular object from the table and nodded. "I know," he said, adjusting something on the back of it. "I will only give you a small dose the first time—"

"What are you talking about?" Marina interrupted hastily, backing away.

Sammell was still making his adjustments and didn't see the panic sweeping over her face.

"You aren't giving me a dose of anything," she warned, reaching for something to defend herself with. Her groping fingers found a heavy metal object on the counter behind her. She lifted it and brandished it in his direction threateningly.

Sammell glanced up as she raised it above her head. "What are you doing?" he asked instantly, his eyes on the object in her hand. "Put that down!" he shouted.

Marina's eyes widened. He'd fooled her by pretending an equanimity that was obviously only skin deep. But she had his number now. If he came one step closer, she'd ...

"Put that down," Sammell repeated in a quieter voice, realizing he must have frightened her. "Please," he murmured softly, "put it down—very gently—on the rack where you got it."

Marina looked at the cylinder. He seemed awfully concerned that she was holding it and not the fact that she was threatening him with it.

"What is this?" she asked with a curious dread.

"A very compact tube of fuel. Please, lay it on the table—gently."

"Fuel?" Her eyes widened in alarm. "Y-you mean as in gas?"

"I mean as in meltanium, a benign material that becomes highly volatile when exposed to air. Put it down—please, I will not give you the injection if you do not want it."

She eyed him narrowly. "Are you lying to me?"

Withdrawing his eyes as though with great difficulty from the cylinder, he met her glance. "Why should I lie? If you do not want the nutrient injection, I will not give it to you."

"Nutrient?"

"Yes," he answered, his eyes again on the cylinder in her hand. "We nourish our bodies with injections of nutrients."

"What about eating?"

"We have evolved past using food for consumption. It is really only the vitamins and minerals that our bodies need and they are in the injection."

Marina was even more puzzled by this than by the nightmares she'd had on her arrival. Was this guy for real?

"Please," he said again, "put the cylinder in the rack and we will continue our conversation."

Not really certain she believed the object in her hand to be dangerous, yet wondering in these strange surroundings if anything was what it seemed, she decided to humor him. Placing the cylinder carefully in the rack where she'd found it, she moved away from the counter.

"What would have happened it I had dropped it?" she asked skeptically, watching as her host hurried to pick it up and painstakingly examine it.

"The end seals are thin so it can be used as an injection fuel. You could have destroyed the entire population of this city sector," he answered solemnly, securing it in the rack with several others like it and placing the rack out of reach in a cabinet.

"Are you serious?" Marina asked with a dubious frown.

"Absolutely."

Clenching her hands against a sudden attack of nerves, she began to shake all over. What if she *had* accidentally dropped the cylinder? How could anything so harmless looking be so lethal? And what was it doing here, where anyone could pick it up?

Was he a criminal? A terrorist?

"What are you doing with that?" She indicated the cabinet where he'd secured the fuel, with a nod. "Aren't there laws governing the use of such dangerous material?" She was becoming angry, holding him responsible for what might have happened if she had unwittingly dropped the thing.

"I use it in my work."

"You're a rocket scientist, right?"

"No, I am a physicist. I am working on the feasibility of traveling in time."

Marina shot him a withering glance. "And I'm Dorothy, the squirrel is Toto and this is the land of Oz."

"No," he answered slowly, "this is the Western Hemisphere of the World State Government. And the year is 2393 A.D."

Chapter 3

"I'm supposed to believe that I went to sleep in the twentieth century and awoke in the twenty-fourth?"

"Did you go to sleep?" Sammell asked curiously. "When? Right away, or later?"

Marina's blue gaze narrowed on his averted face. "I don't think we're on the same wavelength here," she muttered, suddenly at a loss. Obviously the man had a screw loose somewhere—oh! why did she feel so...

"What is it?" Sammell asked anxiously.

Marina frowned, knees shaking, and reached for the counter behind her, doing her best to keep his face in focus. "I don't feel very well," she said, putting a hand to her forehead as the floor suddenly rose up to meet her.

Sammell caught her before she fell. Picking her up awkwardly, he carried her to the Recep and placed her on the floor. She was such a mystery to him. As he knelt beside her, his gaze slowly traveled over the whole of her. He noted the shape of her pale lips, the fine blue veins on the lids of her closed eyes, the delicate bones of her shoulders and the hollow of her neck, the rounded curve of her hips and the long shapely thighs.

She looked fragile, and for the first time since her arrival, Sammell really began to feel the weight of responsibility that was his for bringing her here. Was this sudden faint a result of her trip through the barriers of time, or due to lack of nourishment?

If anything happened to her, it would be his fault for bringing her here. And her presence couldn't have come at a worse time for him. He needed all his powers of concentration for the work ahead, both in his secret work at home and his work at the government lab.

If he was under investigation as he suspected, he could be arrested and charged at any time. If that happened they'd soon ferret out all the material he'd appropriated from the state archives for his own use. And if they discovered that his MDAT was a working machine and not a mock-up of the machine in the state lab, they couldn't help but realize that he'd been sabotaging their project from the start.

Arrest meant termination. There were no prisons on planet Earth. It would be even worse for the woman. The government would have a live subject to study and experiment on. Not even the color of her eyes would be able to save her.

The thought caused him no little discomfort and that surprised him. He felt protective toward her. Just as she felt protective toward her small traveling companion.

This was a new experience for him. He'd never felt responsible for the safety of another. He'd always felt an obligation to try to save his people from the tyranny under which they existed—that's why he was willing to risk his life by building a machine to travel back in time and try to save them. But he'd never taken on the responsibility of one person's safety.

His was a society that didn't encourage closeness in its people. Physical contact was forbidden. Yet he found himself fascinated by the differences between this woman's physical appearance and those of the women of his own time.

He didn't know what to make of her. She acted in a manner completely foreign to him, distrusted him and disrupted his life, but she fascinated him. And in the time it took to get MDAT ready to send her back to her own time, he hoped to learn more about her and more about her society.

He'd learned about her society from the Government Archives, but he'd learned very little about the people themselves. And one of the things he didn't know was how often they needed to take nourishment. By his reckoning it had been about thirty hours since she'd arrived in his lab. But he didn't know how long she'd gone without nourishment before getting caught up in the Recep. Before losing consciousness she'd mentioned that she hadn't eaten in a while. How long was a while?

He glanced at the nutrameter on the table, wondering if he should go ahead and give her the injection. The one thing stopping him was the realization that he knew nothing about her physiology. What if something in the nutrient didn't agree with her system? He was a physicist, not a biologist. He had known enough about biochemistry to isolate, identify and remove the substance the government added to the injections to induce obedience in its people, but that was all. The nutrients themselves could be poisonous to her system.

There was no way around it. He would have to go out and get her some food.

Marina opened her eyes and stared at the ceiling. "Oh, no, not again," she muttered testily. This was becoming a habit she would dearly have loved to break. Why couldn't she have awakened at home in her own bed to find that this whole scenario was nothing more than a particularly nasty nightmare?

A slight sound interrupted her unhappy musings and she sat up, hunting for Monday. But he was nowhere in sight. Her jailer had neglected to turn on the energy field—or whatever he'd called it—and he'd left the room, except where she sat, in darkness.

Marina had no idea where the sounds she'd heard had originated, but all at once she was frightened. Yet she couldn't work up enough nerve to cry out. She didn't want to know any more about this bizarre place and its inhabitants than she already knew. She just wanted to go home.

The sound came again, closer this time. And she finally recognized it as a scraping noise, like metal against the walls or floor.

"Is someone there?" she asked haltingly. She was on her hands and knees, working her way to her feet, when something was shoved into sight on the floor. It looked like a hubcap turned upside down and filled with colored balls.

Inching closer, she realized the colored balls were actually a variety of fruits and vegetables. The metal object still resembled a hubcap, but the fruit looked real.

"Is that you?" she called softly. "Why are you sneaking around like this in the dark? I already know what you look like, so this isn't going to help you when you're caught—" She broke off, recalling the strange conversation they'd had earlier before she'd ... passed out?

Pulling the hubcap quickly toward her, she sat down and crossed her legs. "Don't think this is going to put you in my good books," she warned, contemplating the array of fruit. "Just because you've decided to feed me," she added, mouth watering, "won't get you off when you're arrested for kidnapping."

She picked up in one hand one of the largest reddest apples she'd ever seen and in the other a tomato of the same size and beauty. Her mouth filled with saliva and her jaws ached as she tried to decide which one to eat first.

She had never seen fresh fruit or vegetables equal to these in any of the stores she'd frequented at home. Her stomach growled. She rubbed the apple against her blouse, preparing to take a bite, then hesitated. This was interesting fare from a man who said the people around here didn't eat real food.

Monday stepped suddenly into view. "Where have you been?" she asked curiously. "Oh, well," she said, shrugging, "I guess it doesn't matter. See what our host has provided for our enjoyment?" She picked up a handful of acorns and placed them on the floor near the squirrel. "I think these were meant for you."

Again she lifted the shiny apple to her lips and again she hesitated. Her ears detected another sound. She turned to see another object had appeared within the circle of light. This time it was a glass of water.

"I won't ask you to join us," Marina said with a hint of vexation, "since you seem determined to make this as impersonal a meal as possible. But nevertheless I do thank you for the food and drink."

She listened hard, but got no reply, nor did she hear the patter of footsteps as her provider walked away. But then, she thought wryly, if this was indeed the age of time travel as he'd indicated earlier, he probably induced the food and water to appear on their own without human assistance.

She tasted the apple, closing her eyes and savoring its sweet juicy flavor. So much for a place with inhabitants that grew food they never intended to eat. As if she really believed that. Why would they go to the trouble of producing something so delicious if they were simply going to let it rot on the tree?

On the other side of the laboratory wall, Sammell sat watching her small white teeth tear into the tender skin of the apple. He expected to feel repulsed by the sight. She did it with such primitive enthusiasm that down deep inside some small part of him did indeed respond with passion, but the sentiment was not recognizable as revulsion.

Juice ran down her chin, and Sammell watched the tip of a small pink tongue dart out to capture it. What she missed with her tongue, she used the back of one hand to wipe away. The small white teeth continued to bite and chew, bite and chew, and with every bite she took, something inside Sammell responded to the act. In no time at all only a narrow core remained of the apple. And the uneasiness without a name inside the man watching her had grown to uncomfortable proportions.

He'd thought it was her fragrance causing this disruptive feeling inside him. That's why he'd decided to keep her at a distance. But now he realized it wasn't only that. He was fully aware of her in every facet of his body. It seemed as though she touched him, despite their being on different sides of the same wall.

What was it about her that disturbed him so? The length and color of her hair? It was of a color and texture he'd never seen in his world, but he had tested its softness once. So why did he feel compelled to run his fingers through it each time she was near?

And her scent. It weakened him. It took away his will. Made him feel less a free man than the restrictions placed on him by his own government. Why was that? Would she reveal its secret to him if he asked?

There was of course the color of her eyes, but . . . Marina had picked up a tomato and taken a bite. Juice and seeds slid down her chin and again the pink tongue darted out to capture them and return them to the dark secret of her mouth.

Sammell's palms itched. He stared at them, at the moisture collected on them, and felt again a strange tightness in his lower abdomen. He'd never felt like this before. With one hand clutched against his middle and the other clenched in a tight fist, he stared at the woman.

Had she brought a new strain of virus into his world? Did that explain these alien sensations attacking his body?

Sammell's gaze roamed the woman's figure. She looked healthy enough now that the paleness, possibly caused from lack of nourishment, had disappeared.

His glance lingered on her upper torso, where the outline of full breasts pressed against the tunic she wore. He felt a sudden dryness at the back of his throat. The fingers of his right hand tingled. He recalled having touched one of those breasts and how soft it had felt.

Tearing his gaze from the woman, he moved away from the wall. This was getting him nowhere. And he knew better than to think he was suffering from an illness. His immune system could fight off anything that wasn't carrying a laser-blaster or a cylinder of meltanium ready to explode.

The woman had been fed and given water. He had switched on EWS immediately on returning to his cell after gathering food for her and the squirrel. She would do well for the night.

Stalking to his sleep chamber, he threw himself onto the bed. Rest—that was what he needed. He'd had little sleep since he'd decided to do a test run with MDAT. And now, with the unexpected arrival of the two in the lab, he'd managed even less. It was no doubt the lack of sleep affecting his thought processes and causing his present physical disturbances. A few hours of unconsciousness would put things back into perspective.

But sleep no longer came easily. Normally a few moments of silence were all he required to fall into a heavy doze. But now nothing worked, not even his determination to put the woman and the trouble she caused out of his head. Thoughts of her drifted like wispy clouds through his mind, and once again Sammell felt that strange gnawing in his middle.

He remembered the woman clutching at her own abdomen, when she'd complained of hunger. Was this troublesome feeling hunger? He'd never experienced it before—and didn't much like it.

Since his mind refused to be switched off, he let his thinking process have its way. In a few moments he would check on the woman one last time before properly retiring for the night.

He considered the problem of MDAT. He'd discovered a blown circuit when he had examined it earlier that night, while the woman had slept. MDAT would need some repair before he could send his guests back to their own time.

Apparently it was the unaccounted mass of woman and squirrel that had caused the problem. It had overloaded the system, causing a short in the computer's memory board. That meant another unauthorized trip to the storage room at Government House to steal supplies for the repair. With the way things were turning out, he'd probably get caught....

Marina finished her meal and drank the water. Her hunger appeased, now she was bored and restless. She'd been cooped up in this room without sunlight and fresh air for—she didn't know how long. She didn't have a watch, so she couldn't be certain of the exact time she'd spent here, but it felt like days.

And she didn't know any more about how she'd got here, or why she'd been brought here, than when she'd first awakened. If her elusive host was to be believed, she'd traveled through nearly half a millennium in a matter of—what? Seconds? Minutes? Hours?

Everyone knew that time travel was an illusion, a notion science-fiction writers used to play around with history. She was not a science-fiction fan. And if her host believed what he'd told her, then he needed to see a doctor.

If she could get out of this room and get a good look at the topography of the area, something about it might give her a clue about her location. And that was important. She needed to know *where* she was almost more than she needed to know why she was here.

She was coming to realize that there was no feeling as mind-numbing as being lost, truly lost, without a clue to your location. It made her feel as though she'd lost her identity as a person.

All kinds of outrageous thoughts had been running through her mind. She'd read about people being used by the government, without their permission, as guinea pigs in all kinds of research experiments. She'd wondered at first if this is what was happening to her.

But she'd also seen a few documentaries about people who'd supposedly been picked up by alien spacecraft. And after having met the man holding her prisoner, she was more willing to believe in the alien theory than his explanation of traveling through time.

She wanted out! Unable to sit still, she rose and moved toward the edge of light. Peering into the darkness, she realized that it wasn't as all-encompassing as it appeared. The light where she stood made the relative darkness of the rest of the room seem total, when in fact it was not.

Curiosity sent her hurrying away from the place she'd come to think of as a haven of safety and into the darkness. There she discovered small regions of lighted space at intervals around the room. The nearest one was centered over what looked like a very compact computer.

She was familiar with notebook computers. She'd even owned one for a short time, though nothing, not even a college computer class, had helped her fully understand how they functioned. This one was half the size of a laptop computer and the monitor about eight inches in diameter.

Peering close, she looked for a brand name, hoping it would be one she recognized. She didn't know how that would help her present situation, but seeing something familiar would at least reinforce her theory that everything she'd been told by her host was utter nonsense.

But there was nothing to see. Except for the numbers and letters on the keyboard, there was no other writing. She wondered if he'd removed the brand name to foster her feeling of disorientation, thinking she'd be more willing to go along with whatever he wanted because he was the only human contact she'd be allowed.

That made her angry. She'd heard about the bond formed between a kidnap victim and his captor, forged by the victim's need to relate to someone familiar. That wasn't going to happen to her! Somehow she was going to get away.

The thought of finding a telephone popped into her mind, giving her new direction. The chance that he'd leave one lying around where she could get to it was slim but not completely outside the realm of possibility.

Twenty minutes later she had to revise that thought. She'd looked through every cabinet and drawer, picked up anything that half resembled what she knew as a telephone—even the sometimes ridiculously cutesy ones like footballs and shoes—and found nothing. It seemed he'd outsmarted her.

Her frustration level growing, Marina plopped down on the chair near the computer and angrily contemplated the floor. It looked as if she was stuck here unless she could find a way to outsmart him.

Sometimes she was able to work out a solution to a problem while she slept. But not this time. She'd already spent several hours in sleep and was now wide-awake. Her thoughts came back to the question of how long she'd been imprisoned. Surely it had been long enough for friends and co-workers to miss her.

But not long enough for her family to have become concerned. They lived in the Midwest and were conditioned to go for weeks at a time without hearing from her. It wasn't that she didn't love and miss them, it was just that their lives had taken separate roads.

Sighing, she straightened. This was getting her nowhere. She was tired of waiting. If she waited for him to come to her, she might still be waiting this time next year.

She wanted out! So far, she'd been what she called fairly civilized about this damned charade. But her patience had evaporated.

Jumping to her feet, Marina began to pound her fists on the table before her. Picking up the nearest object, examining it to make certain it wasn't something that would explode in her hand, she began to beat it against the table, yelling at the top of her voice.

Sammell awakened abruptly, still caught up in the threads of a disturbing dream that placed him in the time machine with the woman. They were hurtling down through history out of control and he couldn't stop them.

A second later, he realized he was in his own bed and something had wakened him. Cocking his head, he realized immediately that it was the woman, creating a racket that could endanger both their lives. If the people living around

him were alerted to her presence in his cell, a squad of police would be at his door in moments.

Vaulting from the bed, he hastened down the hallway to
the two-way mirror in the wall of the lab. "Silence!" Sammell called loudly. "Silence! Do you want to awaken everyone?"

She must have heard him over the clamor she was making, because she suddenly stopped. For a moment she sat
perfectly still before turning to search the room.

"What do you want?" he demanded. "I have given you
water and food. What more do you require?"

"Oh, no you don't, buster," she replied angrily. "I want
to talk to you face-to-face."

Buster? "I need rest," he said irritably.

"Oh, is that right? You mean you haven't figured a way
to do without that, too?"

"No. I require eight hours of sleep in a twenty-four-hour
period. But for several days now, I have not been getting
more than two or three hours each rest period. I am very
tired," he added on a deeper note.

She was a prisoner! Was she supposed to feel sorry for
him because he'd lost sleep making her one?

"Well, that's just too bad. If you don't let me out of here,
I'm going to continue making this racket—in fact I'll make
one even louder," she promised. "I'll make so much noise
I'll wake up this whole damned town. And then let's see you
explain to the police about how you kidnapped me and are
keeping me a prisoner against my will!"

For a while there was complete silence. Marina felt like
crying, but she wouldn't because she didn't want to give her
jailer the satisfaction of knowing he'd brought her to tears.

"I'm losing my patience!" she yelled threateningly,
swallowing a dry sob.

"And so am I," Sammell muttered. In fact, he'd never
felt like this in all his life. His insides were coiled in a tight
knot, and his breath came only with difficulty. He glanced
down at his clenched hands, unfolded them, and stared at
the small pink indentations the nails had made in the skin of

his palms. He felt as though something inside was trying to force its way out.

Breathing heavily, shaking all over, Sammell almost lunged toward the control panel beneath the identa panel on the wall. An instant later, the lab lay in total darkness.

Again there was absolute silence in the cell. It fluttered against Sammell's ears with gentle wings. He took a deep breath, let it out, swallowed and forced himself to keep taking slow even breaths. The tightness coiled in his middle began to disappear.

Tomorrow he had to find a way to get into the storage room at work without anyone's seeing him and get the circuit he needed to repair the computer. His safety, and that of the woman, would only be ensured if he could get her back where she belonged.

He didn't like leaving her loose in his lab, but knew she was far too upset to listen to reason. And he didn't know what she was capable of, so he didn't want to take a chance by going into the lab and having her get loose inside the cell.

Maybe, if he gave her some time, she'd fall asleep. Then he could go into the lab and secure her in the Recep. As for the police, he could only wait and hope that the noise hadn't penetrated to the nearby cells. He'd know for certain within the next few minutes.

After a while, when it looked as though they were safe for the moment, he gave one last quick glance into the darkened room and moved away from the mirror toward his sleep chamber. The morning would again come too soon for him.

A few minutes later Sammell was lying peacefully on his side when the racket began all over again.

Chapter 4

The lights flashed on and a door opened in the wall. Marina looked up to see the man responsible for her nightmare enter the room.

"Where were you?" she demanded angrily.

"In my sleep chamber." He came a few steps into the room and stopped near the door.

"I suppose you were lying on a nice soft bed," she rebuked him, arms folded across her chest, "while I lay on the cold hard floor."

Sammell frowned. "I thought that is what you wanted. You did not say anything."

"Well, I'm telling you now. And I want to know where I am, why you brought me here and what you intend doing with me."

Sammell smoothed a hand over his tired face. "I told you where you are, but you do not believe me."

"The year 2393 A.D., if I remember correctly," she muttered contemptuously. "Come on, this joke has gone on long enough. I don't know what your game is, but if you expect to get a lot of money for me, you're in for a shock.

I'm a schoolteacher. I don't make big money. And my family are working people—not millionaires.''

Sammell shook his head and the light got caught up in the golden strands. "Millionaires?"

"All right," Marina murmured with a sigh of resignation, "have it your way—you brought me here from the past. Why are you keeping me locked up?"

"For your safety." All he wanted was a few hours of rest... "If I let you out and you were seen—like that—" he gestured to her person "—you would be arrested—"

"For what?"

"Just for being," Sammell spluttered. She made him feel so... He didn't have a word for the sensations she provoked in him.

"Just for being," Marina repeated softly. "Well, that clears that up nicely." Arms at her side, fists clenched, she took a step toward him. "I want out of here—now!"

"Can you not understand me, woman? They would take you to a government lab and experiment on you!"

He was shouting! Lowering his voice, he explained once more, "I keep you here for your own safety—nothing more."

"All right," she said in a deceptively calm voice, "if you brought me here, then why can't you send me back?"

"Believe me, I wish I could," he muttered. "I will," he said in a louder voice, "but not yet."

"Why not?"

"When you came through, something happened to MDAT."

"MDAT?"

Sammell turned to the machine beside him. "This is MDAT."

And this is my chance, Marina thought suddenly. He could be anything from an insane mass murderer to a white slaver, but she wasn't sticking around long enough to find out. Picking up a mallet lying on the table beside her, she lunged at him, striking him on the side of the head.

The blow only stunned him, but it gave Marina her chance. Hurrying out the door, she found herself in an ultramodern living room that looked as stark as the bathroom. She didn't have time to give it more than a cursory glance. She was looking for the door.

She found it. But to her sad surprise, there didn't appear to be a way to open it, not a handle or knob in sight. Sliding her fingers over the panels, she alternately felt and pounded it in frustration. The damned thing had to open somehow—

"I do not wish to hurt you," Sammell said through clenched teeth from somewhere close behind, "so, please, come back to the lab."

"I won't!" Marina shouted angrily over her shoulder. He didn't look all that strong, and a few years back, she'd been a real scrapper with her three older brothers.

"Yes," he told her succinctly, edging closer, "you will." His head hurt abominably and he was completely out of patience with this woman.

Marina took a long, deep look into the glittering brown eyes and she suddenly knew it was time to throw in the towel—for tonight, anyway.

"All right, I'll come back to the lab—but only if you promise to tell me the truth. And don't feed me any of that garbage about this being the twenty-fourth century."

Sammell stayed out of her reach but managed to move her in the right direction. "If you do not wish to hear the truth, then I have nothing to say," he said flatly, stationing himself between her and the door once she was safely inside.

"The truth," Marina murmured thoughtfully. She could still feel his fingers like iron claws on her shoulders as he had turned her around a moment ago. "Whose truth—yours or mine?"

"Is there a difference?"

"All right," she yielded momentarily, backing up to lean against a table, "tell me your truth."

"My name is Sammell—"

"Sammell what?"

"Just...Sammell. I am a research scientist. I built a time machine in my lab and in my first attempt to break the time barrier I sent a vase into the twentieth century. When it returned, the squirrel—" he nodded at Monday, who had remained a silent watcher during Marina's bid for freedom "—and you came with it."

"Just like that?" Marina asked, motioning with her hands. "Poof, you send something into the past, and poof, we arrive?"

Sammell frowned. "I do not understand the term *poof*." He gestured to the machine he'd called MDAT. "I sent the vase into the past with MDAT and it brought you here."

Marina studied the machine in silence. It looked like a very short and narrow telescope, mounted on a mechanical arm attached to the wall. It didn't look impressive enough to control centuries of time and space.

"If that's true, then why don't you send us back right now?" she asked, still studying the machine. "We'll be out of your hair and you will not only have successfully sent a vase into the past and brought it back again, but you'll have done the same with two living creatures," she added in satisfaction.

"I cannot," Sammell admitted reluctantly.

Marina's head whipped in his direction. "What do you mean? If you brought us here, then you should be able to send us back."

"I sent a very small object into the past in that first experiment. You and the squirrel returned with it. The machine was not equipped for mass transportation.

"Somehow it managed to accommodate both of you, but the added stress of your combined mass overloaded the circuits. I was surprised to see the squirrel come through all in one piece," he added without thinking, "but as for you..."

"A circuit blew?" Marina asked with questionable calm. "Are you telling me that my life was dependent on a circuit? That I could have been floating out there—" she gestured with one hand "—somewhere in time—in little bits and pieces?"

"Not exactly. Molecules are very small and cannot be seen with the naked eye—"

"Molecules?"

"Yes. MDAT—"

"You said that before," she said impatiently. "What does it stand for?"

"Molecular displacement activator and transfer. MDAT converts an object to its basic structure, transports it to whatever setting has been programmed into the computer and then converts it to its original form."

Marina examined her hands and arms. He was telling her he'd disassembled her into...molecules? "That isn't possible," she whispered softly.

"Certainly not in your world. And not in mine...until now."

This was getting them nowhere. Marina was beginning to realize the man did indeed live in a different world. One of his own devising. How far would he go with this preposterous charade?

"All right, tell me about your world," she demanded.

"What would you like to know?"

"Everything," Marina said. "How is your world different from mine?"

Sammell moved to the chair and sat down, putting a hand to the swelling on the side of his head. It still hurt.

Marina pulled herself up onto a nearby table and sat with her legs dangling over the edge.

"I do not know a lot about your world," Sammell said, "only what I have read in the Government Archives. And that is very little. We are not allowed to study the past."

"Why not?"

"I am not certain. Maybe because they do not want us to realize life on Earth under their regime is not the paradise they would like us to believe. And the past is not the hell they make it out to be."

Marina felt a stirring of unease. "Is Earth a paradise?"

"It depends on your interpretation of paradise. Disease has been stamped out. People live long lives—"

"How long?"

"A hundred years. Famine, overpopulation and war have been abolished, but—"

"But?" Marina prompted.

"I do not want to talk about me and my world." He sat forward in the chair. This was his chance to find out about the past. And if he was to accomplish his mission, he needed to learn all he could about the twentieth century. "Tell me about you. Tell me what life is like for you."

"My life is boring. You wouldn't find it in the least bit interesting."

"No?" He studied her carefully. The riotous feelings inside had settled. He could even look into her blue eyes without experiencing that terrible apprehension.

He was very curious about this woman. She showed great courage—a thing his people knew little about. "What are you called?"

"You mean my name?"

He nodded.

"Marina—Marina Ross."

"Two names. You have two names?"

"My given name and my family name." She played along with him. "When I marry, my last name—my family name—will change to that of my husband's."

"Why is that?" Sammell asked with a frown.

Marina thought a minute. "I don't really know—that's just the way it is. Of course," she added an instant later, thoroughly confusing her listener, "I don't have to change it if I don't want to. Some women don't."

"Will you?" he asked, watching the changing expressions flit across her face.

She shrugged, a curious light filling the blue eyes. And then she said, "Yes, I rather think I will. Taking my husband's name would mean that I was leaving my past life behind and starting a new one with my husband. I think that's what marriage is all about."

"I like that," Sammell found himself saying. "When do you take a . . . husband?" he asked uncertainly.

"I don't know. When I find someone to love, who loves me."

"Love?"

"Yes." Marina cocked her head and stared at him through her lashes. "Don't tell me you don't know anything about love?"

"No."

"But...you do marry?"

"We are matched with a mate."

"Matched? Who matches you?"

"The State Computer."

"Computer?"

"Yes. Everyone is required to marry at age thirty."

"A computer-arranged marriage," Marina murmured thoughtfully. "That's interesting."

"Who will pick your mate?"

"I will."

"How will you know whom to pick?"

"I'll know."

"How?"

"When I fall in love."

"That word again. Can you—"

"Tell me more about your world," Marina interrupted quickly. She wasn't about to get into a discussion about love. He almost sounded sincere. But could he keep up the pretense?

"What is a day like in your world?"

"You would not like my world," Sammell said. "Most of the day is filled with work and then we return to our cell and sleep."

"Cell?"

"Here." He spread out his hands. "Our living space—our cell."

"What do you do during your free time?"

"Read technical books or watch television."

Television—now that was a familiar term. "What do you watch? Mysteries? Game shows? Sitcoms?"

"Sitcoms?" He looked thoroughly puzzled. "The programs are educational programs chosen by the government."

"How long is your work week?" Marina asked, becoming interested in spite of herself.

"Six days. On the seventh day we rest."

"Just like in the Bible."

"Bible?"

"Our religious book. Do you go to church?"

"Yes, twice on Sunday."

"When do you have time to do what you want?"

"According to the state, that is what we want."

Detecting a note of bitterness in his voice, Marina asked, "And is it?"

"No." Sammell stood and crossed the room to her. "I know you do not believe these things I have told you, but I am telling you the truth. This is not your world, it is mine, and you are in great danger here."

It was hard not to believe him. Yet it still sounded too fantastic to be real.

"I wish you no harm. Do you at least believe that?"

Marina studied his face, noting the smooth lines of his forehead and the earnest expression in the dark eyes. Suddenly she wanted to believe him. If he'd wanted to hurt her, he could have by now.

"I believe that," she conceded. "I just want to go home."

And he meant to send her there as soon as possible, before her presence was discovered by the government. There was another reason, too. He'd been giving a great deal of thought to the explosion of the vase. And he was beginning to wonder if it had resulted from an overloaded circuit or a miscalculation on his part.

The woman apparently hadn't noticed yet, but the squirrel wasn't eating. And it was acting rather odd. That could have been a result of being confined in a building or symptoms of something having gone wrong in the transfer.

But that wasn't his only worry. He'd taken MDAT's mother board to work that morning so he could duplicate the circuit. But there had been such a heavy concentration of guards everywhere he looked that he'd been unable to gain entrance to the storage room without a written order from Bartell.

Was this further proof that he was under investigation by the government? Until today he'd been able to remove from stock the needed components for their work without written consent. And on the way home, before they had reached the city sector, he'd seen a group of people being herded into a wagon by a squad of police.

It was becoming evident that the government's veneer of freedom for all was wearing thin. Would his people soon be reduced to living in a military state, where it would not be safe to walk down the street without fear of arrest?

His mission to the past was becoming crucial. Yet he couldn't begin it until the woman and her small companion were safely back where they belonged.

"It will take some time to repair MDAT. When it is ready, I will send you and your furry friend back to your own time."

"How long will that take?" She went along with him, and it seemed to appease him. That gave her hope that eventually he would tire of his game and set her free.

"I do not know. We are watched closely at work. And even here. That is why I protect you and the animal with the shield built into the Recep."

"Recep?"

"There." He pointed to where she'd first awakened to find herself lying on the floor. "That is the Recep. From there the vase departed on its long journey, and it is there that you and your companion appeared."

Marina looked with a jaundiced eye to the place where he pointed. "It looks like a metal frame," she said flatly.

"But it is an extraordinary frame. It keeps everything contained so nothing splits apart and gets lost during transference."

Marina shivered. The idea of any part of her anatomy splitting off and getting lost in another realm of time was too unpleasant to contemplate even in jest.

"That's all very interesting. But if your machine doesn't work, why can't you sneak Monday and me into your lab at work and beam us home?"

"There are strict security measures at work. You would never be allowed into Government House. And the machine there is not capable of getting you back all in one rpiece."

"What do you mean? I thought you said you worked on—"

"I do. But I have made greater progress with my machine than the one in the government lab."

Marina had a sudden unpalatable thought. "Are you telling me you're a *criminal?*"

Sammell stared at her without answering.

"You are, aren't you?" And by his own admission.

"The state would terminate me if they knew about MDAT," he admitted. "But it is nothing compared to what they would do to you," he reminded her in a voice edged with steel.

Marina gasped. "What do you mean?"

"I told you, in this *paradise* you would be... different... individual. The state does not like individuality. Conformity—that is what it breeds."

Sammell turned and paced away from her. "You want to know what my world is really like?"

He strode back to within a foot of her, the dark eyes glittering with resentment. "I will tell you. We dress alike, we look alike, we talk alike, we act alike.

"Everything we do is decided upon by the state. We go to school, study, work and mate according to the state.

"The state keeps telling us it has freed us from the need to make choices so we may live long lives of happiness and fulfillment. But in truth, for nearly four hundred years we have lived in chains of bondage forged by one man's desire to free us, only to make us *his* prisoners. And that is why I built MDAT.''

''Who is this man?''

''Our Founding Father, Carson B. Wyndom, president of the United States of America. He wanted to be king of the world and he succeeded. We are his subjects, subject to whatever whim he desires to make law. That is the only past we are allowed to know. It is taught to us while we are children in school.''

''Wait a minute! I thought you only had one name.''

''We do, but the royal family have two.''

''One man, nearly four hundred years old and still king? Do you expect me to believe that?''

''It is true. He lives and breathes—I have seen him.''

''That's fantastic.'' Marina shook her head in disbelief. He'd had her there for a while with his speech, but this was a bit too much to believe.

''It is true. When he became president, he was already a very powerful man. He had been a scientist himself before he turned to politics. And he had been working on several drugs that were to change the course of history.

''Before his election he turned the work over to the other scientists who were his trusted confederates. One of the drugs was a Methuselah drug—one that prolonged life. Another was a drug that controlled men's minds, rendering them incapable of insurrection. I call it the Wyndom drug, named after the monster who first discovered it. It is responsible for making my people slaves to King Wyndom.''

''What can *you* do about it?'' This was all slightly more than Marina could swallow.

''I will stop him before he destroys the past as he has destroyed the future.''

Kneeling before her, eyes blazing, he said in earnest, ''You see, in my time, there are no new peoples to conquer on planet Earth. Wyndom has spread his poison throughout the world.''

Marina shivered and drew back, frightened as much by his intensity as by what he was saying.

Sammell continued. "Now Wyndom wants to travel back in time and conquer the people of the past. We here are all robots and he would make robots of everyone down through history."

"Are you serious?" she asked with fear-widened eyes. But it was obvious that he believed it. And somehow, despite herself, she was beginning to take what he said seriously.

"Deadly so."

"What can one man do? How will a time machine help free your people?"

"In order to free my people, I must go back to the time when this all began. I must prevent Wyndom from developing his drug."

"But I thought you couldn't change the past." Marina dredged up what she'd learned in college about the fabric of time. "Isn't there something about creating a paradox that prohibits time from being changed?"

"That is an out-of-date theory. Time is like a cloth made of living thread. If you snag a thread, pull it or break it, another thread simply moves into place, thereby eliminating the hole and propagating the continuity of the cloth."

"I'm not certain I understand."

"Time itself cannot be changed, but events can be altered. The fabric of time merely flows around them."

She looked puzzled, so he tried to explain. "If you were to remain here for a period, then made a short visit back to your own time, you would find that you were no longer a part of that life. All evidence of your existence would be wiped out. But in this time you would have a past—a beginning—and a future."

"What if I were supposed to have married and have children? What of my family?"

"That would no longer be your fate. How could it, when you are here? Those children would be born to someone else and they would live out their lives as planned. You see? Time absorbs change, thereby creating a new space for a new event and absorbing an aborted one."

"You sound very certain of that. But how can you be, when you yourself said that you've never traveled in time?"

"You do not have to be a part of a machine to know how it works."

"Are you telling me that if I don't get back before long, all trace of my existence—my life—will disappear?"

Sammell couldn't look at her. He was overwhelmed by guilt for bringing her here and not wholly convinced that he could get her back. But he hadn't meant to add to her fears.

Instead of answering, he shrugged. It was a gesture he'd seen her make and it seemed appropriate in the circumstances.

Marina decided she would have to think about this conversation. It wasn't something she could assimilate all at once. She wasn't even certain she believed half of what he had said. It was all so... outside her previous realm of thought and understanding.

Was he telling her that fate was fate and you couldn't change it? That whatever happened—even if it was something so uncommonly bizarre as what was happening to her right now—it was all part of the great plan?

"I'm very tired," she murmured faintly. "I'm hungry again, too."

"I will get you more food."

"Apples and tomatoes?" she asked with a marked lack of enthusiasm. What she wouldn't give for a nice thick juicy steak.

"You would like something else?" He had no idea where he would get anything else, but if she wanted something in particular, he would try to find it. He owed her that.

"No, the fruit is fine. But where do you get it? I thought you didn't eat."

"We do not. But fruit and vegetables grow in abundance in the public gardens not far from here."

Sudden interest lit her eyes. "Public gardens?"

"Yes."

"Can we go? Please," she added before he could refuse. "I need fresh air and so does Monday." She turned to look for the squirrel. "Look, he's moping about like he's lost his best friend." She looked back at Sammell to see him eyeing her curiously. "Please?"

He gave a slight nod. "Tomorrow night—I will take you and your little friend out tomorrow night."

"At night?" Marina asked, suspicion returning to her voice. "Why at night?"

"It would not be safe for you in the daylight. You…" He stumbled over an explanation. "You are not like the women of my world."

"You mean my clothes?"

"Yes, but that is not all."

"No?" Marina slid off the table and stood with her hands on her hips. "Then what?"

"Well, there is all that hair." He motioned toward her head. "And the color."

Marina put a hand to her head. "What about the color? It's natural, I assure you."

"We do not have hair that color. Everyone has my color of hair."

"Everyone?" she asked skeptically.

"All except the ruling class." His glance touched on and skittered away from her chest. "And you are fuller—" he motioned with his hand "—up here."

Marina folded her arms across her chest in sudden embarrassment.

"And down here." Sammell indicated his own narrow hips.

"Are you trying to tell me I'm fat?" Marina demanded peevishly.

"No—there is just more of you. The women in my world are like this." He held his hands out a few inches apart. "You see? They are more like this."

"I would like to see them."

"No," Sammell said quickly. "We must go out at night to prevent that happening, not only because of your hair, but because of the color of your eyes."

"My eyes?"

"Only the high born—those who are descendants of the group who formed the original government coalition with Wyndom—have blue eyes."

"But...how is that possible?"

"Through genetics. They wanted a symbol of their royalty and they chose blue eyes and dark hair. Everyone else has eyes and hair the color of mine."

"You mean everyone has brown eyes and blond hair?" Marina asked in disbelief.

Sammell allowed his gaze to linger on her red curls as he nodded.

"I guess I'd stand out like a sore thumb among your people," she said with a half laugh. "In my time, I'm pretty ordinary. We have many different hair and eye colors. Some natural and quite a few artificial."

Sammell glanced down at both his thumbs, raising an eyebrow, then shrugged. "Artificial?"

"Yes. In my time, if you don't like the color of your hair, you can change it by dying it another color. And you can get colored contacts to change the color of your eyes."

All this surprised and interested Sammell, but there was more that he needed to tell her for her own safety. "There is another thing I must tell you. There is a curfew. It starts at seven in the evening and lasts until seven the next morning.

"Anyone caught outside their cell during that time is arrested. We must be very careful tomorrow night."

"But why? Is there crime? Somehow, I thought things like that didn't exist in your world."

"There is no crime. It is the law."

"What happens when you get arrested?"

"Termination."

"Termination? As in killed? What about prison?"

Sammell shrugged. "There are no prisons."

"None?"

"None."

Marina shuddered. She'd never thought the time would come when she'd be upset because someone told her prisons no longer existed and neither did crime.

She didn't like the picture he painted of his world. She would be glad to get back to her own—if any of this were true, and if he wasn't planning to kill her and dispose of her body somewhere in the dark tomorrow night.

"We must rest."

Marina nodded, suddenly exhausted.

"I would let you sleep in my chamber, but it would not be safe. I have a security device installed to warn me about visits by the police, but it would not give me enough time to ensure your safety before they arrived. In here I can shield you from discovery. Out there I cannot."

Marina nodded. She wouldn't mind sleeping on the floor tonight. She had a lot to think about.

Sammell left quickly. A few moments later, he returned carrying a pile of blankets and two pillows.

"These will make the floor a little less hard."

Marina took them from him and their fingers touched. Sammell drew back hastily from the contact, but she didn't notice. She was thinking how glad she was to have something to cover her, because suddenly she was feeling very cold.

Sammell left her to make her bed. He hadn't jerked away because he feared her touch; on the contrary, there was something very pleasant about the feel of her skin next to his. And that was why he couldn't sustain the contact.

Outside the lab he watched as she moved from the necessary to the Recep. When she sat down on the blankets and put two hands to the edge of her tank top, he turned on the energy shield and turned away. Now that she was becoming less an end product of an experiment that had gone awry, and more of a person to him, watching her without her knowledge seemed somehow wrong.

Chapter 5

The next day at work, Sammell spent a long time thinking about the woman and their conversation the night before. He didn't understand some of the things she said, but he liked talking to her. He was even beginning to look forward to spending more time with her.

Since he was planning a trip to the twentieth century, he needed to know how to interact with the people of her era. By spending time with her, he could learn many things he would need to know about the past and its people. And, too, there were many *good* things about his world that he would like to teach her.

Their planned trip to the public gardens that night would give him opportunity to study her closer. It would also give him a chance to prove that all he'd told her about his world was true. He suspected she wasn't convinced that she'd traveled nearly four hundred years into the future, and for her own safety she needed to believe it.

The trip to the gardens would be dangerous—it was always dangerous trying to evade the state police—but he'd done it many times alone. Tonight he would have to be extra careful, because it wasn't only his life he'd be risking.

He was surprised to realize that he was looking forward to it—to the time they'd spend together away from his lab in surroundings that she would undoubtedly find more to her liking. And he couldn't help wondering if she was looking forward to it—to spending more time with him, too.

As the day progressed, Sammell realized that Larkin was trying to get his attention without being obvious about it. But he avoided eye contact with the man. Since their conversation two days ago, he'd made no attempt to speak privately with him. Sammell knew he couldn't put Larkin off indefinitely, but at the moment he had more important matters on his mind.

He'd read through Larkin's notes from the day before, and there had been nothing in them about the plasma jet. That meant Sammell's secret was safe a little while longer. But he was worried. Last night after retiring, questions about Larkin's sudden desire for a private conversation about their work had plagued him. Had Larkin stumbled onto the fact that Sammell was deliberately delaying progress on project Deliverance? If so, why hadn't he gone to Bartell with his knowledge? What did he hope to gain from Sammell by his silence?

Until now there had been no indication that Larkin *wasn't* under the influence of the Wyndom drug. And though Sammell would have welcomed the man's input on his project at home, with these new developments both at home and at work, he couldn't take the chance. Not now, not with the woman's safety at stake.

The day passed slowly, and Sammell found himself inspecting the faces of everyone in the lab, wondering who—if any—had taken MDAT's mother board from his desk. He found himself delving past the slightly glazed look in their eyes caused by the drug and trying to ferret out what lay beneath. But he soon realized how impossible it was for him to know with any amount of certainty whether their sub-

missive air was a result of the drug, or only a skillfully
drawn mask, like his own.

He had to consider the possibility that the board had been
taken by someone other than a member of his own team.
Bartell could be the culprit. Not he himself—he wouldn't do
such a menial task, but he might have sent one of his minions to do it.

It wouldn't be the first time he'd done such a thing. But
there was a problem with that theory, too. To an untrained
eye, the mother board looked like all the others in Sammell's drawer. There was only one difference—one very important difference. And the thief had recognized it.

Sammell glanced up to see Gissel and Darryn with their
heads close together near the model of the plasma jet. His
eyes narrowed on the pair. It was not unusual to see a male
and female working closely on a project, despite government restrictions on their contact outside of work, but there
was something about these two.... Was their closeness only
in the lab?

Since the day it had appeared as though the pair was trying to listen to the private conversation he and Larkin had
been having, Sammell had been studying them keenly. He
noticed the manner in which they now stood close together
without touching, and he sensed something more between
them than a shared interest in their work.

A vision of the woman in his lab rose before his mind's
eye, and Sammell felt a tightening in his lower abdomen.
The feeling was becoming all too familiar. And though he
tried his best to disregard it, the feeling persisted.

The accidental brush of hands between Gissel and Darryn registered somewhere at the back of his mind, but Sammell's thoughts were on Marina. His lips mouthed the name.
He'd never spoken it aloud, but he'd wanted to.

Marina awoke with a feeling of unease. She no longer
awoke feeling disoriented. This place and the man who held
her captive now followed her into her dreams. But this sen-

sation was different. Something in the lab was different. Had her jailer returned?

She cocked an ear to listen. Someone was definitely in the lab—*but it wasn't Sammell!* There was more than one pair of footsteps!

Her first instinct was to shout for help. She even got to her knees with that thought in mind. But as her lips parted, Sammell's voice rang inside her head. *"I keep you here for your own safety...."*

Marina hesitated. What if he was telling the truth? What if her safety depended on no one else's knowing about her presence in his lab?

Footsteps crossed the floor and came close to where she sat huddled in the Recep. Goose flesh pebbled her arms and legs. She felt so vulnerable. Where was Sammell?

He'd told her that he protected her with some kind of energy shield, but she didn't understand any of that. It was all part of the fantastic story he wanted her to swallow about having been transported to the future.

She stared apprehensively at the wall around her. It was like no other wall she'd ever seen. It appeared to have no substance, unlike brick or wood, yet it was opaque and resistant to outside pressure. Somehow it made her feel as though she was trapped inside a living thing.

Should she make her presence known?

What if everything he'd told her was true? No, that was impossible! But why would he lie? Maybe he was crazy.

It was just all so incredible. How could an ordinary woman get caught up in something so implausible by simply going for an afternoon stroll in the park to feed the squirrels? Things like this just didn't happen!

Wrapping her arms around herself, Marina shivered. Surely whoever was in the lab could see this curtain—or energy field, or whatever it was around her.

What would happen if they found her? Would she be arrested as Sammell had said? She blocked the rest of what he'd said from her mind. She was learning things about

herself in this place that she had never known, like the fact
that she had a very graphic imagination.

As the footsteps grew closer and seemed to be right outside the wall shielding her from view, Marina clamped a
hand over her mouth to keep from crying out. A part of her
wanted to shout at the top of her lungs for them to let her
out of this prison, but another part of her wanted to shout
for Sammell to come and save her from this new threat.

"It appears that Lord Bartell is mistaken," someone said
behind the wall opposite Marina's head. She jerked around
to stare at the spot where she thought they had to be standing. "I see nothing out of the ordinary here."

Marina heard a click as though something had been
switched on, but no sound followed.

"I agree," a second, deeper voice responded. The click
came again. "Lord Bartell imagines subversion in everything he sees or hears. I think his desire to leave Government House and reside in Summit House has unbalanced his
thinking."

"Maybe it is caused by something in his food," another
voice suggested wryly. A short brittle silence followed, and
then the room erupted in laughter.

"Yes," the first voice commented dryly, "perhaps that is
it. Come, let us go, we have more *legitimate* duties to per-
form."

Crouched in her hiding place, Marina listened to the
footsteps cross the floor. When she could no longer hear
them, she removed her hands from her mouth and threw
herself facedown on the pillows.

What had she done? The opportunity to make a bid for
freedom had been within her grasp, and she'd let it slip away
without so much as a peep.

Maybe *she* was the one who was crazy.

"Who is Lord Bartell?"

Sammell's movements became arrested. "Where did you
hear that name?" he finally asked, looking up from trying
to coax Monday into his arms.

"Who is he?"

"The director of project Deliverance."

"That's the time travel thing you're working on?"

"Yes."

"Why is it called Deliverance?"

"King Wyndom intends delivering the people of the past from their bondage."

"Bondage?" Marina frowned. "What kind of bondage?"

"The bondage caused by having to make decisions."

"That's called freedom where I come from. Do you believe in this project?"

Still on his knees, Sammell turned to face her. "No."

"Then why are you working on it?"

"I told you last night, I have no choice."

"Someone was here today," she said abruptly. "I think it was three men. They mentioned a *Lord* Bartell."

"One of Bartell's inspection squads," Sammell said flatly.

"Is that who it was?" She scrutinized his face closely. "It wasn't a few friends you sent over to try to convince me this whole crazy story you've told me is true?"

"Is that what you believe?"

"Is there any reason I shouldn't?"

"I have no friends."

"Then maybe you promised some *acquaintances* money to do a little play-acting."

Sammell smiled. "We have no money."

Marina noted his smile with a little shock of surprise. He was a handsome man; he should smile more often. "What are you saying—you don't use money? How do you pay for things?"

"What *things?* Everything we need is provided by the state."

"Everything?"

"Yes."

"But you know what money is." Her glance narrowed. "How is that?"

"Money is a rate of exchange used in your world." He crossed the floor to one of the shelves along the wall, opened a door and removed a small box. Opening it, he removed a pile of papers. "That information is here—you can read it for yourself." He held the box out to her. When she didn't move, he closed the box and returned it to the cabinet.

"It is getting late," Sammell said. "The security patrol is making its rounds on the other side of the city at this moment. If we hurry, we can get into the woods before they reach this sector."

Marina hesitated. "I am not moving until you tell me who *Lord* Bartell is."

"He is the king's representative. He governs the Western Hemisphere of the World State. And he is the director of project Deliverance."

"You mean he's your boss?"

Sammell looked affronted. "He is a man I do not trust."

Scooping Monday up in her arms—the animal had refused to go to Sammell—she followed him across the room to the door.

In the viewing room, she stood back and watched as Sammell placed his hand against a panel high in the center of the door. It began to glow with an amber light. A moment later, it changed to a pale green and the door slid soundlessly open.

"Hurry," Sammell said in hushed tones. "We must get into the woods without being seen. And from here on, do not speak unless you must."

Marina peered into the darkness. She didn't know what she had expected in light of all that Sammell had told her, but she certainly wasn't expecting the normality of a moonlit sky filled with radiant stars. Nor was she prepared for the sight of lights shining in the windows of cottagelike houses scattered among the trees.

Where was this world of the future Sammell had prepared her for with his talk of wonder drugs and time travel?

Sammell moved swiftly over the ground, darting from shadow to shadow with Marina on his heels, keeping pace.

But after a while she began to have difficulty keeping up with him. In no time at all she was out of breath and lagging behind.

"W-where are w-we going?" she panted, galloping to catch up with him.

Sammell paused to wait for her. "To the public gardens."

"Where are th-they, in the next county?"

"County?"

"N-never mind. How m-much farther to the g-gardens?"

"To the center of town."

"C-center of town?" Frowning, Marina stopped short. "If you're trying to s-stay away from the p-police, why are we going to the center of t-town?"

Sammell slowed, turned toward her stationary figure and backpedaled. "That is where we will find food for you and your little friend. Come—hurry, we have a long way to go."

A few minutes later they were deep in a thick woods. Marina stumbled over a vine and would have fallen if she hadn't grabbed at Sammell's back.

"What is wrong?"

"You're g-going too fast. I can't keep up with you. And besides—" she put a hand to her forehead "—I feel a little dizzy."

"Perhaps it is the air. I believe you had a pollution problem in your century. Our air is clean and pure," he said proudly.

"Nonsense," Marina muttered. She'd seen the mountains in the distance. "It's the altitude. Where are we, anyway?"

"You would know this place as Colorado."

"Colorado?" Marina stopped short. "I've never been to Colorado."

"You are there now. Come," he said, motioning for her to follow, "we have not reached our destination."

On the move again, they hugged the trees, stopping every few minutes so Sammell could pull a pair of strange-looking glasses down over his eyes and examine the woods around them. It was taking longer than he'd planned for them to reach the gardens. He should have realized the woman at his side would not be in the same physical condition as one of his own people.

"Why couldn't we have taken a car?" Marina asked petulantly.

Pushing the infrared goggles onto his forehead with one hand, he frowned at her. "Car?"

"Yes, you know, those things you put gas in and drive wherever you want to go. I'm all for exercise, but I hadn't planned on taking part in a marathon."

"Oh, yes, you mean the vehicles with gasoline-driven engines."

"That's what I said—cars."

"We do not use those kinds of conveyances."

"Then how do you get from one place to another? Surely you don't walk everywhere."

"Walking is good exercise. So is riding a bicycle and riding horseback."

Marina came to a sudden stop. "Are you kidding?"

"Kidding?"

"You know—no, you probably don't. I mean—gosh! Has mankind progressed right back to the eighteenth century?"

Sammell didn't understand all that she said, but he knew criticism when he heard it. "The gasoline-driven engine was greatly responsible for the pollution in your time," he was quick to point out. "We prefer clean air and healthy bodies. My ancestors found a way to repair the ozone layer your people were responsible for damaging," he added arrogantly. "We want to keep it intact."

"Do you mean to tell me that a society that can live without eating has to depend on dumb animals to get them where they want to go?"

"We ride bicycles," he reminded her.

"What about long distances? Are you telling me there are no mechanized vehicles in your world?"

"The king has a solar-powered airplane and the police use solar-powered vehicles. But we do not own such things. Our king has made it so that we have no use for them."

Dumbfounded, Marina let herself be led farther into the trees. If he was telling the truth...

Sammell felt something bounce against the back of his hand and the woman slipped her cold fingers into his. For an instant, he resisted, then closed his larger fingers around her smaller ones and they continued on their way in silence, the only sound the crunch of leaves and brush beneath their feet.

Very conscious of the fingers clutching his, Sammell kept an eye out for signs of a government patrol, hoping they would complete their journey without encountering one. Another fifteen minutes had passed before they came to the edge of the thick woods and Sammell halted to study their surroundings.

Marina gawked at the quaint locale in surprise. If she didn't know better, she'd think she had stepped into a Currier and Ives print. Gaslight lamps lined a wide cobblestone street. The street was clean, the grass at its side neatly trimmed and the night air drenched with an intoxicating perfume. Her glance moved to the entrance to the gardens where a profusion of flowering vines trailed beneath tall leafy trees swaying in the gentle evening breeze. She recognized magnolia and mimosa...and suddenly caught herself. Since when did magnolia trees grow in Colorado?

"Is that our destination?" Marina asked.

"Yes." The word was little more than the stirring of air as it passed over her ears.

"It's beautiful," she whispered in awe. "What are we waiting for?"

"That," Sammell breathed, nodding toward the end of the street as he pulled her down into the cover of bushes.

Marina peered through the branches, straining to catch a glimpse of what the man at her side had seen through his glasses. And then her ears picked up the clippety-clop of horses' hooves on the cobblestone street. But it was several seconds before she could actually discern the figures emerging from the blackness into the light.

Her eyes widened on four men riding abreast, mounted on horses as black as India ink. As they passed into the light, Marina saw that they were all dressed alike. From the tops of their golden blond heads to the black form-fitting tunic and tight black trousers tucked into shiny black thigh boots, nothing distinguished one from the other.

As they drew closer, she saw they were wearing goggles similar to those that Sammell wore. Her glance settled on the peculiar-looking weapons holstered on their hips, and a wave of revulsion washed over her. The four horsemen reminded her of Hitler's SS troops. The only thing missing was the red armband with a black swastika on a white background.

"Who are they?" Marina asked through stiff lips as she moved closer to Sammell.

"Security patrol."

"I don't think I'm hungry anymore." She stared at the end of the dark street where the mounted men had disappeared.

"We have exactly thirty minutes until the next patrol comes along," Sammell said. "And that one goes into the gardens to search for curfew breakers."

Grasping her hand tighter, he pulled her along as he crouched low, looked up and down the street, then hurried across it to the gardens.

Once they were in the gardens, Marina's fear slowly faded and delight took its place as she noted the stone benches, colorfully lighted fountains and small waterfalls, fish ponds and a variety of flowers she couldn't even begin to name. And then, centered in a maze at the middle of the gardens, they came upon something so utterly at odds with the natural beauty of their surroundings that Marina was unnerved.

In a circular clearing, a monument rose the height of a two-story building. It depicted men, women and children in the throes of agony, deformed, bleeding and dying, their faces frozen in eternal grimaces of such pain and suffering that it was hard to look at their agony.

"My God, what is that?" Marina asked backing away.

"That is your world."

"What?" Marina jerked a questioning glance at his face.

"That is a reminder from our good King Wyndom of what the world was like before he brought peace and order to the people and restored life to the Earth."

"You've got to be kidding. My world looks nothing like that," she said angrily. "Suffering exists and we do what we can to alleviate it, but life is beautiful and good," she added earnestly. It seemed very important all at once for him to realize that her world was not a thing of horror as his king would have him believe.

"There were things I would have changed about it," she admitted, "but it wasn't all bad. In fact, there are a lot of wonderful things you should know about. Like picnics, and music, and Christmas, and friends, and babies—"

"Is something wrong?" Sammell asked, when she suddenly stopped speaking.

"I said *were*—I said there *were* things I would like to have changed...."

Her eyes widened in anxiety. Did that mean she believed him—believed that her terrible-wonderful world was gone? And this—her eyes quickly scaled the monument—this is what had taken its place?

"That thing should be destroyed," she said angrily. "It's loathsome!"

Monday scrambled out of her arms and up onto her shoulder, reminding her that all was not lost. They were merely visitors to this place of horrors. The man beside her had promised to send them home.

"I think your little friend is hungry," Sammell said, hoping to take her mind off unhappy things. "Here." He indicated a spot where the underbrush thinned out and the trees and vines provided a sheltered hiding place. "This spot will provide us with protection while we gather food for you and...Monday?" He glanced at her questioningly.

"Yes, Monday. I named him that because that's the day all this began," Marina said over her shoulder, as she scooted through the cramped opening to find herself in a small clearing filled with trees whose limbs were heavy with fruit. Monday scrambled out of her arms and dashed out of sight.

She made as though to dart after him, but Sammell stopped her.

"He knows best what he wants to eat. Let him go. He will come back."

Marina hesitated, then shrugged. He was probably right. And even if he didn't return, it would be better for him to be here than locked up in the lab.

"How do you know this place?" she asked, picking an armful of ripe apples from the ground.

"I have been here before."

Marina sat down with her back against a tree and placed one of the red apples against her lips. After taking a healthy bite, she patted a place beside her. "Come and sit down and tell me why you come to this particular spot, if not to eat the fruit? And why do your people grow such luscious fruit, if not for consumption?"

Sammell hesitated before taking a seat a short distance from her. "It is grown for its beauty. And research."

Marina looked around her. "It is beautiful here." Picking up an apple, she offered it to him. "Are you sure you don't want one?"

He shook his head.

Marina cocked her head and studied him. "So why do you come here, if not to eat?"

"This is the best hiding place in the gardens. I like to sit beneath the trees and think."

Settling more comfortably against her tree, Marina considered his answer. It was a sound one. That's why she went to the park where she'd met Monday. Something in nature made her forget all the petty trials and tribulations she faced day to day and helped her remember the good things in life.

"Tell me more about your world," she invited him, nibbling on the fruit at the core.

"My world," Sammell repeated softly. "Do you believe this is my world and not yours?"

With another apple halfway to her lips, Marina hesitated. "I don't want to," she answered honestly, "but unless this is some elaborate hoax—for which I can see no purpose—then I guess I have to, don't I?"

"Thank you." Sammell felt relief wash over him. It would make things so much simpler if she put aside her doubt and trusted him. And for some reason it had become very important to him that she trust him. "What would you like to know?"

"These drugs you mentioned yesterday—are they real? Is there actually a drug that will keep you from aging?"

"It exists."

"And the stuff you say is in your food—you know for certain that it's there?"

"I know it is there. One day, when I was a boy, I returned to my cell after school to find my parents gone. I broke curfew and went to search for them. I never found them. But I did not want to go back to the empty cell.

"I hid in the woods near the public gardens. It got late and after a while I fell asleep. The next day I knew it was too late to return to the cell. By then the security patrols would be looking for me.

"For several weeks I hid in the woods, and during that time did not take my nutrient injections. As time passed I became weaker and weaker. During the day I observed the animals gather their food.

"One day I saw a bird pull a worm from the ground and eat it. I needed nourishment, so I tried it myself—"

"Ugh," Marina broke into the story, "you ate a worm?"

"I tried many things and almost all of them came back up. But gradually I managed to keep some down and I grew a little stronger.

"More days passed and I began to realize that I was changing. I felt different and I was beginning to view the

world around me with different eyes. Inside me, there wa
this growing curiosity to know about everything. And the
one day I was reckless and the police captured me."

"What did they do to you?" Marina paused in her eat
ing to ask.

"I was questioned about my parents, but I did not know
what had happened to them. Eventually I was placed in the
cell of a government official whose child had grown int
adulthood and left to live in his own cell.

"I think they put me there because they did not believe
did not know where my parents had gone. I lived with the
government official until I left school in my twentieth year
And that is how I know many of the things I know abou
King Wyndom. He was a frequent visitor to my benefac
tor's cell."

"And the drug?"

"For a while I was given my nutrient injections instead o
being allowed to take them myself. I think they wanted to
make certain I got them. The drug must accumulate in the
body over a period of time to reach its maximum effective
ness.

"But a curious thing happened. Even after the injection
were begun again, I still felt different. Observing the other
around me, I soon realized that we were different—except
for the government people.

"Perhaps my parents knew about the drug and had
learned to remove it from our nutrients and that is why they
disappeared.

"When I began taking my own shots again, I gave my
self only half doses. And at night I would sneak out and
come here and eat a few bites of something to supplement
them.

"When I began living in my own cell, I researched the
nutrient injections, isolated the substance placed there by
the government and removed it from my own supply before
taking the injection."

Marina looked at him in amazement. "You must have been one very smart child to put all that together and figure it all out."

"Children have nothing else to do but learn. And perhaps I learned my lessons a little better than some others."

"But why didn't you go to someone and tell them what you had discovered?"

"Who? Everyone is under the drug's influence, except for those directly involved in the government. And they are a part of the conspiracy. I would have been terminated."

"Oh. And you've never trusted anyone enough to tell them about the drug?"

"I trusted you."

The bite of apple she was swallowing became lodged at the back of her throat. She coughed, swallowed and changed the subject.

"How old were you when your parents disappeared?"

"Twelve."

"And you never heard from your parents again?"

"Never."

"Well, didn't you ever wonder about them?"

"Sometimes. But if they left on their own, they chose to leave me behind. And if the police took them away, then they are dead."

"How sad," she murmured. She couldn't imagine living in such a world. Even though she didn't see her family as much as she'd have liked, she loved them and knew they loved her.

A rustling in the bushes heralded the arrival of Monday. Marina laughed as he dropped acorns in a neat pile near her knee before scurrying back through the trees.

She turned to find Sammell's glance on her face. "Do I have juice running down my chin?" she asked self-consciously, wiping the back of one hand across her mouth and chin.

"No," he answered solemnly. But he couldn't seem to take his eyes off her. She was so...different. He wanted to watch and memorize every little thing about her so that when she was gone, he could remember every expression, every movement, every smile.

"Do you really think you can go back in time to prevent the drug from being produced?" Marina asked, wishing he wouldn't stare at her so intently.

"If I do not, your world will become like mine."

"And if you do," she said softly, a hint of something in her voice that he didn't understand, "then this conversation will never take place. Because you won't need to build a time machine and I won't get caught up in it."

"Our time here is growing short," Sammell said abruptly. "Tell me more of your world."

Marina had eaten her fill. She wiped her hands on the grass and stretched out on the ground on her side, cupping her head in one hand. "What would you like to know?"

"Tell me about your life. What was your youth like?"

"Well, I was the youngest of four children. My siblings are all boys. My mother owns a flower shop and my father is a contractor."

"Contractor?"

"He builds things like houses—cells," she amended for his benefit. "I was raised in a big house on the edge of a small town in Indiana. We grew up with Fourth of July celebrations, Labor Day picnics and large family get-togethers at Thanksgiving and Christmas.

"My brothers were overprotective and chased off all my boyfriends until I left home. But I love them, anyway. When I grew up I went to college in Arizona and liked it so much that I decided to stay. I see my family at the holidays."

Sammell had listened attentively to every word she said, not completely understanding all of it because it was so foreign to anything he knew. But the sound of her voice and the play of emotions crossing her delicate features held him in thrall.

"It sounds like a wonderful place, your world. But there is much about it I do not understand. What are holidays and what are picnics?"

"Well, holidays are days you celebrate with family and friends. And we don't go to work or to school." She thought about how to simplify the explanation of a picnic. "You take food and drink to a park or woods and eat sitting like this on the ground."

"We are having a picnic?"

"Well, sort of, except you didn't eat anything—"

"Silence!" Sammell dived toward her, shoving her against the ground, his head cocked in a listening attitude, fear a sheet of ice down his back. He'd seen what the weapons the patrol carried could do one night when he'd stayed in the gardens too long. They homed in on any heat-producing body, identified it in a matter of seconds and if it were human sent a heat-seeking missile to incinerate it. If there hadn't been another curfew breaker on the grounds that night, he probably wouldn't have been here now.

"What is it?" she whispered next to his ear. His upper body lay across her chest, making it hard for her to breathe. She could feel him trembling against her. He was heavier than he looked.

"Patrol," he mouthed almost silently, the words getting stuck at the back of his throat. "They are early."

"What do we do?" Her heart began to pound at the thought of coming face-to-face with the four men on horseback she'd seen earlier.

Coming up onto his knees beside her, Sammell put an arm beneath her shoulders and helped her up. Together they crawled deeper into the bush. His fear was suddenly so great that he couldn't answer her question. He didn't know what to do.

Marina knew she ought to have been terrified out of her wits. She was closer to death than she'd ever been in her life, but strangely enough she wasn't afraid. She glanced at her companion's rigid profile. He certainly wasn't built along the lines of the traditional hero, yet she trusted him implicitly to get them out of this situation without either of them coming to harm.

She didn't understand how she could put such trust in the man, when only a short time ago she'd thought him her kidnapper. But then neither did she understand the aura of innocence surrounding him, or the sudden desire she felt to know him better. Maybe it was because he was like no man she'd ever known, and after this brief interval in her life she might never know anyone like him again.

Chapter 6

"Sammell, what will they do to us if they find us here?"

He could hear the fear in her voice, feel her closing the distance between them, and suddenly his courage returned.

"They will not find us," he said evenly, straining to see through the trees.

"But what would they do if they did?" she persisted.

"We have broken curfew," he said slowly.

"And?"

"We would be arrested."

"But... you said there are no jails...."

He turned slowly to face her. "I know," he whispered softly, resting his cheek against cool earth, the answer to her question in his dark eyes.

Marina's eyes widened. "You mean they'd... terminate us—just because we're out after curfew?" She could feel panic rising inside her. "But that's ridiculous! You don't kill someone just because—"

"That will not happen," he said across the rising hysteria in her words. "I will get us out of here." He tried to speak calmly, though he felt every bit as anxious as the

woman beside him. But he knew better than to give in to the
fear clawing like a raging beast inside him.

Marina wasn't as successful in her bid for control. Too
much had happened too fast in the past few days, and she
was beginning to feel like an animal trapped in a cage. She
had to get out of the gardens before she gave in to the feelings that had been steadily building since she had awakened in this strange new world, and she began to scream.

As though he sensed what she was feeling, Sammell
moved closer until there was little more than a whisper-thin
current of air between them.

"I will protect you." His eyes looked deeply into hers. He
could see her terror. And though he didn't know how to
calm her, he knew he had to try. Both their lives depended
on his keeping her from giving away their position to the
police.

"I brought you here. I will not let anything happen to
you. Trust me."

He wasn't aware that he'd moved, but suddenly he felt her
soft cheek against his palm. The sensation moved through
him like an electric current. And once the feeling had
started, his hand seemed to have a will of its own. As though
a distant observer, he watched it smooth the tangle of bright
hair from her forehead and remove a red curl stuck to her
lips, threading it behind one small shell-pink ear.

Sammell's glance returned to her mouth. How red her lips
looked. The upper one was delicately bowed at the center,
the bottom one full and trembling.

"I trust you, Sammell," Marina whispered, her face lifting slightly, her glance leveled on his mouth. Was he going
to kiss her?

As though her voice broke whatever spell held him, Sammell gave his head a slight shake and blinked. His hand was
tangled in the red curls, his face hovering near hers.

Jerking his hand from her hair as though from flame,
Sammell shrank from her, confused by the strong mixture
of feeling inside him and the changes he felt taking place in
his body.

Marina frowned. "What's wrong?"

"Nothing." He pulled the goggles over his eyes and turned quickly toward the trees.

"Sammell? What did I do?" she asked in a puzzled voice. She'd never wanted anything so badly as she'd wanted his kiss just now. Had he sensed that and been repulsed by it?

"We must concentrate on getting out of the gardens without being seen." His aura of untouchability was once more firmly in place and it piqued Marina's sense of femininity.

"A moment ago you were concentrating on me," Marina said boldly, risking his disgust. "What happened?"

When he didn't answer, she put a compelling hand on his shoulder. The muscles turned rigid beneath her fingers. She removed her hand slowly, staring at the back of his head in affront. "Sammell..."

"My world is different from yours," he said unevenly. "We do not *touch*."

"You don't touch? What do you mean, you don't touch?"

"We do not touch each other."

"You mean never?"

"Never—not deliberately."

"But what about husbands and wives? Don't they touch?"

"No." He was feeling very uncomfortable. He'd never discussed touching with anyone. And discussing it with her, especially after what had happened just now, made him feel...

"That's the most ridiculous thing I've ever heard," Marina said abruptly. "How can two people living in the same house—two married people—not touch? What about children? How do you get children, if you don't touch?"

"We must discuss this later. The police are very close. This may be our only opportunity to get out of the gardens undetected."

Rising to his feet, he motioned for her to stay behind him. In silence they moved toward the hidden entrance to their hideaway. "Oh, wait! Monday hasn't come back!"

Marina whirled toward the pile of acorns. Sammell was right behind her, reaching for her before he realized it.

"We have to go now!" he said urgently, withdrawing his hand before it made contact. "Your friend will be all right. He has plenty of family in these woods."

"No!" Marina said angrily, searching for a glimpse of the small furry animal through the dense undergrowth. Monday was her only contact with home. She couldn't leave him behind—it would be like giving up the idea of ever seeing her friends and family again.

On her hands and knees, she crawled to the gap in the underbrush where the small squirrel had disappeared. "I have to find him! He has to come back with me."

"Marina—we have no time for this," Sammell whispered desperately. "The police—"

"Don't you understand?" she asked suddenly, stopping her frenzied search to stare up at him with tear-bright eyes. "I have to find him! He's all I have...." Her lips trembled and a tear spilled onto one cheek.

Sammell stared at the drop of moisture in awe. He knew the lacrimal glands had the ability to produce tears, but he'd just never seen one.

A sudden rustling from the bushes drew both their glances. Monday scurried into view.

Marina gave a soft cry of welcome and held out her arms. As though they'd been friends for years, Monday leaped into them and she cradled him against her.

Sammell had never seen anything like the bond between this woman and the animal. He'd never shared such a closeness with another living thing, and it made him feel left out.

Filling his hands with the acorns piled on the ground at their feet, Sammell led the way out of the gardens. They sped along in silence, across the cobblestone road and into the trees at the other side, wary of stumbling on the police.

Sammell was concerned with getting his charges safely behind the walls of his cell, but Marina's thoughts were on Sammell. It helped her to forget her fear by concentrating on something else, and she wanted to know a whole lot more about the man at her side and the world that he lived in.

As they moved like wraiths through the shadows, she studied him at every opportunity, but since leaving the park, he'd kept the goggles pulled over his eyes, preventing her from seeing his expression. It was hard to believe that a person could grow to adulthood without ever knowing the touch of another human being. And the thought of Sammell's never having *touched* anyone—never having kissed or caressed a woman—intrigued her.

She wondered if he'd ever wanted to kiss a woman, despite the restrictions against it. How could men and women live and work together without becoming attracted to each other? What about proximity? It was human nature to become fixated on those with whom one spent a lot of time. What did they do to combat the natural desire to mate?

And then she remembered the drug Sammell had mentioned to her. Could there be something in it that prevented them from feeling the need for a closer relationship with each other? Maybe after years of taking it, it destroyed one's physical capabilities.

Marina eyed her companion speculatively. Was that it? Was Sammell physically incapable of making love to a woman?

"How much farther?" she asked breathlessly, unable to recognize anything familiar in their surroundings.

"Just through those trees," Sammell responded.

And then they were running and Sammell was at the door. He placed his hand in the identaplate, and a second later Marina was leaning against the inside wall of the cell with her eyes closed, trying to catch her breath.

Sammell leaned against the opposite wall, watching her. He'd felt her eyes on him several times on the journey back, and had wondered what she was thinking. Was she comparing him to the men of her world?

"Did you have someone in your world that you...
touched?"

Marina's eyes popped open. "What?"

"Was there someone you were close to in your world,
someone you touched...who touched you?"

Was he asking if she had a boyfriend?

"No." She shook her head emphatically. There had been
no one in her life for a long time. Pushing away from the
wall, she bent to set Monday on his feet.

Straightening, she pushed the hair back from her hot face.
All at once she felt embarrassed by the very personal nature of the thoughts she'd been having about Sammell and
by his query just now. Without looking directly at him, she
said, "I need to visit the bath—necessary room."

Sammell led the way to the lab, watching her disappear
inside. He'd said something wrong. She was angry with him
again.

Going to the cooling unit where water and the nutrient
injections were stored, Sammell poured two glasses of cold
water. A few minutes later Marina joined him, and he offered her a glass.

"Did you enjoy the trip?" He sensed her disquiet. He
wished they could go back to the easy relationship they'd
shared for a brief time in the gardens. He'd never had that
feeling with anyone and he liked it.

"Yes. Thank you for taking me." Marina took a long
drink of water, eyeing him over the rim of the glass. "And
thank you for the fruit. It was delicious." God, she sounded
like a school girl politely thanking her uncle for giving her
a treat. "I only wish I'd thought to bring some of the fruit
with me," she added lamely, uncomfortable beneath his
stare.

"It is better that you did not." Sammell drained his glass
and set it on the table. "It is hard to hide fruit," he explained, catching the puzzled expression flitting over her
face. "It decays. The acorns will not be a problem."

Marina wrinkled her nose. "Oh—yes. I suppose it would be pretty hard to explain having food in your cell when you aren't supposed to eat it."

Finishing the water, she placed her glass alongside his and then she couldn't seem to take her eyes off the two glasses sitting so intimately beside each other. Darting a swift glance at Sammell from the corner of her eye, she noted that he, too, was studying the glasses.

What was he thinking? His expression was unreadable. Was he remembering the way he'd touched her cheek in the gardens?

"You are no doubt tired," he said abruptly, tearing his eyes from the glasses.

"Yes," she answered awkwardly. She hadn't felt this inept since her first date. Yet she didn't really want to be alone.

"You may sleep now, if you would like."

"Yes—thank you."

Sammell followed her into the lab and stood awkwardly while she made herself comfortable on the floor inside the Recep. "I am sorry about this," he said, indicating the sleeping arrangements.

After her experience earlier that day, when the lab had been invaded by one of the government inspection squads, she understood perfectly why she had to stay in the Recep. And after the police she'd seen tonight, she felt glad to be sleeping in a place where she would be protected against discovery by one of them.

"It's okay."

"Okay," Sammell repeated slowly. "At times you have a strange way of speaking."

Marina smiled wryly. *She* had a strange way of speaking?

"Sleep well."

"You too."

A moment later the energy curtain shielded him from view, and Marina felt homesickness swamp her. What would she be doing this minute if she was back in her own world?

"Sammell—are you still there?"

He turned quickly toward the sound of her voice. He felt disinclined to leave her. "Yes."

"Tell me more about the men and women of your world."

"We marry, as I have said before." He could hear her moving around behind the wall. "And we have one child."

"One child? Who makes that decision?"

"The state." He wondered what she was doing.

"The state chooses your mate and decides how many children you can have?"

"Yes."

"What if you want more than one child—or don't want a child at all?"

"The choice is not ours."

"It's just so hard to believe that you don't even know the woman you're going to marry."

"Sometimes we do. Intellect as well as genetics go into the choice. Sometimes the person with whom you work becomes your mate." The rustling sounds had stopped.

"That's positively feudal! Why do you put up with it?"

"The drug."

"Oh—yes, I'd forgotten about that." His mentioning it brought her earlier question to mind, but she hesitated. She hesitated so long that she wondered if he'd left.

"Sammell?"

"Yes."

"What about children?"

He frowned. "I told you—"

"Yes, I know, but how..." How could she put this delicately? "If you aren't allowed to touch, how do you..." She bit her lip. There *was* no delicate way to put it.

Understanding where her question was leading, Sammell answered, "Fertilization takes place in a lab. The man donates and so does his mate. The child is biologically theirs."

"And the child? Does the mother carry it?"

"Carry it?"

"Yes—inside her womb."

"No," he answered after a long pause, putting a hand to his forehead. The skin felt warm and moist. "Gestation takes place in an incubator," he continued, confused by the changes beginning to take place in his body. "After gestation the baby is released to its biological parents."

"And you don't share the same bed—sleep chamber—ever?"

Sammell was uncomfortable talking about this. "No."

"You don't make love?" Marina asked boldly.

"No." Marina heard the reluctance in his voice. "The act of making love was banned a generation ago. It confused people—made them lose control. It kept them from reaching their full potential as useful citizens. Society is now run on a strict regimen of work."

"And do you believe that? Do you believe love is something bad?"

Sammell avoided giving a direct answer. He could not speak intelligently on a subject he knew nothing about. "My world has achieved a high level of existence without the loss of life. Everyone works toward maintaining that level. The government would have us believe that control is necessary to maintain it."

"What about love? Love makes life worth living."

"I know nothing about this thing you call love."

"What's the purpose in all this?" Marina gestured, though he couldn't see her. "Why do you get married? It's a farce. Why have a child, if not to love? Where is the meaning—where is the joy—in your life?"

Sammell had been asking similar questions of himself for a long time. "I do not know. We do as we are told—we have always done as we are told."

"Not always," she corrected. "You told me about a time when you broke the rules. That's how you learned of the drug. And you're planning to destroy it. That certainly isn't following the rules. Are there no others like you?" She couldn't believe everyone had gone along with such a shallow philosophy without protest. "Has no one ever rebelled?"

"I do not know," he answered stiffly. He felt her contempt as though it were directed at him. "I am not aware of such a rebellion."

"My, God! I feel sorry for you," she whispered passionately. "I feel sorry for all of you! I'll take my world with all its problems and imperfections over the sterility of this one, any day. I don't know how you manage to stay alive. I would die here."

Sammell's heart missed a beat. "That is why I built MDAT," he said quickly. He drew closer to the energy curtain, wanting her to know he wasn't like the others. "Can you not understand?" he whispered urgently, wanting her to see him in a different light. "I want to change my world!"

"I hope you can. I hope it isn't too late." After several moments of silence, Marina whispered, "Good night, Sammell. Sleep tight."

"Good night...Marina."

As his footsteps faded, Marina realized that he'd spoken her name, not only just now, but back in the gardens, as well. That realization should have cheered her, but it didn't.

She lay down on her blankets, feeling cold, despite the even temperature of the room. Shivering, she felt Monday snuggle up against her and pulled him close. He was the only thing she understood in this place of contrasts.

How could a society allow itself to be dominated by such inhuman rules? What terrible point had life reached in the past to make such a warped philosophy look good enough to make people want to embrace it?

From all she'd seen so far of the Earth, it appeared healthy and beautiful. The same couldn't be said for its inhabitants, despite their advances in medicine and technology. What a terrible thing that amid Earth's newfound beauty and life, human potential had reached an all-time low.

The thought of this happening to her world made her feel physically ill. It made her want to get back to her own time as quickly as possible before her world was changed into something beyond recognition.

The last thought on her mind before she fell into a fitful doze was a question. What could Sammell really do with his time machine to prevent it from happening? It was going to take more than a trip to the past to prevent this horror. And it would surely take more than one person to accomplish it.

Sammell tossed and turned on the bed, twisting the sheet around his damp body. A low moan broke from his lips, and he sat straight up in bed. Disoriented, he stared around the room, wondering first where he was and second what had awakened him.

Then he remembered the dream. His intellect had been placed inside Monday, Marina's squirrel. But the cold sweat sheathing his body had nothing to do with that part of the dream. It was being held close in the woman's arms that had caused it.

Sitting on the side of the bed, he wiped his face and chest with the sheet before standing. He didn't understand the feelings churning inside him. His heart slammed against his ribs, his breathing came in gasps, and his whole body felt as though every sensory organ had been stimulated, causing a terrible yearning inside him—but a yearning for what?

Without donning the tunic that matched the loose-fitting trousers he slept in, Sammell hurried from the room to the lab. He had to see the woman—Marina.

Setting his hand against the door, he waited for the identapanel to change from red to green. But a yellow glow appeared around his hand and a mechanized voice said, "Identity cannot be established. Please try again."

Sammell lifted his hand, realized his palm was damp with sweat, rubbed it down his pant leg and tried again. This time the panel slid smoothly back. Grabbing the glasses on a shelf near the door, he put them on and stared at Marina's sleeping form.

She rested on her back, the sheet draping her body. One arm lay curled on the pillow above her head, and the other lay across her waist, pulling the sheet tight against her breasts.

Sammell studied their outline, licking suddenly dry lips.
He was beginning to feel warm all over, and hot blood
surged through his veins.

A tingling started in his lower body, spreading upward to
the pit of his stomach and downward to his knees, making
them feel weak. He put a hand against his abdomen, felt an
unnatural hardness in his lower body and jerked it away.
What was happening to him?

He stumbled and stood with his back against the wall,
feeling sick and dizzy. Licking sweat from his upper lip, he
let his head fall back and closed his eyes. Maybe, if he stood
still long enough, it would go away. His legs quivered and
his stomach rolled.

It wasn't working. He took a deep breath, fighting the
urge to turn back to the Recep and the woman lying there.
He couldn't move—*he mustn't move!* The sensation of cloth
stroking his lower body became pure torture.

Bracing his hands against the wall, his head pressed back
against it, eyes closed, he fought to keep a vision of Marina
as she lay among the flowers in the gardens earlier that night
out of his mind. But no matter how hard he fought it, the
image surfaced and remained.

"S-Sammell... is that you?"

He jerked to attention, his glance automatically going to
the Recep.

"Hello?"

His hands clenched as he remembered the softness of her
skin beneath his fingertips. She lay only a few yards away.
If he went to her, she would let him touch her—he knew it.

Biting his lip sharply, hoping the pain would keep him
from making such a foolish move, recalling the beauty of
her lush red mouth, he screwed his eyes tightly shut. A deep
groan worked at the back of his throat.

He licked unsteady lips, tasting the salty metallic flavor of
his own blood and knew he fought a losing battle. His eyes
came open of their own accord. He saw Marina raise herself on one elbow, cocking her head in a listening attitude.

"Sammell?" she whispered again. When he didn't answer, she moved—and the blanket fell to her waist, exposing her breasts to his view.

Sammell swung away. Jerking the glasses from his face, he worked his way along the room and out the door as soundlessly as possible, feeling as though his body no longer belonged to him. It followed a new code he knew nothing about.

Tapping the button that closed the lab's door, he pressed his face against the wall, then his chest and finally his whole body, feeling its coolness penetrate his clothing and soothe heated flesh. The pain in his lower body eased a fraction. Jaws clenched, he hugged the wall, a multitude of feelings racing uncontrollably through him. Suddenly his whole body convulsed as shock wave after shock wave of new sensation washed over and through him.

And then it was over, but he still shook. His knees buckled and Sammell pressed his cheek against the wall as the terrible emotion released its hold on him and he sagged to the floor. Dragging his knees up to his chin, he sat huddled against the wall, quivering.

Chapter 7

When Sammell strode into the lab the next morning, ev
eryone was already there. Taking a seat at his own desk, he
tried to settle his mind to work. But that wasn't easy
Thoughts of Marina had kept him awake far into the night

And so had the memory of his experience outside the lab
after she had retired. He had lost control of his body. No
even the Wyndom drug had ever affected him so com
pletely.

Nothing had been able to settle him down, not even the
hot and cold showers he'd taken afterward. And this morn
ing he'd risen and left the cell without seeing Marina
thinking he needed this time away from her to try to under
stand what was happening to him.

It was becoming obvious that she was responsible for the
physical sensations he now suffered. They had started with
her arrival in his lab. And despite everything, he had
growing need to know if everyone in her world was affected
by a member of the opposite sex as he had been last night
Was she?

Stifling a yawn, he opened the file folder containing the previous day's work. His mind wasn't as sharp as it should have been, but when he picked up Larkin's notes, he knew Marina's effect on him was only one of the problems he was going to have to face very soon.

He stared at the paper in his hand, the words blurring before his eyes. One thought stood out above the rest. Larkin was perilously close to solving the problem with the plasma jet. His equation closely paralleled Sammell's own.

He may have already solved it. And the paper quivering in Sammell's hand could have been no more than a thinly veiled attempt to force him to show Larkin what he knew. If that was the case, what would his next move be? A trip to Bartell's office with his suspicions?

He reread the notes. One very important component to the formula was missing. Was it deliberate? A warning from Larkin that he would not wait much longer?

Sammell felt like an animal with its back against the wall, threat and confusion all around him. One of Bartell's guards stepped up to his desk and handed him a folded paper. He opened it to find a summons to Bartell's office at the end of the workday. Another quarter heard from.

Bartell must have been worried about looking bad to his superiors. After having lived in the home of a government overseer for eight years of his life, Sammell knew King Wyndom expected no less than absolute success from his subordinates. Bartell could lose more than his position if he were to deliver any less.

Yesterday's visit to Sammell's cell by one of Bartell's inspection squads was proof that Bartell was getting desperate. Sammell didn't want to think what his next move might be.

"Good day, Sammell."

Hearing his name from behind, Sammell turned slowly, careful to keep the uneasiness out of his face. "Good day, Larkin."

The man stepped to the side of his chair and leaned close before speaking again. "I have been awaiting word from you."

"Concerning what?" Sammell asked, his expression blank. A few days ago he would have given almost anything to be having this conversation with this man. Now, it was too late, too much rested on his silence.

"We must speak about the matter we discussed two days past," Larkin responded cagily. His voice dropped. "The matter is of the utmost importance." Casting a hurried glance over his shoulder, he added, "Lord Bartell has been asking questions about my work. I know he suspects—"

"Good day, Sammell, Larkin."

Sammell looked up to see Gissel at his elbow. Hiding his annoyance at the interruption, he nodded. "Good day to you." Catching a glimpse of the wary expression on Larkin's face as the man turned away, he asked, "Is there something I can do for you?"

Gissel tore her eyes from Larkin's retreating back to give Sammell a vacant look. "What—oh, no, thank you."

As she departed, she was joined by Darryn. Together they entered the chamber housing MDAT'S clone. Sammell watched the pair with narrowed eyes. Had Gissel overheard Larkin's comments about Bartell?

Why did it seem as though Gissel and Darryn were always around when either he or Larkin wished for a few private words? Had Bartell set the pair to spy on him?

He was more uncertain than ever about the people with whom he worked. It was becoming more obvious each day that he could trust no one.

His thoughts turned to the missing mother board. Whoever took it must have known about the matter-time-sequence chip. Sammell just couldn't believe its theft was one of chance. His glance moved around the room and settled on the back of Larkin's blond head. He, too, was a suspect. Especially, if he thought Sammell was delaying the project's progress for reasons of his own. It would win points with Bartell if Larkin brought him a traitor.

He would have to be extra careful the next few days and that meant he wouldn't be able to steal the components he needed to repair the mother board for his MDAT. Marina's return home would be further delayed—and so would his mission.

As the day wore on, he managed to keep Larkin at a distance. But when the time came for everyone to leave, the other man cornered him near the showers. Everyone was required to take a shower before leaving for the day. Sammell figured it was so the guards could search everyone's clothing to see that nothing was taken from the building.

"We cannot speak now," Sammell said with a glance over his shoulder at the guard standing watch. "I have an appointment with Lord Bartell."

Larkin's eyes widened, then narrowed. "Is he requesting a report on my activities?"

"I have not spoken with him. He sent a note."

"I see. Will you mention the plasma jet?"

Sammell grew taut. "Only if Lord Bartell mentions it first."

"He will not," the other man said with assurance.

Sammell stared at him. "Have you noticed anyone around my desk when I am gone from it?"

"No." Larkin studied him closely. "Why?"

"It is nothing." He didn't want to arouse suspicion. "I must go now. Lord Bartell will be waiting."

"Sammell." Larkin took hold of his arm. "Tomorrow we must talk. After work—when we get off the shuttle. I will meet you near the entrance to the old underground shelter."

Sammell stood frozen, shocked because the other man was so disturbed that he had resorted to physical contact and in front of a guard. "Tomorrow," Sammell agreed, detaching the man's hold as the guard in the doorway turned to stare at them.

The carriage was empty when Sammell pulled himself up the step and took a seat. Bartell was angry. He demanded

results by the end of the week or Sammell would be replaced as project head. If that happened, MDAT would be
removed from his lab and all would be lost. Marina would
never go home, he would be unable to save his world—and
Bartell would learn that his time machine was a real working model and not a mock-up as he thought.

Sammell's thoughts stopped there. He had no desire to
imagine what would happen to him and Marina after that.

He patted the satchel on his lap and glanced nervously out
the window at a passing police patrol. Because Government House had been almost deserted by the time he left
and he'd had a special pass for his talk with Bartell, Sammell had managed to sneak into his lab and secure the components to construct another mother board for MDAT.
Until he had them in his cell, he wouldn't rest easy. All citizens were subject to sudden and unprovoked searches by the
state police.

He reached home without incident, a feeling of relief en-
gulfing him as he strode into the lab. It was quickly replaced by one of concern as his ears picked up a strange
sound coming from the Recep.

Removing the shield, he hastened across the room,
shocked to find Marina sitting curled into a tight ball, her
face hidden against her knees, her upper body shaking con-
vulsively. Monday was stretched out on the floor at her feet,
staring at her with large dark eyes.

"What is wrong?" Sammell asked anxiously, hovering
close, yet maintaining a certain distance between them.
"Are you hungry? Do you need water? Are you in pain?"

Marina lifted her head and wiped at her eyes with the
backs of her hands. "I'm all right. I . . . just . . ." She hic-
cupped and shook her head mutely, embarrassed to be
found crying like a child.

Sammell stood undecided, his hands hanging helplessly
at his sides. "What can I do for you?"

He looked so baffled that Marina almost felt sorry for
him. "Nothing, really, it's . . . I just felt . . . lonely. . . ."

Sammell stared at the pink tip of her nose, the moisture sticking her long dark eyelashes together and the trail of water flowing down both cheeks.

"I'm sorry," she murmured. "This is ridiculous. I feel like a fool." Again she wiped at her eyes.

Fascinated, he moved closer, gesturing toward her face. "May I touch one?"

She didn't understand what he meant. "What?"

"The moisture on your face."

He was referring to her tears. "Why?" she asked warily, drawing away from him.

"Until you arrived, I had never seen this watering of the eyes."

"You've never seen anyone cry?"

"No."

"I don't—" She started to shake her head.

"Please?"

He looked so disappointed that Marina hesitated, then changed her mind. What could it hurt? "Yes—all right." She swallowed and lifted her face toward his, eyelids fluttering as his hand drew near.

"Tears," he tested the new word. "Do they hurt?"

"No. I hurt inside. That's what caused them." In truth it was more anger than pain that had caused them. She was half-angry with him for leaving that morning without speaking to her. The days passed very slowly when there was nothing to do but stare at the ceiling and walls. Not even Monday's presence totally made up for the hours of enforced solitude. A fleeting glance at a friendly face, even if it belonged to her jailer, became very important.

"You are hurt inside?" he asked hastily, crouching near her.

"Not physically—emotionally." Placing a hand against her chest, she said as though to a child, "I ached here and that made me cry." And now she couldn't seem to stop.

Sammell darted a puzzled glance toward her chest, but his eyes returned almost immediately to her wet cheeks. Lifting an unsteady hand, he drew a fingertip down one cheek, stared at it, then lifted it to his mouth.

Marina caught her breath and held very still, as he placed the finger against his lips. The unconscious innocence in the gesture tugged at her heart.

He was a handsome man by anyone's standards, but there was a softness about him that might have been feared by the men of her world. Yet she found it a refreshing change from the macho image most men she knew felt compelled to project.

Needing comfort, she grasped his hand with gentle fingers and pressed it flat against one cheek. "Have you ever felt lost?" she asked throatily, forgetting for a moment to whom she spoke.

"Yes," Sammell responded, "I have felt lost."

Rising to her knees, she swayed closer to him. "Stay with me a little while. Talk to me. I'm tired of being alone."

There was deeper meaning in the words than she at first intended. But as she spoke, she realized it was true—she was tired of being alone . . . in her world as well as his.

Sammell couldn't speak over the sudden pounding of his heart. Something was again stirring inside him that had long been dormant in his race. His insides twisted into knots and a strange weakness caused him to quiver all over. Ripping his hand from her face, he twisted blindly away.

It wasn't that he didn't want to go on touching her . . . but there was something so foreign in his feelings for this woman . . . he had to get away. And, too, he was afraid the terrible changes in his body that he'd experienced the night before might recur. He didn't want Marina to see him that way. How could she trust him with her life if she thought him weak?

Afraid he was going to leave her alone again, Marina said the first thing that came into her mind. "Something is wrong with Monday. He won't eat or drink."

Sammell's glance rested on the animal. It was a relief to have something other than the woman to concentrate on.

"What do you think is wrong with him?"

"I think he misses his freedom even more than I do. He's used to running in the grass and playing among the trees." She paused to let that sink in before following it up with a question. "Can we take him outside again?"

Despite the danger, Sammell found himself agreeing to the outing. Something inside warned him it was a mistake to recklessly put off the work he needed to do on the mother board that would hasten her departure and his own mission, but he refused to listen. He wanted to further explore this thing between himself and this woman. He didn't know what the future would bring and he might never have another opportunity to learn firsthand how people in the past interacted with others.

"Can we go tonight?" Marina asked with an eagerness she found impossible to hide.

"Tonight?"

"Yes—right now?"

"Very well, but we must go quickly and we cannot stay long. There is trouble at work and it would not be beyond reason to expect more visits from Bartell's inspection squads in the near future."

Remembering how they'd almost gotten caught in the gardens the last time, Marina nodded and gathered Monday in her arms. She was eager to breathe fresh air and see the trees and grass again even if it was by moonlight.

Once outside his cell, she expected Sammell to follow the same route they'd taken the first night. But he turned in another direction and moved to the back of his cell.

"We aren't going to the gardens?"

"No, there is a sheltered clearing in the woods much closer than the gardens. I thought you might like to walk along the water's edge."

The night air was redolent of roses. A row of bushes with dark red blossoms flourished along the side of Sammell's cell. Marina stopped to sniff a large bloom before following on his heels.

Throwing her head back, she gazed up at the stars. Did they look larger and brighter than she remembered, or was it only her imagination? The temperature was somewhere in the seventies and a gentle wind blew the hair back from her forehead and cheeks and kissed her bare shoulders and legs. If not for the peculiar circumstances surrounding her presence here, Marina would have thought herself in paradise.

"Tell me," she said, eyeing the cloudless sky, "does it ever rain here?"

"Yes, once a week."

"Once a week?" she asked with a raised eyebrow.

"Yes, on Friday at curfew."

"Are you serious?"

His look asked her why she asked such a question.

"But... I don't understand. How do you know it's going to rain on Friday at curfew? And every Friday?"

"Because that is when it is scheduled. Everyone is home from school and work. Everyone is inside because of the curfew."

"Scheduled?"

"Yes."

"Let me see if I have this right. You control the weather?"

"Not me personally, but, yes, we control our environment. That is why we are able to grow fruits and vegetables and flowers in such abundance."

"How fantastic." She didn't know if she liked the idea of controlled rain, though the thought of never getting caught in a thunderstorm without an umbrella was appealing.

Sammell held back a thick leafy branch, and Marina ducked beneath it. They were near the stream and hadn't passed a single patrol.

"Where," she asked as Sammell ducked beneath the branch and joined her in the small clearing near the water's edge, "are all the cops?"

"Cops?"

"Patrols."

"Why don't you put your friend on the ground and see if he is happy to be outside?" Sammell asked, seemingly ignoring the question.

Marina stooped and gently placed Monday at her feet. He stood for a moment, tail lying along the ground. All at once his tail came up against his back and he scampered off into the trees.

Marina laughed softly, watching his antics as he ran back and forth across the clearing before finally disappearing from view. When he was gone, she looked up to find Sammell staring at her.

"What are you thinking?" she asked abruptly, the laughter dying.

"You make such a pleasant sound when you are happy. I like hearing it."

Marina felt her cheeks grow warm. Holding his glance, she asked, "What about the patrols? You didn't answer my question. Why haven't we passed any? Are there none here in this part of the city?"

"There are patrols, but not as many as near the gardens. And they are not as eager to search this sector as they are to search the sectors near the center of town."

"Then why didn't we come here the other night?" she asked with narrowed eyes.

"I wanted you to realize the danger of your situation...and I wanted you to believe what I had told you about where you were," he added in softer tones.

"Why was it so important that I believe you?"

"Your safety—"

"Is that your only concern?" she asked, interrupting him.

Sammell couldn't meet her eyes. He strode toward the water and stood at its edge, staring into the night.

"Sammell," Marina moved up behind him, "why do you never call me by name?"

"I have spoken your name."

"Yes," she agreed, recalling the incidents, "but not as a friend. Why do you hold yourself so stiffly from me? Do you dislike me? Are you angry because I'm here? I know you didn't *want* me here, but...can't we be friends?

"I know we come from different worlds, but...friends don't have to be alike. I could use a friend. How about you?"

"Friendship is not allowed—" he began.

"Well, who's to know?" she said, cutting him off. "Who but us? And I thought you wanted to change all that? Shouldn't change begin at home? I will be your friend, if you will be mine."

After a long silence, she stepped closer and put a light hand on his back. "Don't you want to be my friend?"

Sammell turned, dislodging her hand, to find her only a few inches away. Taking a hurried step back, he felt his heel slip on the mud and struggled to retain his balance without appearing to have lost it.

For some reason it was very important for him to appear in complete control. Recovering his balance, he swallowed dryly and tried to decide how to explain things to her. It would be difficult for someone who knew next to nothing about life in his time to fully understand the contrast between their worlds.

"I have lived almost thirty years knowing there was something more to life than what we have here. But until I met you..." His voice faded as his eyes became fixed on her uplifted face. The night made dark hollows of her eyes and mouth while the silver moonlight gave her skin an odd luminescence, making her appear unearthly.

"Yes," Marina probed, "until you met me?"

Sammell swallowed again and tore his gaze from her face. "What I have learned from you makes my mission to save my people very real. You have something my people do not know enough to dream about. Freedom, true freedom.

"It must be wonderful to walk the streets without fear of arrest, to stop and talk to people whenever you like, to have friends—to choose a mate of your own."

"It isn't all wonderful," Marina said. "And you have good things in your world, too."

"Yes," he readily agreed, "but we are kept from enjoying them!"

Marina shivered at the suppressed anger in his voice. "Do you really think you can stop this world from coming into existence?"

"I must."

"When do you go?" It was unnatural to be discussing time travel as though it were nothing more than a Sunday-afternoon excursion by car. Yet now she believed in it.

"As soon as I have returned you to your own time."

"Do you know what year the drug was first manufactured?"

"Not yet, but I will find out. The information is in the archives at Government House."

"It will be dangerous, traveling in a time you've never known. Have you thought about that? What if something happens to you?"

Sammell shrugged.

"Surely there are others who feel as you do."

"I do not know."

"If you discovered the drug, couldn't other people have discovered it, too?"

"I do not know."

"Have you never heard about anyone rebelling?"

"My government does not tolerate rebellion. Insurrectionists would be terminated."

"But—have you tried to find others like yourself?"

"No," Sammell had to admit. "I have always been afraid of discovery. I did not know whom to trust. There is one man at work whom I once would have trusted, but..."

"There, you see?" Marina said. "Why haven't you taken him into your confidence?"

"It is not safe to trust anyone. People curry favor by informing on others. In any case—" Sammell put an end to the conversation "—that is not your problem, it is mine."

"Yes," Marina agreed, stung by his curt dismissal, "it is. When are you planning to send Monday and me home?"

"I have acquired the components needed to restore MDAT to full power. It will take a little while, but soon I

hope to send you home. I know you will be glad to get back
to your life." He watched her face for signs of denial.

"Yes," Marina agreed without enthusiasm, "I will."

But would she? What awaited her there? Her work, certainly. And her family. But no one special. No one pacing
the floor and ringing her telephone at all hours of the day
and night, worried because he hadn't heard from her.

Sensing something behind her words, Sammell said, "You
do not appear as concerned about getting home as you did
yesterday."

"Yesterday I thought you were a fiend who'd kidnapped
me for an unknown reason."

"Fiend?"

"Yes. Someone who wanted to do me harm."

"And now that you know I'm not a . . . fiend?"

"Now I'd kind of like to stick around and find out what
happens." Seeing the protest hovering on his lips, she added,
"I could be of help to you. Have you considered that?"

"Help? How?"

That was a good question. Until she'd said it just now, she
hadn't realized that she even wanted to stick around. "I
know how things work in my time. I know the people. I
could help you plan how to go about destroying the Wyndom drug."

"But what about your friends and family?" he asked.
"Are you not eager to return to them?"

"Yes—I want to see them again. But you need me. And
their lives won't be changed by my remaining gone for a little while longer."

"No?" He appeared surprised by her answer. "But I
thought people were closer to each other in your world."

"That's true. But getting together in many cases is left to
the holidays."

"Yes, I remember about holidays—and picnics," he
added, reminding her of their last outing. "Tell me about
families," he said. "What are they like?"

"Families," Marina murmured, forgetting her argument
for the moment, "that's a hard one. They love one another

nd share things." She shrugged. How did you explain a family? "They help and stand by each other through the bad imes as well as the good."

"I would like to know a family."

"You mean be a part of one?" Marina asked.

"Yes, I would like to be a part of a family."

"We could be friends," Marina again suggested. "Sometimes friends become like family."

"Do you love friends?" he asked, staring at her intently.

Marina swallowed. "Yes, friends love each other."

"And do friends touch?"

"Yes."

"Then I would like to be your friend."

"Friends sometimes kiss each other, too."

"Kiss?"

"A touching of the lips." She pressed a finger against her wn lips and touched it to his. "That is a kiss."

Sammell fingered his tingling lips. A kiss. He liked it.

Chapter 8

Sammell strolled along the stream with his back to Marina. He'd followed its course many times in the past but had never been so aware of its charm as now. How had he missed the beauty of moonlight on water, the delight of fresh warm air blowing against his skin, the sense of absolute peace in the silence of the woods?

He knew this new sense of awareness was due to the woman at his side. Since she'd arrived, his view of life had gradually been changing. Though he'd always been aware of the beauty around him, he'd never taken much pleasure in it.

Is that what it was like in Marina's world? Were her people free to walk and enjoy the secrets of the night without fear of arrest?

From the corner of his eye, Sammell saw Marina sit down on the river bank and remove her strange footwear, held on by a strap between her toes. And then she was scooting eagerly toward the water.

Looking up at him, she smiled and said, "Take off your shoes and join me."

"We have to get back," he protested mildly. What new feat was this?

"Not yet. Come on, relax and come into the water—or is bathing another thing you don't do?" she asked teasingly.

"We bathe," Sammell said dryly, "but not with our clothes on."

Marina laughed. "Don't be an old stick-in-the-mud. The water feels great!"

In truth the water was chilly, but Marina didn't want to go back yet. Away from the bleakness of his living quarters, Sammell acted more like a human being and less like a robot.

She was starved for conversation and Sammell was her only choice. Besides, he was a paradox. Sometimes he acted in a manner completely foreign to the men of her time, yet at other times the inbred arrogance of his gender came out in full force. And she wanted to know which was the real Sammell—or was he a combination of both?

"Come on," she urged, "relax. Take off your shoes and roll up your pants—come wading with me."

"Wading?"

"Yes." She tromped back and forth in the water, splashing it up around her bare legs. "It's fun. Come on." She reached for him. "I'll help you."

But he refused to be coaxed.

Marina put her hands on her hips in exasperation and asked, "Don't you ever do anything just for fun?"

"Fun?"

"Yes. Something that makes you feel good."

"No," Sammell replied solemnly. And then he was sitting on the grass removing his boots and socks and rolling up his pant legs.

His first steps into the water were tentative. Its icy shock almost drove him back to the grassy bank. But the rocks on the bottom were slippery with lichen and he slipped.

Marina caught hold of him around the waist and helped keep him upright until he could regain his footing.

Gazing down on her moonlit face, Sammell suddenl[y]
wanted to be closer, not only physically, but mentally, a[s]
well. "Is this what you do with your brothers? Do you g[o]
wading with them?"

Marina grinned. She supposed she shouldn't tell hi[m]
about the skinny-dipping they'd all taken part in when the[y]
were younger. He probably wouldn't approve.

"This was one of our favorite things to do on hot sum[-]
mer days when we were kids," she answered with a smile.

"Kids?"

"Young—children."

"Oh." He wondered if she was aware that her arm wa[s]
still around his waist. He was—very much so. And instea[d]
of feeling repulsed by it . . . he liked it.

"What kind of things did you do when you were young?"
Marina asked curiously.

"Studied."

"All the time?"

"No. On Sundays we went for boat rides or walks in th[e]
public gardens."

"What kind of games did you play?"

"Games?"

"Never mind."

"We should go," Sammell murmured abruptly, sensin[g]
that in some way he'd disappointed her. "A patrol is boun[d]
to come by before long."

"Yes, all right," Marina agreed offhandedly. "Tell m[e]
do you like this?"

Sammell met her glance. "The wading?"

"Yes." But she was wondering if he liked being with he[r.]
Staring into her eyes, he murmured, "I like it very much.[”]

The wave of blond hair that always seemed to be neatl[y]
swept back from his face lay across his forehead almost i[n]
his eyes. It made him look younger, less stern and slightl[y]
raffish. Marina liked that. She shivered, suddenly very muc[h]
aware of how close they were standing.

"You are cold," Sammell said, his arms automaticall[y]
coming up to her shoulders.

"No..." she started to protest, then said, "well, only a little." She liked the feel of his arms around her. It made her feel protected.

Sammell didn't know what to do with his hands. They rested on her shoulders, then slowly slipped down her arms. This "touching" was new to him and he wasn't at all comfortable with it.

A dark shape darted past them in the water and he jerked in surprise. "There is something in the water," he said curiously, bending to peer into its murky depths.

"Of course there is, silly," Marina laughed, "They're called fish."

"Oh—yes." He glanced at her self-consciously and Marina laughed harder.

"Did you think it was a monster?"

"No," he answered seriously. "I had forgotten about them, that is all."

When he'd bent to look into the water, he'd drawn her against his side. And now she was very much aware of his lithe body plastered down the front of hers. His hip pressed against her pelvic bone and her legs rested one on either side of his.

"Sam—may I call you that?"

"Why?"

"Because it sounds less formal than Sammell. And friends are easy with each other."

"You may call me Sam if you like."

"May I ask you something?"

He nodded.

"Have you ever held a girl in your arms?"

"No. Why," he asked quickly, "am I doing something I should not?"

"No, you're doing fine," she answered swiftly, thinking that she'd very much like him to kiss her.

As if he'd read her mind, his arm tightened around her. She could feel his body tense and the air around them suddenly felt charged with electricity. Marina moved against him, pushing her hands up his chest to his shoulders, her eyes locked with his. What was he feeling to cause such panic in the depths of his dark eyes?

"What are the women in your world like?"

"I do not know," he answered falteringly, feeling a surge of those sensations from the other night.

"What do you mean, you don't know? Are they beautiful?"

"No," he said uncertainly, "I do not think so. Not the way you are beautiful."

"You think I'm beautiful?"

"Yes," he answered on an uneven breath.

"But you see the women of your world every day. Surely you know if you like looking at them."

"They look no different from me."

"Really?" she asked, not really believing him. "Look, I know you said you have no choice in who your mate will be...." She hesitated. "But haven't you ever wanted to get close to one—just to see what it would be like?"

"No."

"No?"

"No. I work with them. They keep to their place and I keep to mine."

She didn't like the sound of that. Was male chauvinism alive even in the twenty-fourth century?

"But surely you've noticed the differences between your self and a woman."

Sammell stiffened. He'd noticed the differences between himself and the woman flattened against his chest.

"Relax," Marina whispered drawing away. "This is supposed to be enjoyable—we're having a conversation."

"And that is good?"

"If you want to learn more about my world, it's not only good, it's necessary. Friends talk to each other."

"I want to be your friend, and I would very much like to know more about your world."

"Then do as I said. Relax." Marina smoothed her hand down his chest, telling herself to heed her own advice. She was using him shamelessly, but she couldn't seem to stop herself.

"Do friends stand like this—with their arms around each other?" Sammell asked.

"Yes," she whispered, "and more."

Moonlight had turned his hair into a silver halo around his head and made his eyes two dark pools of mystery. Her eyes moved to his mouth and she licked suddenly dry lips.

"What more?" Sammell asked huskily, his senses throbbing with the strength and feel and scent of her.

Marina felt him tremble against her, and it sent fire through every nerve in her body. There was a hunger in him that he wasn't even aware of, and it made her heart thud like a drum. She liked the curve of his mouth, the gentleness in his eyes, the graceful strength of his hands at her waist, the feel of his growing hardness against her thigh. Suddenly becoming dizzy, she lost her footing.

Sammell jerked her tighter against him to keep her from falling. But now the strange new sensations were too much for him. Propelling her from him, steadying her while she regained her balance, he dropped his hands and climbed from the water, hastening to put on his boots and socks.

Marina stood in the water feeling embarrassed. What was the matter with her? She'd practically forced him to kiss her and now she'd driven him away.

"Hurry," Sammell whispered tautly, crouching toward her, "there's a patrol in the woods."

Marina was out of the water in a flash, grabbing her shoes in one hand and reaching for Sammell's hand with the other. Monday scampered into the clearing and Marina hesitated, torn with the thought of leaving him behind, but without the heart to take him back to the lab.

"Sam, can we leave Monday here? He belongs in these trees, not locked up in the lab. I think he'd be just as happy here as he was in Arizona. In fact, he's probably better off here. Are there hunters here?"

"Hunters?" he asked, listening with one ear for sounds of the patrol.

"Men with guns who shoot animals for sport," she explained.

"No," he answered in shock. "The animals are all protected. No one is allowed to harm them."

"Good. Then this is definitely the place for him."

On her knees, she held out her hands and Monday ran into them. Holding him close, she explained what she was planning to do and told him a quick goodbye. Then she set him on the ground and hurried to where Sammell was waiting, holding the heavy tree branch that helped hide the small clearing from view.

"I am doing the right thing, aren't I?"

"Yes," Sammell assured her, "your little friend is better off here."

Sammell led them out of the woods and along the winding path toward his cell. After a few minutes, when they had left the patrol behind, he noticed Marina was being very quiet.

"You are already missing your friend."

"Yes. He's all I had of home."

"I am sorry."

Several times in the short period it took to return to his cell, Sammell glanced curiously at Marina. To display so much feeling for another creature, and especially one not of her own kind, amazed him.

The new and strange sensations he'd been experiencing since her arrival confused and frightened him. Would a time ever come when he could give in to those feelings without guilt or misgiving?

Just for a moment, he wondered what it would be like to have Marina feel about him the way she felt about Monday. Such thoughts caused a churning in his middle, and Sammell quickly put them out of his mind.

Once safely inside his cell, they leaned against the closed door, breathing heavily. Their glances touched, tangled and parted. Both were very much aware that something had changed between them, but neither was ready to put a name to it.

"It is late." Sammell took a quick breath and swallowed. "I am certain you are tired. I know I am. Tomorrow, after work, I will repair MDAT for your journey home."

Marina nodded silently. Yes, it was time she went home. Before the feelings churning inside got way out of hand.

When they were inside the lab and Sammell was preparing to switch on the energy shield, he hesitated. An impossible idea had taken root in his mind and refused to be put aside. It was beyond all reason, but with Marina looking at him with those big blue eyes, he couldn't let it go without mentioning it.

"Your world is very different from mine."

"Yes, it is," Marina agreed.

"But, someday, my world will be free like yours."

"I hope for your sake that it is."

"When that happens . . . do you suppose we might meet again?"

A warmth spread through Marina. "I'd like that."

"You would?"

"Yes, very much."

"Yes," Sammell whispered huskily, "so would I."

"Good night."

"Good night."

Sammell was in the process of changing for sleep when a soft whirring sound floated to his ears. He froze. It was the sound of a hand-held teleporter in use.

Then he remembered that he'd forgotten to turn on the Telebloc, a device that prevented teleportation directly into one's life cell without a warning. *Marina*—no, he breathed a sigh of relief, she was safely concealed behind the energy shield.

"Sammell? Sammell—where are you?"

In amazement, Sammell recognized Larkin's voice coming from the viewing room. What was he doing out at this time of night?

Exiting the room, Sammell hurried down the hall. "Larkin? What are you doing here? It is well past curfew."

"I know, but I had to speak with you, and we never seem able to find the time at work. Besides, it is safer here, without Bartell's guards lurking about."

"What is so important that you chanced arrest to come here?"

"I must know what you think about the new formula I worked out for the plasma jet. Am I close to the correct answer?"

Sammell nearly fell into the trap baited by the man's words. It was the studied glance Larkin gave him that warned him to consider his answer very carefully.

"Until we put it to the test, I cannot answer that with any degree of certainty." He disciplined his voice to remain neutral, but Larkin was an intelligent man—very little slipped by him. "It does look good, and it's obvious that you have worked very hard."

"Yes," Larkin agreed impatiently.

"Please be seated," Sammell offered.

"No, thank you, I will stand." Larkin moved around the room, stopping before the door to Sammell's lab. "This is where you work at home." It was a statement, not a question.

Sammell nodded. To his knowledge Larkin had never been in his cell. How did he know where the lab was located?

"May I have a look inside?"

Sammell hesitated. He didn't want the other man inside the lab with Marina there, but if he refused it would look odd. Hoping Marina wasn't asleep and would hear both their voices and remain quiet, he opened the door and preceded the other man inside.

"I see you have a model of MDAT," Larkin commented.

Sammell nodded, watching as Larkin examined the equipment.

"Of course this one has no mother board," Larkin mused, studying the computer. "Sammell, are you satisfied with your life? Are you content to be squeezed beneath the iron fist of our government? A government that cares little about us or our real needs?''

Sammell stiffened. This was sedition. Even to discuss the government between themselves would mean termination if word of it reached Bartell's ears.

"What do you mean?" Sammell asked.

"Come—" the other man whirled to face him "—I know you are aware of the secret drug."

Sammell felt as though the breath had been knocked out of him. "What do you mean?"

"I mean the whole population has been emasculated for nearly four hundred years. When Wyndom took over the world, he made robots of us all."

"How do you come by such knowledge?" Sammell asked guardedly.

"The archives. Surely you know that the world archives are preserved at Government House."

"How have you seen them? No one is allowed access to them."

Larkin smiled, but the smile didn't reach his eyes. "I am tired of doing the bidding of others. I want to live free." He stared at Sammell through narrowed eyes. "What about you? Are you ready to be a free man?"

"Your words confuse me. Why have you come here tonight?"

"I came to warn you that Gissel and Darryn are watching you. Remember, you asked if I had seen anyone around your desk? Well, yesterday, just before I left, I caught them going through your notes. I could not tell you this at work because they listen to everything said."

"Thank you for the warning, but I have nothing to hide."

"No?" Larkin quirked a heavy eyebrow.

"No."

"I know of a group who would very much like to get their hands on a working model of MDAT."

"Who?"

"Freedom fighters. Some are descendants of those who were not exposed to the drug. Some have discovered the drug on their own. They are gathering in the hills outside the city. They work toward a common goal—freedom for all. Do you not want to be a part of that?''

"How do they plan to achieve it?'' Sammell asked, ignoring the question.

Larkin drew himself up straight, his eyes darting nervously toward MDAT. "I cannot say. Not this time. Another time we will discuss more important matters. I must go now, before the patrols become concentrated near my cell.''

"Wait! What about Bartell? He expects a trial run by the end of the week. If you continue working along the same lines at work, I am certain you must hit on the right formula. How does that tie in with your desire for freedom?''

"I do not want to arouse suspicion. I must appear loyal. Just as you must appear loyal,'' he added suggestively.

A moment later he was gone. Sammell stared with furrowed brow at the spot where he'd stood. What had been the purpose of his visit? Had he come to warn him about Gissel and Darryn? Or had he come to ferret out what Sammell had in his laboratory?

"Sam?''

He heard Marina call his name and hurried toward the Recep. "Is something wrong?''

"I heard voices. Did you have a visitor?''

"Yes. It was Larkin, the man I told you about from the lab.''

"The man you trust.''

"The man I would like to trust—yes.''

"What did he want?''

"I am not certain,'' Sammell replied thoughtfully.

"Is he gone?''

"Yes.''

"Are you going to bed now?''

"In a few minutes. First I am going to give you a device with which to call me if you need me—without having to bang anything on the floor,'' he added ironically.

"That would be nice.''

He could hear the smile in her voice and knew he was smiling, too. He touched his lips with his fingers, remembering the kiss Marina had given him near the stream. Like the kiss, it felt good. A few moments later, he turned off the energy shield and handed her a small round disk. "Attach it to your clothing like this," he said and proceeded to press it against the shoulder of her blouse. "All you have to do is rub your finger over it to speak to me, then tap it once so you can hear my reply."

"Thank you. How far will it reach?"

"Only within the cell."

"How did your friend get here?" she asked abruptly, curious about the man. She would have liked to be introduced to him. "Did he dodge the Gestapo the way we did?"

"Gestapo?"

"Nasty police soldiers from my past who liked to hurt people," she explained concisely.

"Oh. No, he did not walk. He used a teleporter."

"Teleporter?"

"Yes. It is possible to teleport anywhere within the city."

"You don't mean it?" she asked in amazement. "You mean in a blink of an eye you're anywhere you want to be?"

"Yes. Would you like to try it sometime?"

"No," she answered instantly. "Traveling through time was enough for me. Besides," she reminded him, "I doubt I'll be around long enough to use it. Where would I go? You said I would be arrested if anyone saw me."

"Yes, that is correct." But he didn't like being reminded that she would soon be gone from his life. "It was a foolish suggestion. And now, I think I will go to bed. Tomorrow will be very busy, both at work and here in the lab."

"Good night, Sam."

"Good night...Marina."

"Sam! Sam, are you there?" Marina pulled the shoulder of her blouse up against her cheek so she could speak directly into the small communication device attached to it.

"Wake up!" she whispered urgently. She was terrified. Someone must have learned about MDAT and was trying to steal it, because someone was trying to get into the lab.

How would she get home if the machine was stolen? And what had the bastard done to Sammell?

"Why don't you answer?" she said desperately. "Someone is trying to get into the lab. Oh, God, I can hear them right outside!"

Sammell lifted an eyelid and sat up in bed, rubbing the sleep from his eyes. "Marina? Are you in distress?"

"Oh, thank God," she cried in relief. "I was so afraid you'd been injured. Someone is trying to get into the lab!"

He was instantly alert. "I'll be right there. Remember, you are safe from detection—"

"It isn't me I'm worried about," she interrupted him. "It's MDAT . . . and you. Don't do anything foolish and get yourself killed."

Sammell paused at the side of the bed. "You would be sorry if I died?"

"Yes, of course I would. How would I get home without you?"

"Oh."

Marina heard the disappointment in his voice and wished she had given a little more thought to her answer. "I wouldn't want anything to happen to you in any case," she amended. "We're friends, remember?"

"Yes," he answered gravely, "we are friends. Do not worry, I will be all right and you are safe as long as you remain quiet. Remember, no matter what happens, stay quiet."

Marina sat on her knees, wishing she could help him. She shouldn't have made him think she was only worried about herself. It's just that she'd been so frightened that she didn't know what she was saying.

The furtive sounds at the door intensified. Whoever wanted to get inside was beginning to sound desperate. They must be after MDAT. Her fear grew. What would happen to her if the time machine was stolen or destroyed? Samnell had said that if she was missing from her own time for too long, time would knit a new strand, leaving her out.

What would happen to her then? Would she belong nowhere?

Somewhere outside the room, she heard a loud clatter and the sounds at the door abruptly ceased. Where was the intruder? *Where was Sammell?*

"Sam, are you all right? Sam? Sam—answer me!" She was on her feet, considering how best to tear a hole in the wall of her prison and go to his aid.

"I am here," Sammell answered breathlessly, righting the table he'd stumbled into.

"What happened? Did you see the intruder? Did you catch him? Are you hurt?"

"There was only one and he got away. I saw only his back as he was leaving. I am not injured, and he took nothing with him."

Inside the lab he switched off the energy shield, and Marina rushed into his arms. They closed around her, pulling her tight against him. He could feel the rapid beat of her heart and hear the rasp of her uneven breathing and his own responded in kind.

Hugging him to her, Marina whispered against his chest, "I was so frightened for you—I thought you'd been hurt!"

"It would have mattered so much to you if I had been injured?" he asked, an odd note in his voice.

Leaning back in his arms, Marina stared into his eyes and what she saw there made her heart skip a beat. It made no sense at all, but she wanted him to go on holding her—no, she wanted him to kiss her more than she had ever wanted anything in her life.

She had wanted other men to kiss her, and they had, but... She couldn't explain it even to herself. This man was a stranger. Yet in a sense she felt as though she'd known him all her life—no, longer than that—forever.

It was evident that he, too, was disturbed by their closeness. Evident in the twitch of an eyebrow, the sudden tightening of his jaw and the way he kept his lips pressed firmly together. Did he want to know the touch of her lips as badly as she wanted to know the touch of his?

Heeding an instinct older than time itself, Sammell's head dipped toward hers. Marina lifted her face and closed her eyes. It was the lightest of kisses, a mere meeting of lips, but the flood of sensation it caused sent shock waves throughout her body.

She had wanted to know his kiss and now she knew. But the knowledge was more than she had bargained for. Wrenching herself from his arms, she turned away.

"I'm very tired," she said with an edge to her voice. "I'm glad you're unharmed and nothing was taken. Now I think I'll say good-night."

Stepping into the Recep, she lay down and turned her face to the wall without waiting for him to move away. She'd been playing with fire and she'd gotten burned. She was falling in love with a man who wouldn't be born until centuries after her own death. And she could not exist in his world, because the things she wanted most in life—a husband, a home and a family—were denied to him and his people.

Sammell left her silently, feeling very confused. There was something very different in the kiss she had given him by the stream and the one they had shared just now. Alone in his room, all he could think about was Marina. With his body crying out for a release from the sweet torture her kiss had aroused in him, Sammell threw himself on the bed and stared at the ceiling.

To hold her in his arms again, to feel her lips pressed against his, he would give anything... *almost* anything...

Chapter 9

As he rode to work the next morning, again Sammell's thoughts were filled with Marina. Before leaving, he'd given her a stack of books from his library. The books were all scientific manuals, but without Monday to keep her company, the twelve hours he'd be gone would drag by, and he hoped the books would at least help pass the time.

As he strode down the corridor to the lab, he noted a heavy concentration of armed guards near the transvator leading to the government offices on the next level.

What was Bartell up to now? Since they had started project Deliverance security measures had been stepped up twice already.

Had the missing files from the archives been discovered? His feet moved a little faster and his eyes remained straight ahead as he passed the heavily armed men. Time was growing short. He had to make his move and soon. No matter how much he wanted to prolong his time with Marina and learn from her, he had to send her back very soon.

The realization filled him with more than disappointment—it wrenched him apart inside. He'd shared more with her than he'd ever thought to share with another human being. She more than anything had made him realize the importance of his mission.

Stopping in the doorway to the lab, Sammell let his eyes rove the room. Gissel and Darryn were at their desks, heads bowed over their work. Lab technicians were scattered about the room, conducting experiments on altered formulas. Everything looked as usual—no, something was different! With a bump of alarm, Sammell saw that a new face had been added to the team. An armed guard stood at the entrance to the time chamber housing MDAT's twin.

As he moved toward his own desk, Sammell noted that one chair was empty. Where was Larkin? Had his unauthorized trip to Sammell's cell been discovered? Was he even now under arrest? If he talked, Marina's life would be in danger and so would Sammell's mission.

Sammell knew that whoever had broken into his cell last night had used an antiteleblock to override the security system he had installed to warn against such an intrusion. Only the police had access to such devices. He had a feeling that if he found the intruder, he'd probably have found the thief who had stolen MDAT's mother board from his desk drawer.

His eyes clung to Gissel's straight back. She'd been acting strange the past few days—and so had Darryn.

Taking his seat, he caught Gissel's eye and motioned her over to him. "Where is Larkin?" he asked, disregarding the standard formal greeting.

"No one knows. Lord Bartell has already been here looking for him. He said—"

"Sammell! In my office immediately!"

Sammell pushed away from his desk and stood, Bartell's guttural voice ringing in his ears. "Do you know what this is all about?" he asked Gissel.

Her eyes widened at his tone. "I know there was trouble in one of the city sectors last night. After curfew, a storage unit on the east side containing nutrient was vaporized."

For a split second, a dark premonition held him still. Larkin had been out last night after curfew. Could he have had something to do with it?

What if Bartell knew about Larkin's visit to his cell? He might think Sammell was involved in the affair. Moving stiffly around Gissel, he headed for the door. The thought of making a run for it entered his head, but he knew he wouldn't get far before one of the guard's Maser-weapons took him down. He decided he'd have a better chance using his wits to escape.

"Good day, Lord Bartell," he said after knocking and entering at the other man's command.

"I want a test run in four days," Bartell said without preamble.

"Four days? But—"

"Four days! Have Gissel enter the binary code today."

"The plasma jet—"

"I believe Larkin was working on the formula for that. Turn the work over to Darryn."

"But Darryn isn't qualified—"

"Then do it yourself!" the other man growled. "I want a test in four days. Do I make myself clear?"

"Very clear, sir."

"Where is Larkin?"

Sammell stiffened. "I do not know. I was surprised to arrive and not see him at his desk."

"When did you last speak with him?"

"Yesterday—I have not seen him since yesterday."

Bartell examined Sammell's face thoroughly before granting him a nod of dismissal.

"I expect results," was his final comment. "Do not disappoint me."

Back in the lab, Sammell delegated the work as Bartell had demanded. Before Gissel entered the binary codes in MDAT'S computer, Sammell opened the back to make certain everything inside was in working order. As he looked closer, something about the mother board looked wrong. Removing it, he studied each circuit carefully. And then he realized what was bothering him. The board had an extra chip.

On closer examination, Sammell realized it was his chip, the one he'd developed and added for the matter-time-sequence program. *This was his missing mother board!* Whoever had stolen it must have placed it in the computer.

"Is something wrong?" Gissel stood at his side, looking over his shoulder curiously.

"No. I was just checking the circuits."

"Is there a problem? Larkin went over them carefully yesterday."

"Yesterday?" Sammell shot her a look of surprise.

"Yes. You were helping one of the techs next door. He said you had told him there was a problem with one of the circuits."

"Did he say which one?"

"No. I could tell he did not want me bothering him, so I left. But a few minutes later Lord Bartell sent for him." She moved a step closer and lowered her voice. "Do you know what has happened to Larkin? Has he been arrested?"

"No. Why would you ask that?"

"The two guards I heard talking about the vaporization said someone from Government House had been breaking curfew. Larkin has been acting strange lately. I thought maybe..."

"The guards could have been discussing someone in another lab—they probably were. Larkin has not been arrested or we would know about it. Bartell would have replaced him by now. And as for his loyalty, you should not question it. Now, please, let me get on with my work."

"Yes. I am sorry."

When she was gone, Sammell studied the mother board in indecision. If he removed the chip, when Larkin returned he'd have proof that Sammell had tampered with the computer, because yesterday the man could not have failed to notice the added chip.

That, no doubt, was why he'd made the visit to Sammell's cell so late. And if the chip was removed, and Larkin returned to work, all he would have to do was speak to Gissel and he'd know Sammell had been inspecting the computer's insides.

Then again, Larkin might never return. It seemed no one knew where he'd gone. Maybe he had joined the freedom fighters he'd mentioned last night. Maybe he *was* responsible for the vaporization.

In any case, Sammell couldn't take the chance on running a test in four days and its being successful. He'd have to damage the chip in some way and hope no one realized it before he'd had the opportunity to use his MDAT to send Marina home. He couldn't do it now because there were too many people around, but before he left work that day, he would find an opportunity to get at it again.

This was not how he had planned things. He'd hoped to avoid exposing himself to Bartell before he had the opportunity to fulfill his own mission, in case there were things he would still need from the lab or the archives, but now it looked as though he might have to disappear once Marina was safely out of danger. And there would be no doubt in Bartell's mind why he'd gone.

Everyone was required to shower before leaving work because of the possibility of contamination. Sammell was invariably the last one to do so.

He was just finishing up when he heard someone enter the room. The lights suddenly went out and someone whispered, "Do not trust Larkin. He is not a friend."

Before Sammell could get his bearings, the lights came on and he was alone. What was that supposed to mean? Friendship was not allowed in their society. Who would suggest such a thing to him and why? The voice had been unrecognizable.

Was Bartell behind the message? Or had it been Gissel or Darryn? What did they hope to accomplish by such a warning?

Sammell let himself back in to the lab, nodded at the guard as though he had every right to be there and moved past him into the chamber housing MDAT. It took only a moment to remove the cover on the computer, but when he looked at the mother board, he realized this was not his board. While he'd been in the showers, someone had replaced his board with another.

Gissel had been standing behind him when he'd discovered his mother board in the computer. Had he given himself away to her? Had she entered the lab while he was gone and switched boards? Why? Was it possible that she was working for Bartell and wanted to add to Sammell's confusion?

Whoever was responsible for the switch had succeeded beyond their wildest dreams. Sammell didn't know what to do.

An hour later, he let himself into his cell with a feeling of relief. Once he had looked on this place as a prison. But since Marina's arrival it had become a haven. And each evening he looked forward to his time alone with her. For a little while he could even pretend nothing was wrong in his world and Marina belonged in it with him.

It was a dangerous fantasy and he knew it.

He found her sleeping. For a long moment he simply stood and gazed at her. Then, unable to help himself, he moved closer and dropped down beside her. Brushing her cheek with unsteady fingers, he fingered the bright auburn curls lying soft about her forehead and temples, noting how they gleamed with shadows of deep red.

He studied the thick curling eyelashes and dark winged eyebrows several shades darker than her hair. There was both strength and delicacy in her face.

Suddenly he frowned. What had happened to the pink bloom in her cheeks when he'd first seen her? The small spots of brown had begun to fade from her skin, too. Was she sick?

Illness still existed in her world. Could she have been infected with some disease when he'd unwittingly transported her into the future? Or worse still, was there something in his world that was making her ill?

Marina's eyelids fluttered open, and in the instant before recognition lit her eyes, he saw the fear she hid from him with her smiles.

"You're home." She smiled. "I'm glad."

"Are you all right?" he asked anxiously.

"Yes." She rose to a sitting position. "But it was a long day—I miss Monday."

"You need fresh air and sunshine. Sunday we will go out."

Marina frowned. "At night, you mean?"

"No."

"But we can't go out in the daytime, you said—"

"I know what I said. I will take care of it."

Putting a hand on his arm, she said, "I don't want you to get into trouble. I'll be all right without sunshine for a while longer."

"I want you to see my world in the daylight. I want you to see its beauty without having to run from the police."

Covering her hand with one of his, he added, "I want you to love my world as much as I do. It could be a wonderful place to live—the true paradise the government would have us believe it is now—without King Wyndom and all his lies."

Marina was very much aware of the warmth of his fingers squeezing hers and surprised by the gesture. Touching was taboo. Or had he forgotten?

Now that she had realized the extent of her growing attraction to him, being alone with him was going to be difficult. It would be best if they could stay away from the personal and keep the touching to a minimum.

"Tell me about your government and how it works," she said, removing her hand from beneath his and getting to her feet. "In my time we had elected officials."

"I have already told you about King Wyndom," Samnell replied, watching her with a puzzled expression on his face. Was she still angry with him about last night? "King Wyndom has absolute power."

"I suppose he has a crest and coat of arms and all that Do you have to bow and call him Your Majesty?" she aske with a slight grin.

"Yes," he answered solemnly. "And the sector heads at called Lord. Lord Bartell heads this sector."

"He's your boss, isn't he?"

"Yes."

Marina tilted her head and screwed up her eyes. "Yo don't like him."

"No. He is a pompous fool. He would like to be king."

"In this new world you hope to create, would you hav kings and queens?"

"No," he thundered, getting to his feet. "All the peopl would have a say in what happens in their lives."

"Perhaps you will be the first president of your new world."

Sammell studied her pursed lips and innocent eyes. "Yo are...kidding with me?" It was a new concept for him, bu he was learning many things from his association with Ma rina.

Marina's eyes crinkled and her lips turned up at the cor ners. "Yes, in a way, but I was serious, too. You woul make a wonderful president."

"How do you know this?"

She shrugged. "I just do."

"We will see. Now, I want to hear more about your lif and the people who are close to you."

That night passed without incident. He and Marina talke into the early morning hours. And when she went to sleep he worked on MDAT. The machine was ready for Marina' trip home—Sammell was not.

It wasn't until he was lying in his sleep chamber, thinkin back on their conversation, that he realized they had talke mostly of his world, very little about hers and not at a about Marina. She had steered the conversation in a new direction each time he asked something personal.

Sammell sadly faced the fact that though she had said they would be friends, they were not. They were in truth little more than strangers.

The next day at work Larkin was still missing. And as the day came to a close without his being summoned to Barell's chambers, Sammell heaved a sigh of relief.

He took his time getting to the showers so that everyone else would be gone and when he left the building he was carrying several clean jumpsuits in his satchel instead of one.

The next morning Sammell helped Marina bunch her long hair up beneath a turban—an item occasionally worn by the women in his world—and left the room while she slipped into the jumpsuit everyone in his world wore.

A few minutes later, he rejoined her, stopping in his tracks to stare at her in speechless amazement. The turban and jumpsuit, both a buttercup yellow, had never looked on one of his people as they looked on Marina.

"What is it?" she asked quickly. "Do I look awful?"

"No—you look...you look..." His glance moved up her figure from trim ankles to well-rounded hips to her bosom and stopped.

"What?" she asked self-consciously, hardly able to restrain herself from wrapping her arms around her chest to hide it from view.

"You—here." He motioned toward his own upper torso.

"Up here?" she asked, fluttering her hands before her chest.

"And here." He motioned toward her hips.

Marina put a hand on either hip and frowned. "Are you telling me again that I'm too fat?"

"Not fat—rounded. But we can take care of that," he assured her quickly. "I have a larger jumpsuit." He eyed her chest doubtfully. "But I do not know about up there."

"I have an idea," Marina said suddenly. "Do you have a large towel?"

Sammell brought her a towel. And though he'd never seen a safety pin, when she explained what she needed, he managed to fashion something similar from wire.

"I'll need your help," she said with a flush on her cheeks
"My help?" he asked doubtfully.
"Yes. Can you turn your back for a moment?"

Sammell turned around, wondering what she needed him
to do. He was at a loss about how to hide her femininity
He'd thought the jumpsuit able to hide anything, but . . .

Marina slipped the jumpsuit down to her waist, folded th
towel and slipped it beneath her arms, wrapping it tightl
around her breasts. "Okay, you can turn around."

Sammell did so reluctantly, his heart pumping irregu
larly. He remembered the night he'd seen her breasts with
out a covering. Those achingly familiar sensations he'd fe
for the first time that night were beginning to stir, makin
him ill at ease.

"What I want you to do is pull the towel tight."

He had to stand close to do as she asked, and he could fee
the heat from her body all along his front. He ached an
could hardly stand still. Her scent was making his head spi
and his knees were once again acting strange, making it har
for him to stay upright.

"What do I do now?" he asked unsteadily.

His fingers against the skin of her back and shoulders se
a shiver racing down her spine. "Just hold it tight," sh
answered, twisting to face him.

Their glances caught. Marina swallowed tightly an
turned away. She handed him the pins he'd fashioned to h
specifications. "Pin it in place at the back."

"H-here?" His fingers fumbled with the makeshift pir
and the towel was suddenly in danger of slipping.

Marina caught it tight against her, goose bumps din
pling her arms as Sammell's fingers brushed the side of h
breast. "There," she said quickly readjusting the towe
wanting this to be over so she could breathe normall
"Now, can you pin it?"

"Yes."

His warm breath feathered her naked shoulders. Closin
her eyes, she bit her lip and concentrated on keeping h
balance, the uneven tenor of his breathing whistling in h

ear. It felt as if it took hours for him to fasten the towel in place, and by the time he was finished her knees felt weak as water.

Sammell lifted the jumpsuit over her shoulders and smoothed it in place. The act wasn't necessary, but it was an excuse for him to go on touching her—and he wanted to go on touching her very much.

Now that he was losing his reticence about it, he couldn't understand why people didn't touch each other all the time. It caused such strange and remarkable sensations inside.

"Shoes," Marina said abruptly.

Sammell looked taken aback.

"Shoes," Marina repeated, pointing to her bare feet. "I can't wear my sandals—unless your people wear sandals?" he asked hopefully.

"No, but I have more of these." He indicated the boots he wore.

Marina was skeptical about the fit, and sure enough, when he returned with the boots they were at least two sizes too big. But she managed to fix that by putting the technical manuals Sammell had given her to read to good use.

"Put these on." He handed her a pair of wraparound dark glasses and put on a pair of his own. "Do not remove them until we return."

Outside, they hurried away from the house, keeping a sharp eye out for any of Sammell's neighbors. They knew he was not yet mated and he didn't want to arouse their curiosity.

This time they had no need to slip from tree to tree in the thick woods. They walked side by side at the edge of the cobblestone road.

Marina was happy to be walking in leaf-dappled sunshine beneath a blue sky. She felt as if she'd just been released from prison and she couldn't take in enough of the sights. In moonlight the small cottagelike dwellings with their walkways and flower gardens had been picturesque, but in daylight their charm reminded her of home—the home in Indiana where she'd been raised.

"You were right," she murmured, "your world is indee
lovely."

They passed several people, some walking, some ridin
bicycles and a few on horseback, and Marina had to ca
tion herself against familiarity. Everyone nodded whe
passing, but there were no smiles of greeting, no friendl
conversations. And she quickly understood Sammell's he
itation in taking her out without her breasts bound.

The women and men looked very similar. They dresse
alike, had their hair cut in the same style, and except for th
softer bone structure in their faces and the occasional tu
ban, it would have been very difficult to tell man fro
woman. And to her amazement—though Sammell ha
warned her about it—everyone had blond hair and dar
eyes.

Sammell touched Marina lightly on the arm. "We wi
have more privacy down this path."

They had been walking for several minutes in silenc
without seeing anyone else, when Sammell touched her ar
again and motioned behind them. "There are fruit tre
growing back there in a spot that cannot be seen from th
path."

"Good day, Sammell."

Sammell stiffened. "Larkin," he said, turning, "what a
you doing here?"

"Taking the air, same as you."

"You have not been at work for the past two days.
Sammell glanced up and down the path as though expec
ing to see armed guards about to descend on them.

"Do not worry about that. I have taken care of thin
with Bartell."

Sammell's glance sharpened on the other man's fac
"You have been to the lab?"

"Yes. I was in the lab yesterday. I spoke with Bartell, b
he did not want certain people to know I was there."

Sammell frowned. "What are you saying?"

"Oh, I do not think this is the place to discuss work.
Resting his glance on Marina, he stretched his lips in th

acsimile of a smile and offered her a nod. "I have not seen ou before."

"Ah—" Sammell thought quickly. "This is a colleague rom a visiting sector. She is a brilliant research physicist in he field of matter transfer."

"Is that right? Well, why is she not on our team?" Larkin asked.

Sammell saw his glance linger on Marina's chest and reponded quickly, "Perhaps she will be."

"I must go. I will see you tomorrow."

"Larkin!" Sammell stopped him. "Are you aware that a est is scheduled for tomorrow?"

"Yes, I suggested it to Bartell."

"You! Why?"

"I thought it was time."

"Time? I do not understand."

"You will."

Sammell stared at Larkin's retreating back. Marina stared t Sammell's expression. "What is it?" she asked after a ong moment when he didn't move. "What did he mean by hat?"

"I do not know."

A bird began to trill in a tree overhead and Marina rabbed his hand. "Come on. It's too beautiful a day to tand about and frown."

Sammell resisted, his thoughts still on Larkin's cryptic emark. But Marina wasn't having any of that. This was her irst day in the sunshine for far too long and she wasn't going to let it be spoiled.

When he wouldn't budge, she ran away from him. And Sammell could do nothing but give chase before she got into rouble. Before long he was taking the lead. Marina folowed, and soon they were ducking beneath tree branches, queezing through narrow gaps between bushes, stumbling, falling against each other, rolling on the ground and aughing uproariously as they removed leaves and twigs rom their clothing.

Having reached the place he'd told her about, he stopped and pulled her down beneath the cover of bushes. Sobering instantly, he gazed at her, realizing that they were lucky they hadn't been spotted and informed on. By laughing and running, he'd broken the law. And this woman was responsible for it. He should be angry, but he was elated. She made him feel truly glad to be alive.

He reached for the dark glasses shielding her eyes. Removing them, he tossed them aside. "What have you done to me?"

"I beg your pardon?" Marina asked uncertainly.

"You have made me a criminal—no worse than that, you have made me *glad* to be a criminal."

"I'm sorry," she said slowly, staring at him, wondering if he was serious.

"I am not."

She smiled, then focused her attention on the apple tree behind him. The limbs were heavy and the ground beneath it was littered with ripe fallen fruit.

Crawling around him on all fours, she gathered a handful of the shiny red apples and sat cross-legged to wipe one on her sleeve before taking a large bite.

"There's so much of it," she said, staring at the wall of trees around them. "And it's all so delicious."

"All part of the government's plan to keep us happy," Sammell said with a sneer in his voice. "Remember, this is supposed to be paradise."

Marina wiped the juice off her chin with the back of one hand, savoring the sweet taste of the fruit. About to take another bite, she glanced up into Sammell's eyes.

"Oh, sorry, here." Apparently forgetting he didn't eat, she offered him one of the apples.

Sammell stared at the fruit for a long time. Then he shook his head and glanced away. He'd forgotten to take his nutrient injection both last night and this morning, but he didn't want to eat any of what she offered him because sometimes—most times—the first few bites made him ill.

Marina shrugged and took another healthy bite, feeling the juice drench her lips. She was about to lick it away when Sammell reached up and touched her lower lip with his fingers.

Her eyes jumped to his face. They looked at each other for a moment, his fingers quivering against her lip.

Sammell's glance began to waver and he started to withdraw. But Marina grabbed his hand, holding it still, her eyes locking with his as she bent and licked the sweetness from his fingertips.

He didn't dare take a breath. If he did, the tight control he barely maintained on his body would splinter and he was afraid of what might happen then. Filled with a multitude of riotous sensations caused by Marina or simply the thought of her, Sammell was a willing prisoner of his emotions.

Aware of his rigidity, Marina dropped his hand, thinking she had offended him. Sometimes she forgot that the little instinctive things she did were outside his realm of understanding.

"I'm sorry. I—"

Sammell took one of her hands and lifted it to his lips. Her eyes widened in shock as he caressed the soft pads of her fingers with the tip of his tongue.

"What are you doing?" she asked a little breathlessly, withdrawing her hand.

"I want to learn from you. We are friends, are we not?"

"Yes," she answered, swallowing dryly, "we are friends." With her heart in her eyes, she offered him a bite of her apple.

After only a moment's hesitation, he leaned forward and sank his teeth into the fruit. Sitting back, watching her, he chewed slowly and swallowed.

Marina took a bite, smiled and started to wipe her lips. But Sammell stopped her. On his knees at her side, he drew his fingers across her moist lips, then licked the sweetness from them.

Marina chewed, feeling as though the apple expanded rather than diminished in her mouth. She swallowed and Sammell placed his hand over hers and held the apple to her lips.

She looked up at him from beneath long dark eyelashes and he said, "Bite."

Marina bit and his head suddenly swooped to hers. She drew back instinctively, but he followed and she felt the moist tip of his tongue against her lips.

"It tastes better this way," he explained against her lips. When she didn't respond, he drew back. "Is this not permitted?"

"I—yes, it's permitted," she answered a bit unsteadily.

Sammell again lifted the apple to her lips, watched as she took a bite and then took a bite himself. Marina stared at the top of his head, her heart pounding. And then his head curved toward hers.

"We will both taste...what?"

"Sweet," Marina supplied, still in that unsteady tone of voice. "We will both taste the sweetness."

"Yes." His lips brushed hers, a tantalizing invitation for more. "Sweet," he murmured against them.

The apple fell from Marina's fingers and her hands moved to his shoulders. Sammell settled his mouth over hers in a tentative moist kiss. Marina responded by parting her lips in mute invitation, and a small sound of wonder came from his throat.

And then he was pushing her away, staring at her with dark wary eyes. His insides felt on fire. That terrible yearning he'd felt two nights ago, when he had watched her through the protective shield without her knowledge, was tearing him apart.

Marina saw the confusion on his face—and something else. The dark eyes were filled with a raw need that he was trying his best to hide. She opened her arms and he came into them. Drawing him forward, she lay back against the grass. His chest pressed against her breasts and she drew him closer.

All the air expelled from Sammell's lungs in one wild gasp as he felt every inch of her body pressed to his. And then, as though her touch had triggered a primitive response beyond his control, his fingers tangled in her hair, his hips ground against hers and his mouth took hers in a savage hungry caress.

All at once the air was filled with a shrill whistle. Sammell stiffened and jerked away.

"What is it?" Marina asked anxiously.

"A warning signal."

Chapter 10

"Warning signal? What kind of warning signal?" Marina asked.

"It is time to leave the gardens," Sammell hedged. "Come, we must go."

He climbed quickly to his feet and offered her a hand. But something in his attitude alarmed her. This was no simple warning to leave the gardens—it was something far more serious and she knew it.

Marina pulled on his hand and dug her heels into the ground. "I don't believe you. They're looking for us, aren't they?"

He started to deny it, then nodded instead. "I believe so. That was a signal telling the police to switch to a certain channel on their communicators where they will be given details about the criminal, or criminals, at large."

"Us. They're looking for us."

Sammell didn't deny her words. His instincts told him she was right. They were being sought by the police. And he had a hunch the police had exact descriptions of both of them right down to the color of Marina's turban.

"What are we going to do?" She was trying very hard to keep the panic out of her voice.

"The only thing we can do—run."

They ran, but it was useless. They could hear voices in the trees around them. The police were closing in. There was nowhere to run. They didn't have a chance.

"Oh, Sam, what are we going to do?"

"Here!" A voice seemed to rise from the ground almost at their feet.

Marina took a sudden step back, her eyes on the square of grass slowly rising in the air. The top of a blond head became visible in the aperture, and then two eyes peered at them out of the darkness.

A pale hand moved into view and fluttered toward them, motioning for them to hurry. Marina took a hesitant step forward then halted, reaching for Sammell.

Sammell encouraged her to move forward and they both peered down into the face of a man standing on a ladder beneath the earth's surface.

"Hurry!" the stranger motioned. "We have only seconds before the first squad of police arrive."

Sammell helped the man assist Marina onto the ladder, and he was only one step behind as Marina backed down the slippery steps with fear like a live thing gnawing at her insides. Who was this man with his hands at her waist, pulling her down into a darkness so complete it almost smothered her?

"Close the top carefully," the man's voice rose from the darkness. "If the police find the opening, we are finished."

Sammell did as instructed, and an instant later a light flashed on below. He stared down at three faces—Marina, Darryn and Gissel.

"Where did you come from? And how did you know we were here—being sought by the police?" Sammell asked quickly, making his way to them.

"We have been monitoring police calls for months," Gissel answered, taking the lead as they moved away from the ladder and deeper into the tunnel.

"Do you know who alerted the police about our presence in the gardens?" Sammell asked.

"Larkin." Again it was Gissel who did the talking. "I warned you that he was not your friend."

"You warned me," Sammell repeated slowly, his face a study in confusion. "The showers! That was you in the showers?"

"Yes. Now we must hurry. They want this woman very badly."

"Me?" Marina asked abruptly. "How do they know about me?"

Sammell stepped closer to Marina. "This is Gissel and Darryn. They are members of the team working on project Deliverance. And this—" he touched her lightly on the shoulder "—is Marina."

"Yes, we know," Gissel said shortly. "Bartell has been watching you for some time—just as we have. He knows you have made greater advances on project Deliverance than you have acknowledged. And when Larkin told him about this woman—"

"Larkin told him!" Sammell interrupted.

"Yes," Gissel answered. "He communicated with him from the gardens. Larkin has been trying to establish a personal relationship with you for some time on Bartell's instructions so that he could find out how far you had really progressed with the matter transfer device.

"We, too, wanted to contact you, but did not think you were ready."

"Larkin was working for Bartell," Sammell said. "Who are you working for?"

The path was becoming steeper. The walls were damp with moisture, and the passage narrowed as they moved in single file with Gissel in the lead, Marina next and Sammell behind her, while Darryn brought up the rear.

"We work for no one," Gissel said tersely. "We fight for our people so that one day they will call no man master."

"Fight?" Sammell asked quickly.

"Yes, there is fighting in the mountains behind Government House. It has been so for many months."

"There is no fighting," Sammell protested. "We are at peace. We have been at peace for nearly four hundred years."

"The fighting only stopped for fewer than twenty years after the Wyndom regime came into power," Gissel said on a note of contempt. "Not long after his takeover it soon became evident to those of the world who had not been infected with his drug that their neighbors were acting peculiar. Within a year the drug was found in the water, and steps were taken to remove it."

All of this was news to Sammell. He had deluded himself into thinking the world needed him to save it, and all the time others had been busy working to save it without his help.

"So," he said thoughtfully, "we are at war. Who is winning?"

"They are." Darryn spoke for the first time.

"But how can that be?" Sammell asked. "Surely the people are on your side."

"Weapons," Gissel responded. "We have very few weapons. And despite centuries of resistance, we have made little progress against the government armies."

"Armies?" Sammell asked. "It is hard to believe this talk of war and armies. Where is the evidence?"

"The storage unit vaporized last night," Gissel said. "That is evidence, is it not?"

"What do you want from me?" Sammell asked abruptly.

"As I said earlier, we have been watching you for a long time. We know about your nocturnal trips. We know you discovered the drug on your own at a very early age, that you removed it from your own injections and that you have been experimenting with food."

"How do you know all this?" Sammell asked in amazement.

"We have developed a very thorough spy network over the years," Gissel answered, stopping to look over her shoulder. "We know things that would surprise you even more than this.

"Come." She led the way into a huge high-ceilinged chamber and swept out both arms. "Look around you, see our preparations for this war you do not believe exists."

Before he would enter the cavern, Sammell propelled Marina behind him and stood facing Gissel. Though he'd been dissatisfied living in bondage under the present administration, he wasn't certain that he wanted to be a part of an army. And he wasn't sure he understood what Gissel and Darryn expected from him.

"What is it you want from me?" he asked Gissel again.

"We want you to join us. Help us fight our oppressors."

"I am not a soldier. I am a scientist."

"We, too, are scientists," she replied. "We want you to work with us."

"And do what? I know nothing of fighting and making war."

"Your knowledge can help us," Darryn said.

Sammell turned to him. "Are you willing to kill for your beliefs?"

"We will do whatever is necessary," Darryn replied.

"You want MDAT—that is what this is all about, is it not?"

Gissel glanced at the silent Darryn.

"Why?" Sammell asked them both. "Why do you want my time machine?"

"To further our cause for freedom and peace," Gissel answered.

"Don't speak to me of peace when you advocate killing," Sammell said sourly. "Did you violate my privacy, break into my cell and try to break into the lab? Did you try to steal MDAT?"

"No." Gissel stood straight and tall before him, meeting his glance head-on. "We are freedom fighters—revolutionaries—not common thieves!"

Sammell hesitated, studying her set jaw and proud face. "I need time to think, time to consider my position."

"Granted," Gissel said. "Now, come, you must rest while you think."

Sammell reached behind him and felt Marina slip her cold fingers into his. They stepped into the cavern together.

The cavern was enormous, the size of two football fields placed end to end. The walls were worn smooth by aeons of water flowing over the rock. Stalactites hung from the ceiling in intricate shapes in a variety of sizes.

What must have once been a large river was now only a four-foot stream flowing from a fissure in the wall dividing the cavern in two. Equipment and belongings lined the walls on one side and makeshift beds lined the other. Scattered throughout the room were small campfires, their glow pushing against the darkness, adding smoke to air thick with the smell of damp earth.

Marina stared at the empty campfires. A few had pots suspended over them with anonymous liquids bubbling over the edge and the air near them was redolent of cooking. Where were the people?

"Come, I will show you to your quarters." Gissel again took the lead.

At the back of the cavern were a series of small chambers carved out of the rock. A cloth curtain hung across the opening of each one, affording the inhabitants a small measure of privacy.

"The conditions here are primitive," Gissel said without a hint of apology in her voice, "but we live without fear. Rest now and we will speak again later."

After she'd gone, Sammell stood in the center of the small area and stared at the furniture—a phosphorus lamp sitting on the floor in one corner, giving out an eerie green glow, a bed of rough wood and a matching chair. Taking a seat on the chair, he motioned for Marina to sit on the bed.

"I am sorry," he apologized.

"For what?"

"For this." He spread his hands to their surroundings.

"It's all right. At least we haven't been arrested." Sh
looked around the small room. "It's even kind of cozy an
I'm not afraid here."

"I am."

"You are?" Marina asked in surprise. "Of what?"

"All this. I was not happy with my life and the life m
people are forced to live, but I planned a peaceful solution
No one would have been hurt by my going into the past an
preventing the development of the Wyndom drug. Bu
this..." He shook his head. "This is insanity."

"Are you saying you aren't going to join your friends i
their fight?"

"They are not my friends. I have been suspicious of Gis
sel and Darryn for the past several days—but I thought the
worked for Bartell. I never imagined..." He shook his hea
again, the swatch of blond hair tumbling into his eyes.

Marina leaned forward with her hands clasped tightly o
her lap. "Sammell, they're fighting for the same things yo
want—freedom, and the right to make your own choices
How can you not help them?"

"I could not take a life. Nothing is worth the taking o
another's life."

Getting to his feet, he moved around the room, brushin
at his hair with an impatient hand. "If events outside m
control had not occurred," he murmured to himself, "
would not be faced with such a terrible choice."

Marina knew she was one of those "events" and she fel
guilty for causing him such mental anguish, but, still, ther
were some things a person had to be willing to fight for i
this world—anyone's world. And freedom was one of them

Noting her silence, Sammell faced her. "Would yo
fight?" he asked abruptly. "Would you take life for free
dom?"

"Your fri—Gissel said the fighting and killing has bee
going on for nearly four hundred years. The government i

killing your people! How many do you suppose they've killed in the past hundred years? One a day? Ten a day? A hundred? How many thousands does that add up to? Can you let that go on without trying to do something to stop it?"

"You would fight," Sammell said flatly.

"I would do what I had to do. Just like you will do what you have to do," she answered. "From what I've seen and heard about your world, worldwide revolution seems unavoidable. Four hundred years is a long time to live under oppression—especially this kind of oppression."

"Yes," Sammell answered vaguely. His mind was working on another problem, one that had remained fixed at the back of his mind since their earlier conversation with Gissel. If she and Darryn hadn't broken into his cell, then it must have been Larkin.

Did he know about this group? He'd made a comment about freedom fighters being in the hills outside the city. Had that been an attempt to trap Sammell into giving away his own feelings about the government? Or had he been baiting Sammell to find out what he knew about this organization?

Now he knew who had taken MDAT's mother board from his desk—Larkin. And that meant he had the matter-time-sequence chip. He might already have the power to travel back in time. The only thing he lacked was the correct formula for the plasma jet and he'd been perilously close to figuring that out—unless he'd been playing with Sammell by pretending he had only a part of it.

Should he speak with Gissel and tell her about Larkin's veiled comments? The people here might not be as safe as they thought. He was halfway to the door when the first pains struck.

Grabbing his abdomen, he doubled over, catching hold of the chair with one hand to keep from falling to his knees.

"Sam! What is it?" Marina jumped off the bed and rushed to his side. "Here, lean on me." She supported him

to the bed, helped him stretch out on his back and sat dow
beside him.

"What is it?" she asked anxiously.

"Pain," he muttered through clenched teeth, folding h
arms tightly across his middle.

"Your stomach?"

"Yes." Sweat dotted his forehead and upper lip, and
pulse beat at his temple. He'd had little experience of pai
and this pain was bad, but he didn't want Marina to kno
how bad.

"I'll get Gissel—"

"No!" He grabbed her arm and held her still. "Stay wit
me. I do not want or need Gissel. I will be all right—do n
leave me."

"Yes," Marina said, "I'll stay, but don't you think—"

"No," he said, cutting her off, panting with the effort
speech. "I do not want to think. I want you to...stay wit
me...please..."

Marina stayed, and after a while he fell into a fitful doze
But every now and then he'd awaken with a cry on his lip
and dig his fingers into the skin over his abdomen. Marin
took his hands and held them tightly, whispering words
comfort to him. And he soon settled down into anothe
doze.

Time passed, and though she couldn't know for certai
she guessed they must have been here for at least a couple
hours. And though he wouldn't let her leave his side, ha
made her promise to stay, she prayed Gissel or Darry
would appear so they could see how sick he was and he
him.

His face looked flushed, and she tested the skin on h
forehead with the back of one hand. Though it had bee
damp before with perspiration, now it felt hot and dry.

Marina was growing more worried. What he needed wa
a doctor. She gave a half-smothered laugh that almost ende
on a sob. Where did you look for a doctor in a subterra
nean chamber, among people who were never ill?

Her worry turned to anger. How dared these people let themselves come to this. Hiding like rats in a cave! Why hadn't they stood up to this Wyndom person long before now?

If Sammell were to be believed, the man was nearly four hundred years old. How much fight could there be in a four-hundred-year-old man?

Sammell groaned and moved restlessly in his sleep. Marina scooted out of the chair and took a seat on the bed beside him. She had to do something. She couldn't just sit by and watch him in pain. He had a fever. She needed cool water and a cloth to bathe his forehead. At least she could get that. There was a river running practically outside their door.

Outside the chamber she moved among the campfires searching for something to hold water. She didn't waste time looking for Gissel, but couldn't help hoping the woman would show up. She finally found a crudely shaped bowl carved from wood. A further search among the articles stacked along the wall revealed cloth.

Dipping the bowl into the water, she hurried back to Sammell, spilling some as she ran. She halted in the doorway, a cry of alarm on her lips. In her absence he must have awakened and looked for her. He was lying facedown on the floor between the bed and chair.

For a heart-stopping moment, she couldn't move. And then she had to grasp hold of the bedpost to keep from falling herself, because she thought he was dead.

He groaned, the world stopped spinning and she felt her heart kick into its normal rhythm. Setting the bowl of water on the chair, she kneeled beside Sammell and put her arms beneath his shoulders. He didn't look it, but he was very heavy. It took all her strength to move him, but she managed to lift him from a sitting position to his knees and finally onto the bed.

There her strength deserted her and she fell down beside him on the blankets out of breath. What would her friends think of her now, if they could see her?

What would she tell them when she returned to her own
world? There was no question about it. She could never tell
them the truth. Time travel? She hadn't believed it herself
until she'd been shown irrefutable proof.

Sammell turned, threw a leg over one of hers and flopped
an arm across her waist, his hand cupping one breast. Ma
rina caught her breath and started to move away. It would
be an embarrassing position to be found in, should Gissel or
Darryn come to the door. Still she hesitated. It seemed to
comfort Sammell to be close to her. And that was more im
portant than what two strangers might think of her, so Ma
rina lay still beneath his hand, listening to him breathe,
feeling her nipple grow taut against his warm palm.

Settling herself more comfortably against him, she let her
mind drift. If he were not ill...if they were not running from
the police...if his world was not in a state of war...this
could be paradise....

When she awoke, it was to find Sammell's hot face
pressed to the side of her neck. He was burning with fever.

Disengaging herself, Marina climbed carefully from the
bed and picked up the water and cloth from the chair. This
was all she had to help him, and it was precious little. He
needed more. *She would not let him die!*

She bathed his face and neck repeatedly, then decided it
would help more if she could bathe his chest and back.
Rolling him onto his side, she managed to pull the clothing
off his shoulders and down to his waist. With soft gentle
strokes she smoothed the cloth over his face and chest until
his skin began to feel cooler.

Just when she was beginning to relax a little, he began to
shiver with chills. Marina removed his boots and lifted his
feet beneath the blanket, drawing it up to his chin. And then
she just sat in the chair and watched him, memorizing his
face.

His features were so symmetrical that any more delicacy
would have made him too beautiful for a man. He was saved
from that by the square jaw, slight dent in his chin and
firm mouth.

Pain had carved merciless lines on his face, and the shadow of his beard gave him a manly aura that until now had only been hinted at because of his unisex style of dress. Moisture clung to the damp blond hair lying over his forehead, turning the ends dark. Marina brushed them back from his forehead with a gentle hand. He looked so pale and defenseless. But she remembered the glint in his eyes a few days ago when he'd pleaded with her to trust him.

A few days ago... that's all it had been since she'd awakened to find herself his prisoner. Prisoner...she was still his prisoner, but in ways he couldn't begin to imagine.

Sammell stirred and opened his eyes. She smiled and he tried to return it but bit his lips against the pain. A spot of blood appeared at the corner of his mouth, and she closed her eyes, wishing she could do something more to help him.

His face grew paler and his body shook with chills. Marina put a hand to his forehead and felt the clammy skin.

"Sam? Can you hear me?" she asked softly. "I'm going for Gissel. She may have something to help you."

"N-no." His hand tightened on hers. "I need nothing but you."

Once again he fell into a fitful doze and for a little while she thought he was getting better. But then a spasm of pain hit him and he moaned, turning onto his side and drawing his knees to his chest.

Marina couldn't stand it any longer. Easing her hand from his, she moved to the door, pulled the curtain aside and stepped into the main cavern.

Almost immediately she spotted Gissel on the far side of the cavern. "Please..." Marina called, motioning for her to come closer. "You must help Sam—he's in terrible pain."

Gissel strode across the cavern, her feet making hollow sounds on the rock floor. She dodged around Marina without waiting for further explanation and hastened into the room. Taking a quick look at Sammell's contorted body, she asked, "Has he eaten anything?"

"W-what?" The question came so unexpectedly that Marina needed a moment to assimilate it.

"Has he eaten anything?" Gissel asked again, turning to face the other woman, impatience in the dark eyes.

"Part of an apple—he ate part of an apple—earlier, when we were...up there." She pointed toward the ceiling.

Gissel nodded as if that was what she had expected to hear. "I will return shortly."

Marina took her seat at the side of the bed and began to sponge Sammell off again. His eyelids twitched, but other than that he gave no sign that he knew she was there.

Guilt engulfed her. This was her fault. She'd offered him the apple. What if the fruit had somehow poisoned him? She knew nothing about how his digestive system worked. She shouldn't have tempted him. Tears burned her eyes.

Oh, God, what if he died? The thought struck terror to her heart, and not because she was afraid she wouldn't get back to her own time. She didn't want anything to happen to him because...she was falling in love with him.

It should have come as a shock for her to realize that her feelings for him had grown so strong in such a short time. But it had happened so gradually.

As she smoothed the damp hair back from his forehead, a tear spilled onto her cheek and her lips moved in a silent prayer. Her heart wrenched at the sight of the dark circles beneath his eyes and the line of white around his pale lips.

What if it wasn't the apple? What if she had brought a virus with her from the past—something they were not immune to in this century? That's how the settlers had annihilated many Indian tribes in the 1800s.

And that made her remember that before long she would be leaving. The thing she'd wanted most in life lay before her—but he could never be hers. The old adage about coming from different worlds had never been more true.

They came from different worlds, but she was beginning to think she'd be glad to give up her place in her world if she could be assured a place in Sammell's. It would mean leaving her family behind forever and never seeing any of her friends again.... But they had all found their places in life

Marina was still searching for hers. She'd always felt as though she was never quite in step with the rest of the world. She'd wanted a husband, home and family, the kind of life her parents had found together.

But society's values had changed a great deal since her parents had first married. The men she dated weren't interested in a family. And if one stuck around long enough to discover that she wanted one, she got a lecture on how men were no longer looking for a "little woman."

The men of today wanted a woman with a high-powered career. One who could help provide those European vacations, expensive sports cars and membership fees to elite social clubs. Life was meant to be enjoyed in between making corporate decisions and social statements. And if the marriage didn't work, divorce was the next step.

There was nothing wrong with that way of life—if that's what you wanted. Marina didn't. She wanted a man with whom to share the rest of her life. She wanted a lifetime commitment and everything that went with it, including children. She'd always hoped that somewhere there was a man wanting the same thing and someday their paths would cross.

Her glance found Sammell. Is this what it was really all about? Was she willing to give up her dreams of a home and security for a gun? If he chose to fight, would he expect her to fight right alongside him?

She'd told him she would do what she had to do in his situation. But could she really pull the trigger of a gun, knowing it would result in the death of another human being?

And what about that family she wanted? In a world where babies were created in test tubes and incubated like eggs in a chicken house, where did that leave her?

Sammell might not even be capable of making love. Remembering the way he'd pulled away from her in the gardens just as their kiss was beginning to grow into something more intense, she sighed heavily. And what about making her pregnant?

She looked at him lying so pale and still beneath the covers and wondered what a child of theirs might be like. Red and blond hair together—what did that make . . . orange?

Sammell said his mate would be chosen by a computer according to genetics and intelligence. Well, that left her out of the running. She wasn't stupid, but she didn't come anywhere near to being on the same IQ level as a man who could develop a time machine that really worked.

He'd been defensive about his world, wanting her to love it as much as he loved it. Marina loved her own. Could she ever grow to love this one as much?

There would be so many things she'd have to give up besides her family and friends. And what about her career? She was a teacher, and she'd always thought that after her babies reached a certain age she'd want to go back to teaching. But then again, in a brave new world teachers would be needed.

Sammell stirred and Marina quieted him with a gentle hand against his cheek. He snuggled against it like a child seeking comfort, and a warmth spread through her.

How could she not stay? Her own words came back to haunt her. She'd told Sammell that by the taking of her husband's name she would be leaving her old life behind and creating a new one. Isn't that what she would be doing here?

Only here it would really be a *new world*. Their world, hers and Sammell's, one they had truly helped forge with their own two hands.

But what about what Sammell wanted? She was taking a lot for granted in thinking he'd want her to stay. All she'd heard from him since she'd arrived was his plan to send her back as soon as his machine was repaired.

And what about love? Sammell didn't know the first thing about love. Admittedly the thought of teaching him intrigued her. But it might not intrigue him. He'd shown a curiosity about it, but still . . .

And what about children? She'd never heard him mention anything about them, except when she'd asked him. He would make a good father—she'd bet on it. But was she willing to bet the rest of her life?

Husband, father, lover—these were all roles foreign to Sammell's nature. She could teach him the rudiments of each role, but what about what was inside him? Was the instinct for each role there? Without it all her teaching would be wasted. Some things could be learned and some could not.

Chapter 11

"How is he?" Gissel asked as she pushed through the curtain.

"I think he's still in a lot of pain," Marina answered, standing up and moving back to give the other woman access to the man on the bed.

"Do you know if he has missed his nutrient injections in the past two days?"

"I don't know."

Gissel nodded. "I have brought something that will help him. He is not going to want to drink it, but he must. His system is not yet used to solid food. It will take time for him to adjust."

She eyed Marina speculatively before continuing. "I do not know how much you know about our society, but the government adds a drug to the nutrient injections they supply us with before we get them. It makes our people more *amenable* to their control. The chemicals are incompatible with food—deliberately so," she added with an angry glint in her dark eyes.

"But Sammell removed the drug—the Wyndom drug, he called it."

Gissel smiled, but it was a smile without humor. "The Wyndom drug," she mused. "Yes, that is an appropriate name for it, named after the monster who created it. But that is not the drug I am speaking about. There is more than one drug in the injection. There is also one that removes the natural desire to mate."

Marina's glance darted to Sammell's pale face and she felt her cheeks grow warm.

"They want us subservient to them in every way," Gissel added. "Here." She shoved a small wooden bowl and crudely shaped spoon at Marina. "Spoon this into him until it is all gone. Some of it might come back up, but no matter. He must take it all."

Marina accepted the bowl and spoon with a nod, then wondered what would happen if he were to be sick. She hadn't seen any bathroom facilities. She wanted to ask where they were but hesitated doing it. The woman was brisk and not very friendly. Marina had a feeling Gissel resented her presence.

The other woman was at the curtain preparing to leave when Marina screwed up her courage and asked, "If he becomes sick, where..."

"There." Gissel motioned with one hand toward the back of the small room. And then she was gone.

Marina investigated the area and found a wooden bucket with a lid. She shrugged. It was better than nothing.

Sammell had turned over onto his back when Marina moved to the side of the bed. Placing the bowl and spoon on the chair, she took a seat beside him and felt his forehead. It still felt cold and clammy. She hoped the stuff in the bowl Gissel had given her would help. As an adolescent she'd had her share of tummyaches, but none that had affected her like this. But then she hadn't spent her entire life sticking needles into her arm instead of cramming food down her throat, either.

Placing an arm beneath his head, she lifted his head and shoulders off the pillow. "Sam, can you hear me? I want you to drink this." She held the spoon to his lips awkwardly, hoping he would cooperate so she wouldn't have to force the spoon into his mouth.

Sammell's eyes fluttered open, then closed. Marina bit her lip, thinking she was going to have to force the liquid down his throat. What would she do if he choked?

Suddenly his lips parted and she quickly tilted the spoon to them. With the first swallow he gagged, and Marina remembered the bucket with the lid sitting only a few feet away. And then he swallowed again and it looked as though everything was going to be all right.

"What—" he muttered, turning his head aside.

"Medicine," Marina said. "Gissel brought it and said you had to drink it all."

"What medicine?" he asked weakly, keeping his head turned aside and his lips tightly closed.

"I don't know. She didn't tell me its name. She said it would help—but you have to drink it all."

"No." Sammell shook his head stubbornly. "Take it away."

Marina raised an eyebrow. He was acting like a baby. "I will not," she said firmly. "Shame on you. You're acting like a child. You will drink every drop of this willingly—whatever it is—or I'll...I'll hold your nose and force it down your throat."

Sammell turned his head slowly and looked up at her. "Is this how you treat people who are ill in your world?"

Marina bit her lip. He was very sick and she was practically yelling at him.

"I'm only concerned about you," she said quickly. "You need the medicine in this bowl. Gissel seemed to understand what was wrong with you right away, so apparently they have treated this kind of thing before. How can you work if you are ill? And there is much work for you to do among your people. Please, if you won't take it for me—think of your people."

Sammell studied her silently. And just when she thought it was a lost cause, he lifted his head and opened his mouth.

Within the next half hour she managed to get all but a small amount of the liquid down him. She had no idea what was in it—it had no odor and she couldn't bring herself to taste it—but whatever it was, it seemed to help. In what seemed like no time at all the lines of pain around Sammell's mouth and eyes began to disappear and he began to look drowsy. But before he fell asleep, he murmured something in tones so low that she had to lean down to make out the words.

"I took it for you...perhaps...there is not so much difference in your world and mine...after all...."

Time passed. The cavern outside their room was silent. She had no idea if it was day or night. And it didn't matter. There was a timeless quality about this place, and she found herself adjusting to it without difficulty. She was with Sammell, he was getting better and for the moment that was all that mattered.

Her head drooped and her eyes closed. Sometime later she awoke and looked around the room in bewilderment. Where was she—oh, yes, the cavern. Her eyes darted to the bed and she heaved a sigh of relief. Sammell was sleeping peacefully.

All at once she shivered and clasped her arms together, hugging her shoulders. The temperature above ground might be a constant seventy-two degrees, but it was at least ten degrees cooler down here.

She could go into the main room and get a blanket. She'd seen a stack of them against the wall, but... Her eyes moved to the bed and the man lying on it. What she wouldn't give to be able to lie down. But there was only one bed in the room, and Sammell occupied it. Come to think of it, Gissel and Darryn had placed them here knowing that. She lifted an eyebrow. How long, she wondered wryly, had Gissel and Darryn known about the other drugs in the nutrient injections?

It seemed they might be fully aware of the benefits of combined body heat. Studying the bed, she realized there was plenty of room for two. And there was no place else for her to sleep—unless she wanted to stretch out on the floor.

Ugh! She frowned in revulsion at the thought, staring at the hard stone floor at her feet. It would be nothing like sleeping on the floor of Sammell's laboratory. There might be bugs and things down here. *Rats?*

She glanced back at the bed. What would Sammell think if he were to awaken and find her lying beside him?

Another shiver raced through her and Marina decided she was about to find out. Removing the towel binding her breasts, she slipped from the chair to the side of the bed and lay down on her side, snuggling against Sammell for warmth and pulling the blanket over both of them. She'd just managed to find the perfect spot for her head against Sammell's shoulder when she floated from consciousness to sleep without even realizing it.

Sometime later she cast aside the thick layers of sleep one at a time to feel a featherlike touch on her cheek. She lifted a hand and batted at it until it went away. A moment later it was back.

Opening her eyes with a frown, she gazed into Sammell's dark eyes. He was lying on his side facing her, and it was one of his fingers that had been tickling her cheek.

Seeing that she was awake, he quickly removed his hand. But then he didn't seem to know where to put it. There was very little space between them—so little, in fact, that Marina could feel the heat of his body all down her length.

They studied each other silently. Marina noted the vulnerability in his eyes and wished there was something she could say that would make him feel more relaxed.

Was he always going to feel the restrictions his society put on a man and a woman? Why couldn't he forget them and go with his feelings? Maybe that was the problem. Maybe he didn't feel anything for her, not like what she felt for him.

There were so many things about him that attracted her, like the curve of his mouth, the gentleness in his eyes and the strength of his hands. She wanted very much to touch him, stroke his brow, feel the blond bristles on his cheeks and chin. She flushed at the thought and dropped her gaze.

Sammell was trying to still the wild pounding of his own heart. When he'd awakened to find her lying so close, the heat from her body scorching him, a jolt of pain in his nether regions had taken his breath away. The feeling was new, but he was beginning to recognize it for what it was, the heavy ache of male desire. Since his first sight of her, he'd suffered the torment of her presence.

And now he ached to know what it was that men and women did together—how they showed that they cared for each other. He wanted to know about this thing Marina had mentioned called *love*. But how did one begin?

"I..." He swallowed, feeling inept. "I have this need...I do not understand..." He shook his head, his glance darting from her face to the wall above her head.

Marina felt her pulse quicken. "Tell me about it—about this...need."

Sammell glanced at her. Her nearness affected him so completely. His heart pounded, it was difficult to breathe and his body acted curiously—as though it had a will of its own.

"When I first saw you...I had never seen a creature like you...I touched you—"

Marina felt her heart lurch. "You...touched me?"

"Yes...there." He indicated her breast.

Picking up his hand, she placed it over her heart. "Like this?"

Sammell swallowed and nodded because he couldn't speak. A fire was growing in his loins and it was slowly burning him up. His insides were twisted in knots and a strange tingling began low in his body.

"Is that all you did?" she asked softly, pressing his hand firmly against her.

"Y-yes."

"Did you want to do more?"

"No!" He looked shocked, and then his eyes darkened.
"Yes," he answered slowly.

"What?"

He opened his mouth, then shook his head mutely. He
didn't know what—only that it wasn't enough to just look
and touch her breast.

Marina unfastened the front of her jumpsuit and slipped
his hand inside against her breast. She felt him tense as his
palm covered her distended nipple and a shiver of excitement raced through her.

"I like having you touch me," she whispered, her eyes
closing.

"You do?" he asked wonderingly.

"Oh, yes!" she breathed, a liquid warmth spreading
through her.

"The kiss...would you..."

Marina leaned forward and gently pressed her lips to his.
"Is that what you want?"

"Yes." It was just like before—he felt the same electri-
fying sensations inside him at the touch of her lips.

He wanted to feel her lips again. As though reading his
thoughts, Marina put a finger to his chin and exerted a gentle pressure, separating his bottom lip from his top.

"It's even better like this," she whispered, leaning against
his chest to press her mouth over his.

Sammell gasped at the feel of her tongue against his teeth
and jerked back, his eyes wide with surprise.

Thinking she had offended him, she drew back and apologized. "I'm sorry...I thought—"

But Sammell didn't give her the chance to finish what she
was about to say. He propelled himself forward and fastened his mouth to hers. This time when their lips met,
Sammell felt the kiss all the way to his toes. His hand tightened on her breast and his fingers began to knead it gently.

It took a few minutes for him to get the hang of it, but
Marina realized Sammell was going to be a great kisser. He
put all of himself into it. His mouth clung to hers, tasting
her, sipping her, drinking from her lips as though she were

a fine wine and he'd reached the bottom of the glass and wanted to consume every last drop.

But kissing wasn't enough. Sammell's body still burned with a heat that scorched his clothing. That terrible wonderful feeling he'd experienced for the first time a few nights ago was sweeping over him, changing the contours of his body, demanding something more than the meeting of lips.

Acting purely on instinct, he glided closer, until the length of his body pressed completely against hers. Sammell removed his hand from her breast and slipped it beneath her shoulders, drawing her to him.

Her breasts now jutted against his chest and ragged whimpers of sheer torture escaped his taut lips. And still it wasn't enough. That raging fire started in his loins was consuming him a little at a time. It had reached his middle and his insides felt blistered by it, every system affected by this insistent need for release.

Knowing he was reaching the point of no return, Marina slid her fingers across his shoulders to his chest toward the hot pulsing ache low in his body.

Closing his eyes, Sammell caught his breath and waited, but her fingers stopped at his waist. And then he realized she was unfastening his coverall. In a moment his chest had been laid bare and Marina was pressing soft kisses against his collarbone and chest.

Marina began to pull the jumpsuit down his body, and Sammell raised himself to his knees and helped her. But when they were below his waist, he grasped her hands and held them still.

Marina looked up at him and saw the fear in his eyes.

"Don't be afraid," she said gently.

"I am not afraid." He hesitated, unable to meet her eyes. "What if I am not like the men of your world?" he asked with difficulty. "What if I have been altered in some way?"

"I don't think you need worry about that," she tried to reassure him. But she could see her words hadn't helped. "Would you rather not..."

"No!" he said quickly. "I want to..."

"Then trust me," she said, pressing her lips against his.

Sammell leaned into the kiss, already adept at returning her kiss. When he drew back, his head was spinning and his heart hurt in his chest.

"If it will make you feel better, I'll take mine off, too." Marina unfastened her jumpsuit and began to slide it down her shoulders. Sammell's breath caught in the back of his throat as her breasts came into view.

Two creamy white globes with pale mauve centers. He remembered the night of her arrival when he'd touched them and just now when she'd placed his hand over one, and he longed to touch them again.

Marina could read the desire in his eyes. "It's all right," she whispered, taking his hands and placing them against her.

Sammell squeezed their softness gently. "So beautiful," he murmured. "I have never seen anything so beautiful." As his hands moved over their softness, he felt the small pebblelike hardness at their center and pulled one hand back to investigate its cause.

He moved his thumb back and forth over it curiously and felt Marina shiver. He looked up into her face and saw that her eyes were partially closed, a slight smile parting her lips. The tip of a pink tongue smoothed her lower lip, and Sammell felt a jolt somewhere inside.

Marina cupped the back of his head and gently nudged his head forward so that his lips were against one breast. Sammell seemed to know what to do without further prodding. His lips opened and the tip of his tongue slid gently across one proud nipple.

Marina's hands were in his hair, across his shoulders, sliding inside the jumpsuit and moving against his hips. Now she was on fire for him. Pulling his head up to her mouth, she opened her lips over his and pressed her tongue flat against his teeth, feeling them open as she tasted the warm dark recesses of his mouth.

Sammell felt a wrenching in his lower body and pressed her back against the bed, coming down half over her. His hands slid against the smoothness of her belly, and he began to shake and quiver, panting, the veins standing out in forehead and neck. And in his eyes was an expression that Marina had never seen in all her life. She couldn't describe it even to herself. It was part wonder, part pain, part embarrassment and part of some emotion she couldn't interpret.

Sammell lay against her, panting, his muscles quivering. Marina felt him stiffen and start to withdraw, his face turned away from her.

"It's all right." She smoothed a hand up his shoulder to the side of his face, feeling the bristles of his beard, the fine sheen of sweat on his skin. "It's a normal reaction."

Sammell looked at her. His eyes probed hers.

"It's true, I swear." Reaching for his hand she raised it to her lips. "Touch me," she murmured against his palm. "Please...I want you to."

With her hand over his, she guided it down her chin and neck, between her breasts, across her concave belly to her hip and the inside of her thigh. Drawing his head down to her, she took his lips in an openmouthed kiss.

Sammell was amazed. His body was hardening again, and the tingly, breathless feeling was fluttering in his chest.

Marina pushed at his jumpsuit until it lay around his ankles. "Take it off," she said.

Sammell did her bidding, still very shy about his body, but Marina refused to let him hide himself from her. She slipped her own jumpsuit down to her ankles, but before she could remove it herself Sammell was at her feet pulling it over her toes.

He just sat there for a moment, staring at her, his eyes taking in the full breasts, narrow waist, rounded hips and long curving thighs. So this is what a woman looked like beneath her clothes.

"Come, lie beside me," Marina said, patting the mattress at her side.

Sammell lay down, turning to face her, and once again his body was scorched by her heat. He was so disturbed by their nakedness that the muscles jumped in his arms and legs and the muscles in his jaws began to quiver.

Thinking he was cold, Marina was about to draw the blanket over them, but Sammell reached for her.

"I want to feel your skin against mine," he said unsteadily.

Marina slid a leg over his hips and lay flat against him. "Is this what you want?"

"Oh—yes!" Sammell's hands moved from her shoulders down her back and up again. But he wanted something more—his body cried out for something more.

"Please," he whispered, "please ... I want ... I need—" He broke off and shook his head back and forth against the pillow. There was no name for what he wanted. If one existed, he didn't know it.

Marina understood. Pushing him onto his back, she moved over him, gently enfolding him in warmth. Sammell gasped, raised his head off the pillow to look at her—at them, joined together as one.

"This," he whispered, "this is ..."

"Making love," Marina whispered, leaning forward to place her lips over his. For a long moment, she lay against him unmoving, their flesh as one and then she began to move slowly, giving him time to experience each new sensation before a new one took its place, crowding the old one out.

As the kiss deepened, his hands came up to her breasts and then to her face, his fingers tangled in the red curls. Marina began to move her hips in a gentle back-and-forth motion and the man beneath her shuddered, opened his mouth to hers, gasped and reached for her hips to press her tighter against him.

Soon he joined her in the strange rocking motion. The rhythm increased, his hands grasped her hips tighter and his whole body felt as though it was building toward some kind of an explosion. And the sensations were so terrible—so wonderful—that he wanted to slow down and enjoy them but he couldn't. Something inside drove him on to greater speed, greater heights of feeling and the need grew inside him. Nothing in his life had prepared him for such an experience. A sound began to grow somewhere down low in his body. It reached his chest and worked its way up to the back of his throat, straining at his vocal chords until it had to be let out.

Rearing up on the bed, clasping Marina to his sweat-slickened chest, his mouth opened wide and Marina bent to press her lips to his, taking the sound from them. Sammell jerked against her, held her tighter and kissed her over and over as his body shuddered and shook in the aftermath of their joining.

When it was over and they lay side by side, he studied her inquisitively. "That is love?" he asked softly.

"That is lovemaking," Marina answered.

"Can we do it again?"

"Now?"

"Soon."

"Yes."

"And will it be like that?"

"Maybe even better," she promised, resting her head against his chest, the heavy thrum of his heart echoing in her ear.

"Better?" he asked in amazement. "How can it be better?"

"Sammell! Are you awake?"

At the sound of Gissel's voice, Sammell sat up. "Yes, I am awake. Is something wrong?"

"When you and the woman are ready, we would like the two of you to join us."

"Give us a little time."

"You will find a place to bathe at the end of this great hall, where the river flows through the wall. There is nourishment at any of the campfires. Take yours slowly. We will supplement it with an injection until you get used to eating. Afterward, please join us."

"Where?"

"Where we came in yesterday, you will find an opening on the right. We will be waiting for you there."

When she'd gone, Marina slipped into her jumpsuit and the two of them went searching for the bathing place. They found a small waterfall and pool in another chamber by stepping through the spot where the river flowed into the cavern. Bars of crude soap and towels were stacked on the rocks near the water's edge.

The place was deserted. In this new setting Marina and Sammell were shy with each other, but soon got over it, taking turns bathing each other's back. It was another new experience for Sammell. Only it wasn't just her back he wanted to bathe.

While they played and laughed among the bubbles, they forgot the seriousness of their present situation. And then Marina slipped on the rocks and Sammell grabbed for her. Together they tumbled into the water.

Excitement coursed through Marina as Sammell's gaze focused on her lips. Her arms came up around his neck and his lips descended on hers. They sank beneath the water, locked together in a strong embrace.

As Marina had predicted, Sammell was becoming a good kisser. His was a wild and hungry kiss full of passion and need. And as their lips clung together, Sammell became aware of a coiling tightness low in his body. He would have intensified the embrace, but Marina stopped him.

Separating, they floated to the surface, treading water. Sammell would have pulled her into his arms, but Marina resisted. Pushing the wet hair from her eyes, she said, "It's too open here. Someone could see us."

She could see the disappointment in his eyes, but he nodded. "You are right. I am sorry."

Marina touched his cheek with gentle fingers. "We have plenty of time."

All the time in the world—two worlds, his and hers. But something in Sammell's expression reminded her that her days here were numbered and that number was growing smaller all the time.

"Sammell, I don't want to leave," she said abruptly.

"We must go. It is time to speak with Darryn and the others."

"No. That isn't what I meant. I mean I don't want to leave here. I want to stay with you—if you want me," she added uncertainly.

For a brief moment a blinding light blazed in the dark eyes above hers, and then it was quickly extinguished. Sammell turned away and climbed from the water. Wrapping a towel around his waist, keeping his back to her so she couldn't see his face, he bent to pick up his clothes.

"You don't belong here," he said gravely. "You belong in your own time, among your own people. There is trouble here. And I am a part of that trouble. But it is mine—not yours."

Marina left the pool with a heavy heart. She had been afraid he would say something like that. How could she make him understand that whatever affected him now affected her, too?

They had shared something beautiful and it had bound them together, made them a part of each other in a way that nothing could ever change. Wrapping herself in a towel, she stepped in front of him so that he was forced to look at her.

"I'm a part of this, too. It isn't only you the people up here are chasing. They want me, too."

"No. Bartell is looking for me," he emphasized. "All of his police are looking for me. They want my knowledge and if they have that, they will not need you. This is not a safe place for you. You must go back. Your life can then continue in peace."

Marina opened her mouth to protest, but Sammell took her hands and pressed them against his chest, holding them there, his eyes holding hers. "I do not want anything to happen to you. It would give me great peace of mind to know you were safe in your own world, going about your daily life. Perhaps, someday, we will meet again—"

"But I care about you," she interrupted. "We care about each other." She pulled a hand from his and touched the slight hollow in his chin, smoothed a finger along his eyebrow, down the side of his nose.

"I..." She wanted to say she loved him, but she wasn't certain he'd understand all that that entailed. "We are one now. Don't you understand? I can never be happy away from you."

Sammell covered her lips with his fingers. "This feeling between us is a new thing for me." He struggled for the right words. "I like it." His hands tightened on hers and he pressed them harder against his chest. "I would like it to continue, but if anything happened to you—if your life was ended by one of Bartell's men—I would want mine to end, too.

"This way, if you go back to your own time, I will know you are safe. I will think of you with your family, sitting on the ground beneath a tree, sharing a picnic as we did and that will give me great joy."

"But..."

"That is the way it must be," Sammell said with a note of finality in his voice, dropping her hands and stepping away from her.

She knew by the set of his shoulders that further protest would be to no avail. She was being sent home and that was all there was to it.

A little while later they followed the directions Gissel had given them and made their way to the chamber where Darryn and Gissel awaited them. Marina had eaten some fruit before they left the main cavern, but Sammell had taken nothing except a little water.

Stepping through the narrow entrance, they stood facing ten people sitting in a semicircle around a small fire. "I am here," Sammell announced quietly, studying the ring of faces in the firelight.

Chapter 12

Gissel stood and motioned for Sammell and Marina to take a seat facing the group whose members were evenly divided into both sexes. When they were seated, she resumed her own seat and looked at Darryn.

"You have thought about our invitation?" he asked.

"I have thought about it," Sammell replied. "I have questions that need answers before I make my decision."

"Proceed," Darryn said.

"First, I want to know if you agree to my sending Marina back to her own time as soon as it can be arranged. Second, I want to know if you expect me to take up arms against our people."

Darryn, who seemed to be the leader of this group of rebels, studied Sammell for a long moment in the flickering firelight before answering. "We do not *force* our brethren to do what they cannot do in good conscience. We are not like the Wyndom regime. Our people are not divided by disloyalty and fear. We are not one voice. Do what you feel is right for you."

"That is agreeable with everyone?" Sammell asked, studying each face in turn.

Darryn looked down the row of people to his left and each man or woman nodded in turn. He looked to his right and again each one nodded in agreement.

"You have your answer," he said, spreading his arms to encompass his companions. "We are all in agreement. It will be as you say."

"Then I will join you. But I will not raise my hand against another of my people."

The group rose as one and came forward to greet Sammell and Marina individually. Afterward, Darryn asked them to follow and led them into the large chamber divided by the river.

"This," Darryn said, "is Great Hall. And these are your people." He spread his hands as he spoke and people began to emerge from the shadows into the firelight. More than a hundred people soon stood staring at them.

Contrary to the rebels depicted in movies of her time, Marina saw that these people were clean and well dressed. Very few of them wore the standard jumpsuit she and Sammell wore. Instead they wore what was obviously home-made breeches and jerkins that laced up the front.

She was pleased to see that there were several children in the group, but an inspection of their faces surprised her. Unlike the children she was used to teaching, these stood in an unnatural silence watching and listening to the adults, wearing expressions too old for their faces.

"This," Gissel announced in a loud voice, indicating the pair beside of her, "is Sammell and his companion . . ."

"Marina," Sammell supplied.

"Marina," Gissel continued. "They are friends. Welcome them into our midst."

A roar of welcome came from the group as a whole, and then several individual greetings were called out to them. A few of the people came forward and offered their hands. And everywhere she looked, Marina saw shy smiles of welcome. Her own lips curved in response.

"Look!" someone cried abruptly, backing away from her. "Her eyes! She has the royal eyes!"

"Her hair!" someone else cried, "it is on fire!"

Marina raised a self-conscious hand to her head as a taut silence fell over the throng. She shrank beneath the feeling of bitter hostility directed at her. Did they think her a spy? What would they do if they thought she was one of Wyndom's people?

Sammell turned to see that her hair had dried since their bath in the pool and it now gleamed with bright flame. Knowing he had to stop this before it got out of hand, he stepped in front of her and raised a hand for silence.

"Hear me, please." He spoke clearly and with authority. "This woman has nothing to do with the house of Wyndom. She is a traveler—a time traveler. She's come to help us in our fight against the tyranny we face at Wyndom's hands.

"Do not fear her—welcome her. She is a brave woman." Stepping aside, he reached for her hand and drew her forward so they could get a good look at her. "In her time," he continued, "eyes and hair are of many different colors. You can change these things yourself."

The people stirred, a note of disbelief in their voices, suspicion on all their faces. How could this be? After gestation these things could not be changed.

"Liar!" someone called. "This is a trick!"

"The woman is a spy!" someone else shouted. "Seize her! She will bring the death squad to our door!"

"King Wyndom is up to his old tricks!" the first voice shouted. "And if the woman is one of his minions, the man must be one, too."

"Yes," another voice joined in the denunciation, "we have two traitors in our midst—and we know what to do with traitors."

Gissel stepped up beside Sammell, aligning herself with him. "No! What Sammell has said is true," she called loudly over the discordant voices. "The woman is a time

traveler. Sammell brought her here in his time machine
They have come to help us.

"Do not be afraid. The time for fear is past. We must b
one without fear, united in the cause of freedom. If we ai
to create a brave new world in which we all can live in peac
and harmony, we must love and trust each other."

The group whispered among themselves, casting uncei
tain glances Marina's way. And then someone at the bac
called out a welcome. The air of tension lessened and soo
the people were once again shouting friendly greetings t
their two new members.

As Gissel motioned for Sammell and Marina to follov
her, and the group made a path for them, Marina was awai
of many curious stares directed her way. She walked vei
close to Sammell, keeping her hand in his, knowing that sh
was a curiosity—a never-before-seen oddity to these pec
ple. And she wouldn't soon forget the feeling of fear tha
had swept through her when she'd thought they were abou
to become a lynch mob as of old and take matters into thei
own hands, no matter what anyone else said.

Is this how everyone she met here would perceive her? Sh
didn't know if she could ever become accustomed to bein
stared at with that peculiar mixture of awe and fear she'
seen on every face just now. She glanced at Sammell's grav
profile and her shoulders slumped. Under the circum
stances, she supposed that wouldn't be a problem. As o
now he was probably more determined than ever to send he
away for her own safety.

As they moved among the people, Marina's attention wa
caught by the presence of many pregnant women, some i
greatly advanced stages of pregnancy. Apparently not all o
Sammell's people were as untutored in the ways of love a
he'd been.

Sammell, too, had noticed the protruding bellies on man
of the women. Some were very young and some years olde
than the age of thirty. Puzzlement filled his mind. There wa
a certain look about them...he couldn't name it, but...the
all seemed to glow as with an inner light.

Noting his expression, Darryn said, "Our movement is t new. Our people have been meeting in secret for some ne now and slowly withdrawing from society to form their n community in these caverns."

Sammell was offered a bowl of thin broth by a very pregnt young woman and found it difficult not to stare. He ew that women had once grown the embryos inside them, t to actually see a woman ripe with child...

His glance found Marina. Thanks to her, he not only ew the clinical aspects of reproduction but had expericed its pleasures, as well. She turned to accept a steaming wl of broth, and her unfettered breasts jutted against the n material of the jumpsuit. Sammell's senses stirred, and at once his clothes felt too tight for his body. How would e look ripe with child—his child?

"Let us sit." Darryn motioned for Sammell and Marina take a seat near one of the campfires. When they were ted, he continued, "There are many like us. This group but a small portion of a worldwide movement that has en in existence almost from the beginning of Wyndom's anity.

"When he and his people put their plan to dominate the rld into effect, they were not as smart as they thought. any people in distant lands who did not drink from a blic water supply were not infected by their drug.

"The unaffected people banded together to form small ckets of resistance and fought the soldiers Wyndom sent try to force them to drink the contaminated water.

"Many of our people died, but so did many soldiers. That when Wyndom began to send in his death squads. ousands of our people have been wiped out in the interning years by these devils.

"But despite all Wyndom's efforts, the number of rebels s increased and they continue to fight. Gradually we have ven the soldiers out of the mountains and valleys and into e cities now held in Wyndom's iron fist.

"And our people have done this—managed to fight these avily armed soldiers—with little more than courage and

wit, having only their family's strength to keep them goin,
That is why more than a generation ago Wyndom decide
to separate us by refusing us the close ties of family life. I
family there is strength and hope.''

Several of the group murmured their agreement, son
reaching for the hand of a loved one. Darryn reached f
Gissel's hand and placed it beneath his on his knee.

''When we live alone as we have been forced to do, the
is no hope of unity.'' He raised their joined hands. ''But
family we have strength.''

Sammell felt Marina's shoulder slide against his and kne
the man was right. Already she had become his family. A
soon he would lose her. The thought brought him gre
pain, but her safety was all that mattered. He would su
vive... and so would she.

''We have been fighting our enemy with primitive wea
ons, and though we make progress despite this, we a
growing weary of war. Too many of us die every day.

''That is why we need your help,'' Darryn said, turni
to Sammell. ''You can help us end this war and bring pea
to our land with your time machine. Gissel and I have be
working on such a plan for several years, but it will ta
many more to reach the stage you have already achieved.

''That is why we worked to get assigned on project D
liverance with you. Your brilliance in the field of matt
transfer has become legendary. And your defiance of Wy
dom's laws has been an inspiration to our young people.'

''Why,'' Gissel asked, ''did you never seek out others li
yourself?''

Sammell was amazed by all that he'd heard. And nev
more so to realize that his movements had been closely c
served and approved by these people for a long time.

''I thought there was no one else like me. I knew nothi
of the fighting. I was afraid I would one day disappear li
my parents if I did anything to put myself under sus
cion.''

''Yes,'' Darryn said, nodding, ''your parents. That is s:
They were terminated many years ago. Your father, als

brilliant scientist, was secretly working on the development
of a machine such as MDAT. His work was discovered and
he and your mother were killed.''

Sammell's expression remained unchanged, but Marina
felt his tension in the muscles where her hand rested on his
thigh. If they had been alone, she would have offered him
comfort. All she could do at the moment was squeeze his leg
in sympathy and hope he understood how she felt.

"I often wondered what had happened to them," Sammell murmured, "and why they had left me alone. But why
did the police question me if they were responsible for my
parents' disappearance?"

"Your father knew about the Wyndom drug," Darryn
said. "He had removed it from his and your mother's injections. I think the police wanted to know how much you
knew of his work. But he removed only a portion of the
drug from yours. He was worried that it might be too obvious to others if he removed it completely from yours. It
appears that you reacted differently from most people who
were on the drug—it didn't affect you as totally as it appeared to affect others."

Sammell frowned. "How do you know all this?"

"Your father was my uncle," Darryn replied, meeting
Sammell's incredulous look, "and he was a driving force in
the rebellion in this sector for many years before his death."

"Your uncle? But... how do you know this?"

Darryn smiled. "We have spies in many areas of government who have access to many secret files."

Sammell didn't know how to react. Ever since Marina had
explained the things a family did together, he had wondered what it would be like to be a part of a family. And now
he was, but it was so unexpected that he would have to give
it time to become real to him.

"I must tell you about Larkin," Sammell said, feeling his
way. "I think he must be responsible for stealing the mother
board I first built for MDAT—the one in my lab, not the
state's lab—from my desk at work. And I think he tried to
break into my lab the other night to make certain I did not

have another one with the special chip I developed that makes time travel possible.''

"We know this," Gissel said. "We have been aware of his duplicity for some time now. Bartell suspected you of sedition and set Larkin to find out what he could. He was supposed to trap you into giving yourself away. As I have already said, the government has been aware of your nocturnal journeys for many years.

"We, too, have been aware of them," she added.

"But what you do not know is that Larkin has the mother board with the matter-time sequence chip," Sammell said. "I found it in MDAT's twin the day Bartell demanded a test.''

Gissel looked at Darryn. "Does that mean he has the ability to travel through time?" the man asked.

"He might," Sammell responded. "All he lacks is the correct formula for the plasma jet—and he may have that by now.''

"That is not good," Darryn said. "It makes our need for weapons even more critical.''

"Weapons?" Sammell asked, recalling Gissel's earlier words on the subject.

"We want you to help us gather weapons with your time machine," Darryn continued. "The weapons will help free our people—your people.''

"What good is freedom if it costs you your life?"

"You must look beyond your own personal misgivings about the use of weapons," Gissel said in a stern voice. "Think of the future. With weapons we can defeat Wyndom. We can win back our freedom—our lives—and the lives of our unborn children.''

"I can stop Wyndom's madness without weapons." Sammell leaned forward to stare into Darryn's eyes over the fire. "No one else need die.''

"How?" Darryn asked.

"I can travel back in time and prevent the Wyndom drug from being produced. None of this need ever happen.''

Gissel and Darryn looked at each other. The other members of the group stared at one another.

"You would change time—like Wyndom plans to do?" Darryn finally asked.

"No—not like Wyndom. I would prevent his madness from ever taking place."

"But if you do that," Gissel protested, "we may never exist."

"Yes," Sammell agreed, "that's possible. Then again, maybe not. Carson Wyndom will still be born and he may even become president. If I can stop him from producing the drug, our world will still exist, but without the oppression that we now live under."

There was fear in the look Gissel cast Darryn. "We would be different people." She looked at Sammell. "Would we be different people?"

"Perhaps." He shrugged. "Perhaps not."

"What do you think?" Gissel asked Darryn.

Darryn looked at the people around them. "It is not my decision alone." He turned to Sammell. "You are certain you can do this?"

Sammell hesitated. At the back of his mind was the memory of the vase and its destruction. He felt Marina's hand on his thigh and was reassured. This was a flesh-and-blood woman sitting beside him, and after the first few days, when she'd slept many hours and experienced periods of dizziness—which could have been from hunger—there had been no adverse signs in her condition.

"I brought Marina from the past into our world," he said gravely. "I think I can safely travel into the past and do what must be done."

Darryn stood up and gazed into the faces around them. He motioned for Sammell to stand also. "This man has a plan. I want you all to listen to it."

Sammell spoke in clear carrying tones, his voice reaching to the back of the great hall, bouncing off the ceiling and walls. He explained who he was and what he'd achieved in the past few years. He asked them to consider the reality of

Marina, and then he told them what might happen if he changed an event that would alter the course of history—their history.

He explained that if he accomplished what he set out to do, many lives could be saved. And then he explained how time changed could affect their own lives. When he was finished, he took his seat next to Marina. It was out of his hands. He'd done all that he could.

"You have heard his words," Darryn said. "You know there is a chance that we, and our world as we now know it, will not exist in this new past Sammell will help create.

"But every day more of our people die in this fighting. The decision is yours. The majority will rule. What is it to be? Do we fight? Or do we let Sammell journey to the past and try to prevent the production of the drug?"

For several minutes the people spoke among themselves. And then silence descended over the entire group.

"What is your decision?" Darryn asked. "Do we fight? Or do we let Sammell have his chance?"

"Let him stop Wyndom if he can," someone said.

"Yes," another voice chimed in, "give him a chance. We can still fight if need be."

"Then we are in agreement," Darryn said. "Sammell, you may have your chance."

Marina slipped her arm through his and squeezed it. She wanted him to know she was proud of him and she was on his side. Even knowing the results of his plan, the fact that they would most likely be parted forever, she loved him for the way he had stood his ground—stood by his convictions—holding nothing back in his explanation to these people. It took courage, the kind she wasn't certain that she possessed.

There was a moment of silence, and then Darryn dismissed everyone. Motioning for them to follow, Darryn assisted Gissel to her feet and swept across the floor to the smaller chamber where Sammell had first been summoned.

"So," Darryn asked, once they were alone, "how do we go about this?"

"We must get MDAT from my home lab and bring it here," Sammell said.

"That will be dangerous. Your cell is being watched."

"That is not the worst of it," Sammell continued. "We must find the mother board Larkin stole from me and destroy the machine in the lab."

"So," Gissel said, "Bartell has a working time machine."

"No—not unless, as I said before, Larkin has discovered the correct formula for the plasma jet. In any case, we must get to him quickly."

"I will take some men and go to your cell first and get your machine. Then we will visit Larkin's cell and see if we can recover the mother board he took," Darryn said.

"I will go with you," Sammell said, much to Marina's dismay. She'd seen the wicked-looking weapons the police carried, and she didn't relish having one of them pointed at him. But she held her tongue. She'd encouraged him to join in this fight, and she couldn't ask him not to at the first sign of risk. Besides, she hadn't the right to try and stop him.

"We must go quickly," Sammell repeated. "Time is everything."

It was agreed that Darryn, Sammell and two other men would go. Marina listened to their plans with growing concern, knowing he had to go, but wanting to beg him to stay.

Sammell sensed her fear and it gave him pleasure. He knew it was wrong to get pleasure from another's fear, but knowing her feelings stemmed from her affection for him somewhat appeased his conscience. Drawing her back into the shadows for a moment's privacy, he held her face between his hands and spoke close to her lips.

"Do not worry. You will be safe here and when I return I will have the means to send you home."

"Do you think I care about that?" Marina asked almost angrily. Sliding her hands around his waist, she drew him closer. "I don't want anything to happen to you. Don't you realize how much I care about you?"

"I care for you, too," he whispered softly.

He would have left her then, but Marina hung on to him.
She wanted to ask him to hold her but felt suddenly shy.

"I will return," he promised, disengaging himself and
turning away, anxious about the stirring in his body. Would
a time ever come when being near her would not arouse the
passion so new to him? With a stab of pain, he realized the
time would come all too soon—as soon as he returned from
this mission.

"Sammell!" Marina said quickly.

"Yes?" He refused to turn toward her because he didn't
want her to see the reluctance to leave her that he knew must
be written on his face.

"Please—be careful."

Sammell was surprised, yet unsurprised, to see Darryn
hold Gissel close, touching his lips to hers. The other men
embraced their women, too, before leaving. Only Sammell
held back. And he held back for more than one reason.
What he felt for Marina was very private. It encompassed
his whole being, and he couldn't allow it to be viewed by
others.

Once the men were gone, Marina didn't know what to do
with herself. She would have liked to get to know some of
the other women, but was afraid their attitudes might mirror Gissel's. So far the woman had evidenced very little but
tolerance for her presence in their midst.

Marina stood on the sidelines, watching the others go
about the business of living, and fiddled with her hair. She
didn't have a comb and knew it probably looked like a
bunch of wild snakes had nested on her head.

Suddenly a child of about eight stepped up to her and held
out her hand. Marina hesitated, giving the child a tentative
smile, then looked closer at what she held in her hand. A
comb. The child was offering her a comb. She accepted i
gratefully, thanking her with a smile.

The girl did not smile back. She stared into Marina's eye
for a long silent moment, then quickly vanished in the
crowd.

"I see you are making friends," Gissel said abruptly from behind her.

Marina turned to the other woman. Pulling the comb through the snarls in her long hair, she asked abruptly, "Why don't you like me?"

The other woman's lips quivered, but she steadied them by compressing them. "I neither like nor dislike you. I am indifferent to you. You do not matter. Soon you will be gone."

Marina was taken aback by the woman's almost hostile attitude. What had she ever done to her?

"Would you like to meet some of the other women?"

Surprised at the question, considering her attitude, Marina studied her face before answering. "Yes," she said, when it appeared she'd never get beyond the unyielding barriers in the woman's eyes, "I would."

They moved through the great hall slowly, going from one campfire to another. Marina was introduced to so many people that she couldn't possibly remember all their names. In fact, she remembered very few. But she felt warmed in the glow of smile after smile on the faces of the women. It seemed not all of them resented her for being there.

One thing stood out in her mind—many of the women were pregnant, but there were not many babies or toddlers in the group.

"May I ask you something?"

Gissel nodded.

"Why are there so few younger children?"

Gissel's lips quivered. "Come, let us sit down and I will answer your question."

They made themselves comfortable, and one of the other women brought them something hot to drink. Marina sipped the steamy liquid. It tasted a little like tea, but none that she'd ever drunk before. She wanted to ask what it was, but wasn't certain she wanted to know the answer.

Gissel saw the question in her eyes. "Sassafras," she said, nodding to the bowl in Marina's hand. "That is sassafras tea."

"Really?" She remembered her grandmother had made sassafras tea. She'd always maintained that it cured a number of ailments.

"What did you think it was?" the other woman asked with a hint of contempt in her voice.

Marina shrugged. "I didn't know."

"You asked about the little ones," Gissel said after a moment while she sipped at her own tea. "I am sorry to say that these are all we have. And it's the same in many of the other camps."

"But why? I see many expectant women."

"Yes, but you forget that this is all relatively new to us. In the past few decades we have been so busy developing our technology that we have spent little time learning how to birth babies.

"There are many subjects covered in the archives at Government House—childbearing is not one of them. Unless we simply have not found it yet.

"Many women die when the child comes and so does the child. We know what to do," she said sadly, "we just don't do it well."

Marina's eyes darkened with sympathy. "But surely among the people who were not infected by the drug, there are knowledgeable women who could teach you what you need to know."

"Perhaps. But travel among the various groups around the world is very difficult. And the government has many devices to hunt us down and kill us. If we could all band together, perhaps our numbers would be great enough to make a difference. As it is, we are merely thorns in the side of a great monster who would devour us all.

"With the machine Sammell has developed, we can change all that. But these things take time, and if Bartell has access to MDAT before Sammell can stop him, then we are defeated before we begin." She studied Marina closely. "We need all the help we can get."

Marina raised an eyebrow. "Are you thinking I might be able to help you?"

"Can you?"

"I...don't know. You're far more capable than I am. What could I do?"

"Do you know anything about childbearing?"

"I used to live on a farm when I was growing up and I saw plenty of babies being born—baby animals, that is. And in college I took a course in first aid and another in natural childbirth," she answered doubtfully. "But—"

"Anything you could teach us would be of great value," Gissel said eagerly, losing some of the aloofness with which she'd treated her up to now.

"But I'm only here for a short time," Marina reminded her. "Sammell plans to send me home as soon as he returns with MDAT."

"Do you want to go?" Gissel asked, watching Marina's reaction to the question.

"No," she answered simply. "I want to stay."

"You care for Sammell."

"Yes."

"And he cares for you?"

"He said he does."

"Then why does he want to send you away?"

"Sam is very—" Marina broke off to search for the right words. How could she say what she meant without embarrassing Sammell?

"Ignorant?" Gissel asked, smiling when she saw the indignant expression flash into the other woman's eyes. "I do not mean stupid," she explained hastily, "I mean he does not understand many things—" she gestured to her heart and then toward Marina's. "—the way you and I understand them."

Marina smiled. This woman understood far more than she had given her credit for. Sammell was indeed a fledgling when it came to love and emotion.

"He's afraid for my safety," she explained. "He feels very responsible for my being here."

"But you can help us! And if you go back—" Sitting forward, Gissel suddenly grasped both of Marina's hands.

"If his plan works, you and Sammell will never meet. Has he thought of that?"

"Yes," Marina answered sadly, returning the woman's comforting pressure.

"I will speak to Sammell."

"No!" Marina said quickly. "Don't do that, please. It wouldn't help and..."

"And you do not want him to know about his conversation," Gissel added wisely. "Very well, I will not speak to him of our conversation, but I will help you change his mind."

"You will? Why? I thought you didn't like me."

"Indifferent," the other woman corrected, "I said I am indifferent, not that I dislike you."

"All right, but why do you want to help me?"

Gissel pressed one of Marina's hands flat against her abdomen. "*I* am with child. I do not want my baby to die—do not want to die. If you can prevent that, I would gladly go before King Wyndom himself on my knees.

"Darryn and I were both born in incubators," she said as if that explained everything. "But we are a family now and we hope to have many children."

It was not a testimony to Marina's great charm, but it was an honest answer. And if she were in the other woman's place, Marina thought she'd feel the same way.

"Thank you for wanting to help me. I would be glad to help you in any way possible when the time comes—if I am here."

Later Marina lay on the bed where she and Sammell had made such beautiful love together and prayed for his safe return. She loved him very much, but talking to Gissel had made her think about her own family, her brothers and their wives and children and her mother and father. She would be leaving them all behind if she stayed here. Could she do that? For a little while she'd thought she could, but when it came right down to it—could she?

Life in this world would be very different from her own. ven if the government was overthrown, life here would be ar removed from the idyll she'd planned once she'd found man whom she loved enough to want to settle down and aise a family.

She loved Sammell with her whole heart, but...

No! No buts. She had found the love of her life.

"Sammell," she whispered, a warmth spreading through er at the sound of his name. She hugged the pillow where is head had rested, inhaling a scent that was all his, and felt n ache begin low in her body. Was he thinking of her?

The ache grew until she couldn't stand to lie in the bed if e wasn't lying beside her. She stood and went to the cur- ain. Pulling it aside, she stared out at the people, most of hom were now at rest. A child cried out and a woman loved to its side. Another woman held a baby to her breast, er husband at her side, his arm around her, his head bent watch the suckling child.

Sammell was not her only reason for wanting to stay here. Ie was the main one, of course, but there was a great deal ae could teach these people. Teaching was her profession. nd she was darned good at it.

There was a time when she'd thought about giving it up she got married, but now she knew she couldn't. She re- ized that teaching was a very important part of her. And ere were plenty of children here—not to mention the lults—who could benefit from her tutelage.

She didn't know if it was fate—she didn't even know if e believed in fate—but something had sent her here. And re was where she wanted to stay. These people needed r—Sammell needed her. Now, if she could only get him admit it.

The night dragged on. Marina dozed, sometimes in the air, sometimes in the bed. Sometimes she paced back and rth in the small room. But whether she was awake or leep, Sammell was never far from her thoughts, a prayer r his safe return on her lips.

* * *

Sometime later Gissel came to her door. "Marina, are yo
awake?"

"Yes. Come in." Sitting up on the side of the bed, sh
asked, "What is it? Has there been word from Sammell?"

Gissel came to her and sat beside her, putting an arm
around her shoulders. "There has been a weapons fight in
the city. And an explosion at the lab. Martial law has been
declared."

"Sammell?" Marina asked quickly, jerking away from
her. "What about Sammell—what does that mean? Oh
God, what does that mean?"

"It does not look good."

"Then we have to get help to them," she said quickly,
surging to her feet. "We have to get help to them," she re
peated. "Don't just sit there. Get up! You wanted to fight—
so let's fight! I'll go with you. Come on, we have to fin
them—we have to make certain they're all right."

"There is nothing we can do. If we leave, we jeopardiz
the safety of everyone here. I cannot do that."

"Then I'll go alone!"

Gissel stood. "I am truly sorry, but I cannot allow that."

"You mean you'd try to stop me?"

"I would stop you."

Marina stared at the other woman's uncompromising ex
pression. "You know nothing about love!" she whispere
harshly. "If you did, how could you stand there, carrying
man's child—knowing he is in trouble—and do nothing t
help him?"

"Perhaps, as you say, I know little about this emotion yo
call love, but I am old in the ways of war. We must wait."

"I hate you," Marina said without passion.

"Yes, I know you do. At this moment, I hate me, too."

It was said with such heartbreaking truth that Marin
found herself feeling sorry for the woman. Tears spilled ont
her cheeks. She bit her lower lip against the pain in the othe
woman's eyes and looked away.

If Sammell died...

There was a sound from the other woman and Marina glanced back at her. Tears rolled down Gissel's cheeks. And suddenly they were holding each other close, worry and fear for the safety of the men they loved making them sisters in this dark hour of despair.

Chapter 13

None of the adults got any sleep that night. Gissel le
Marina to the communications room and they sat, drink
ing hot sassafras tea and listening to the police-band radic

They knew Sammell and the others had managed to ge
away from the lab, but one of their number had bee
wounded in the explosion. Marina couldn't meet Gissel'
eyes because of the thoughts running through her mind. Sh
was praying very hard that Sammell hadn't been the one in
jured.

The hours dragged by. They drank a gallon of tea, an
everyone took a turn pacing. And the tension mounted.

As they continued to listen to the radio, they heard that
squad of police had spotted the fugitives huddled in a ditc
beside the road and a vapor bomb had been sent into th
ditch after them. Marina was on her feet and at the doc
with a cry of helpless protest on her lips when Gissel stoppe
her.

"Wait! We have underground passageways all throug
the city. That is how we have managed to run our spy ne

work so efficiently, despite the curfew. Give them a little more time. It is quite possible they have gotten away.''

The woman's words gave Marina new hope. The alternative was unthinkable. And again the hours dragged by and Marina paced the floor. Every now and then her glance would seek out Gissel and she would study the woman's calm demeanor with a feeling of growing impatience. How could she sit there, looking so serene, when the father of her unborn baby might be dead?

About the time her own patience had stretched beyond its limits and she thought she might scream in frustration, a commotion outside the chamber drew everyone's attention. Marina bounded eagerly toward the entrance and then abruptly hung back. If it was bad news, she didn't want to hear it.

Gissel had already left the room. "They are back," she stuck her head in the doorway to cry with relief.

Marina pushed past her and hurried toward the Great Hall, where she could see a group gathered. Two men were carrying a third on a makeshift stretcher. For an instant she thought the injured man was Darryn and couldn't restrain the gladness filling her heart. And then a man stepped forward to give them instructions and she saw Darryn's face in the firelight. Her glance immediately sought the stretcher and Sammell's smoke-blackened face.

He looked dead! She rushed forward to hear Darryn tell Gissel to prepare a place near one of the fires for the injured man. He was in shock.

They placed Sammell near the large central fire and Darryn prepared to examine him. But Marina shouldered her way through the crowd and dropped to her knees at Sammell's side. She did not trust anyone else to examine him—she wanted to do it herself to determine the extent of his injuries.

At first Darryn appeared almost angry at her intrusion. But when it was apparent that she knew what she was doing, he relaxed. And when she called for light to examine

Sammell's eyes for signs of a brain hemorrhage, and cloth
and water to clean the grime from his face and hands, h
sent someone to fetch what she needed.

In a short time Marina had ascertained that Sammell ha
no outward sign of broken bones and no serious lacer:
tions or contusions. But she couldn't be one hundred pe
cent certain about internal injuries without X rays. And h
continued state of unconsciousness worried her.

When she spoke with the other men, she learned that he'
been unconscious since getting caught in the lab explosion
Darryn said that though they had given themselves plenty c
time to leave beforehand, Sammell had been the last t
leave. He'd wanted to make certain beyond any doubt tha
nothing, including the blueprints for MDAT, would r
main.

They'd all been outside when Darryn realized Samme
wasn't with them. He'd gone back to find him and gotte
trapped by a unit of police. Sammell had acted as decoy s
Darryn could get free, but then he'd gotten caught himsel
He'd barely made it to the door when the explosion ha
hurled him into the air. Fortunately he'd landed on the so
ground and not the wide granite walkway that led to th
building.

Sammell had been injured saving Darryn's life. That's th
one fact that stood out in Marina's mind. And she couldn
help feeling resentful of that fact, though she felt ashame
of the feeling and tried not to show it.

When she was finished with her examination, she washe
Sammell's face and hands and attended to the cuts an
bruises. After that, she asked that he be carried to th
chamber they'd been given. She followed the men closel
making certain they handled Sammell with the utmost car
But she needn't have worried. Sammell was a fallen hero i
their eyes and they treated him with reverence.

After the men had gone, she sat on the bed smoothing th
blond hair back from his face and gently exploring th
bruise on his left temple. She had to touch him, feel th

warmth of living flesh beneath her fingertips, to make herself believe that he was here, safe and alive.

"The trip was a success."

Marina turned to find Gissel at her elbow. "I thought you would like to know that all prototypes and blueprints for MDAT have been destroyed along with the government machine. Only Sammell's machine remains."

"I'm glad." But in truth, with her eyes fastened on Sammell's bruised face, she didn't feel much gladness. Still, she knew he would be glad to hear the news when he awakened—*if he awakened.*

Marina felt a hand on her shoulder, and Gissel said encouragingly, "He will recover. You must believe that. I do."

"I hope you're right." She tried a smile, but knew it had to be a sorry example of one.

"I will leave you now," Gissel said. "If you need anything, stick your head outside the curtain. Someone will come."

"Thank you."

The other woman hesitated and turned back. "We leave tomorrow," she said abruptly.

"Leave?" Marina twisted to give her a quick look. This was the first she'd heard about leaving. She'd thought they were only safe if they stayed in this rabbit warren beneath the ground.

"We must move our base of operations away from here now. Soon the government police will find this place. After tonight it is inevitable. They will find the passageway Daryn and the others used to make their escape, and it will eventually lead them here.

"Besides, we have made it a practice to remain in one place for only so long and it has served us well. We have been here longer than any other," she added sadly. "It has begun to feel like home."

"Are you sorry to leave?"

"In a way, yes—in a way, no."

"Where will you go?"

"To the mountains." A smile creased her face. "I look forward to the mountains." Putting a hand on her abdomen, she added, "I want my child to be born in sunshine.

"Besides—" eagerness made her words stumble into each other "—a larger group of our people awaits us there. They have fought their way to us from a far-northern sector. Our numbers will swell to three times what they are now. And with the added force we will be able to mount a large-scale attack and drive the government police from our city."

"You mean fight—as in warfare?" Marina asked quickly. "But I thought you were going to let Sammell try it his way first."

Gissel glanced toward the bed then hurriedly away. "He is not able to do that now. And we must strike while we have the advantage.

"In the raid last night, we managed to secure a few weapons. They are few, but they will help us. The police are still reeling from the victory we scored against them. We must keep the advantage, show them we are strong and that tonight was only the beginning."

"What about Sammell?"

"He will go with us. He is a hero."

"And me?"

"You must come, too. That is what Sammell would want. And perhaps when he awakens and sees what help you have been, he will change his mind about sending you away."

"What about MDAT? I didn't see it when the men returned."

"It is hidden. They could not carry it all the way here and carry an injured man, too. We will recover it from its hiding place when we leave."

Marina nodded. "Good night."

"Good night to you," Gissel replied. "Get some rest. Tomorrow you will need all your strength."

When the other woman had gone, Marina scooted off the bed and took a seat on the chair. Folding her hands on her knees, she gazed at Sammell. A hero. He didn't look much like a hero with all the scratches on his face and the bruise on his left temple, lying so still and pale against the pillows. He looked like . . . Sammell . . . the man she loved.

Leaning forward, she touched his cheek. How cold it felt. The two men who had carried him into the room had removed his jumpsuit and placed a blanket over him, leaving it folded to his waist. Marina pulled it up to his chin, her hand lingering to trace the fullness of his lower lip.

He'd be all right—he *would* be all right! *He had to be!*

The hours dragged by, and Marina's eyes began to grow heavy. Her head drooped on her shoulders. . . .

Marina gave a sudden start, sat up and looked around. All was quiet. Her glance leaped to the man on the bed. With a sinking feeling, she realized that he hadn't moved. Whatever had awakened her, it hadn't been him. Putting a hand to his forehead, she felt the coolness of his skin and pulled the blanket up closer around his neck.

Leaning back in her chair, she realized someone had come in while she slept and placed a blanket over her. Snuggling down into its warmth, she yawned. Her limbs were stiff, her tailbone ached from the hardness of the rough wooden chair and her neck had a permanent crick in it. And though she longed for a bed to stretch out on, she would not even consider leaving Sammell's side. Her glance moved to the empty area beside her love. As she well knew, the bed was plenty big enough for two—and so soft!

Sitting in this hard chair was ridiculous. She was tired and cold—and Sammell was cold, too. They could at least give each other warmth.

Scooting from the chair, she climbed onto the bed beside him and spread both blankets over them. Putting her arms around him, she settled down to sleep with her head against his shoulder, the reassuring beat of his heart echoing in her ear like a lullaby that sang her to sleep.

The next day Sammell's people prepared to leave the caves in groups of two or three. Gissel explained that it would be easier and safer for them to get past the police in small numbers without arousing suspicion.

Marina was shocked to learn that everyone was going to simply walk nonchalantly out of the city as though they were going about their daily business. Everyone except the women who were obviously pregnant. They would travel the same route as Marina and Sammell through the underground tunnels as far as the edge of the city.

Darryn and Gissel went first and alone. No one knew what route they would take. It was safer for them. Over the police radio that morning they had learned that their pictures were being circulated by Bartell. They would travel quickly and in secret.

Everyone would rendezvous at a given spot outside the city. When it came time for Marina and Sammell to leave, they were moved through the tunnels slowly. Some of the turns in the passageways were quite narrow, and it was difficult carrying a stretcher through them.

Marina watched Sammell closely for signs of regaining consciousness or a worsening of his condition, growing more concerned about him with each passing hour. Though not a nurse, she knew that extended unconsciousness was not a good sign, and the longer it lasted the less likely he'd ever regain full consciousness without brain damage.

The trip was tedious and it took all day. They came close to one police guard, but in the cover of trees managed to escape without notice.

As they were waiting to make their way past them, Marina thought about the cloaking device Sammell had used in his lab to prevent anyone from seeing her. It had worked against the police the day they'd invaded Sammell's lab. These people could use something like that. If Sammell...*when* Sammell regained consciousness, she would speak to him about it.

At the rendezvous point, Marina and her party were met by a large group from the caves who assisted them through the winding path up the foothills. By dusk they were at th base camp. This was not their final destination, Marina learned, merely a stopping-off place to rest, eat, spend the night and receive warmer clothing. The temperature in the mountains was not so easily controlled as in the cities.

Marina asked about Gissel and learned that she and Darryn were already on the next leg of their journey. They would catch up with them sometime the next day.

That night they slept on blankets out in the open. Fires were prohibited after dark because they might be seen by a police patrol looking for them.

A mountain lay at their backs, and guards had been posted on the three open sides. And Marina still didn't feel safe. She hadn't felt safe since Sammell had left her to go on his mission and returned to her in this state of suspended animation—lost to her and to the world.

Unable to sleep, she sat with her back against the mountain, studying his face in the firelight, noting the strong thrust of his jaw, the cleft in his chin and the straight line of his nose. Though blond like his hair, in the flickering light, his eyelashes looked like black fans lying against his pale cheeks.

Her heart swelled with emotion. How she loved every dear feature of his face. And how she longed to see that face filled with warmth and expression.

One of the men sleeping nearby rolled to his feet and strolled toward her. "Is there anything you need?"

"No, we're fine," she answered softly. "Thank you."

With a nod, he left her to return to his blankets. Everyone had been very accommodating since they'd arrived at the camp, offering to do anything to help her care for Sammell.

On the other side of the camp, someone removed a pot from the spit over one of the dead fires and poured himself a drink. Marina wondered what Sammell would say if he knew she'd eaten a stew made with meat that night. She hadn't asked what kind, thinking it better not to know.

She'd spooned some of the broth between Sammell's lips
and he'd swallowed it. Or at least she told herself he'd
swallowed some of it. For a little while afterward, his cheek
had seemed pinker, but that could have only been her
imagination.

She wanted him to be better so desperately. Becoming
aware that her hands were clenched so tight that the nails
were biting into her flesh, she forced herself to open her
fingers. Raising her hands to her face, she peered closely at
the half moons indented on both palms.

Trying for a calmness she didn't feel, she took a deep
breath, rested her head against the rock behind her and
raised her eyes to the stars. She found the brightest one and
made a wish.

A strong scent of burning wood lingered in the air, though
the fires had long been extinguished, and in the distance she
heard the lonely howl of a coyote. A shiver raced over her
skin at the sound. That's how she felt . . . alone . . . terribly
alone . . . without Sammell.

"Dear God," she whispered beneath her breath, "let him
be well."

"How did stars get into the cave?"

"Sammell? Sammell!" Marina cast her blankets aside
and launched herself at him. And then, remembering he was
an injured man, she restrained her exuberance and con-
tented herself with kneeling at his side.

"How do you feel?" she asked quickly, touching his
forehead and cheek. "Are you in pain?"

"My head hurts." He lifted a hand to his bruised temple.
"What happened?"

"You were in an accident. Do you remember going with
Darryn and the others to the lab where you worked?"

"No . . . yes . . . yes, I do."

"You didn't make it out of the building before it blew.
There's a bruise on your temple and some scratches on your
face and hands. I've been worried about internal injuries.
How do you feel?"

"I feel all right inside. It is my head—it hurts."

"You took quite a blow, but it will heal."

"Was anyone else injured?"

"No—only you."

"That is good."

"Are you hungry? Would you like something to drink? ou haven't taken much nourishment since the accident. I anaged to get a little broth down you, but you need ore."

"I do not need nourishment or drink, thank you." He oked around the camp. "We are no longer in the cave." It as a statement, not a question.

"No. We're in the mountains. This is a base camp. To-orrow we travel higher."

"Darryn? Gissel? Are they here?"

"No. They have gone on ahead. I understand that we'll atch up with them tomorrow."

"MDAT? Did they get MDAT out all right?"

"Yes. They had to hide it, but Darryn and Gissel have it ow."

"Good. That is good."

"What about Larkin? Did you have to go to his cell to nd the mother board? In the confusion of the moment, I rgot to ask Darryn, and Gissel didn't mention it."

"There was no time." He tried to sit up on his own and farina helped him.

"Well, you destroyed MDAT's twin, so that should be nough. What good is the mother board without the ma-hine?"

Sammell shook his head, winced and paused to let the orld stop spinning before he continued. "You do not know arkin. He is a brilliant scientist. He may have another achine hidden somewhere. Something must be done about im, or we will never be safe."

"What do you mean?"

"I realized tonight—the night we went to the lab—that estroying the government's MDAT and even their blueprints for it was not enough. For our safety Larkin must join us. If he does not . . ." He let the sentence hang and Marina chose not to take him up on its implications. There were other, more immediate, problems to face.

"Sammell, I know this isn't a good time for this, but I think you should know that we are on our way to join a group of rebels from the north. With their help, Darryn is planning a large-scale assault on your city. They aren't waiting for you to travel into the past and complete your mission."

"I was afraid something like this would happen. Tomorrow, when we reach the mountain camp, I will talk with Darryn. Once I have you safely away from here, I will get MDAT and make my journey, no matter what Darryn and the others plan."

"I'm not going," Marina said abruptly, a stubborn note in her voice. "I've decided to stay here. My home is here."

"Your home is a long way from here. And it is my responsibility to see that you get back to it. You are going," he added, matching the stubbornness in her voice.

Pushing the blanket away, he tried to get to his feet. Marina helped him, keeping a hand on his arm to steady him until he'd gotten his bearings.

In a taut silence, they walked a little way from the camp toward the darkness near the edge of the cliff. A guard stepped out of the shadows holding his weapon before him, pointed at them. But when he recognized them, he gave them a brief salute and disappeared silently into the darkness.

"Where did he get the weapon?" Sammell asked.

"A few were taken from Government House last night after the explosion."

Sammell's jaw tightened. Perhaps it was inevitable, but he just couldn't see the good in such things. If he had his way, all the weapons would be vaporized and no one would be allowed to produce more. As long as there were weapons, there would be no peace—no lasting peace.

As they stood looking out over the valley below, which lay mostly in darkness, a sense of tranquility began to weave its way through Sammell despite his misgivings about Daryn's plans. There was so much beauty in the world, and suddenly he very much wanted the time to enjoy it. He'd spent most of his life shut away in a lab working on one government project after another. And when he wasn't doing that, he'd worked on his own inventions and experiments.

Over the years, since his parents' disappearance, he'd stolen away at night whenever he could and gone to the woods, looking for the peace and freedom missing from his life, but he now recognized those times for what they were—acts of defiance against the government.

His glance moved from the valley below up the hillside, where shafts of moonlight silvered the tops of the trees. A deep sigh eased its way up his throat. How picturesque it all looked.

"I don't want to go back," Marina said again, taking up the battle once more. "Sammell, please—I want to stay here with you."

Sammell sighed again, but this time it was a heavy sound filled with despair. "You have not given this enough thought. Do you fully understand the magnitude of what you are saying? You would be giving up home and family to stay in a strange land with people who mean nothing to you."

He turned to her, able to read her expression in the moonlight. "It would be forever. The choice you make will be forever. I have made a decision. Once I have done what I have set out to do—once the drug has been destroyed—I am going to destroy MDAT."

"What?" she asked in alarm. "But that's your life's work—why would you want to destroy it?"

"So no one else can use it to bring harm to others. Do you not understand the temptation?"

He was talking about more than one kind of temptation. Knowing he could get to her even after she was gone would be a temptation he knew he'd be unable to resist. And traveling back and forth in time would be dangerous. Eventually someone—perhaps someone like Wyndom—would learn of it and then this horror, the horror of his world, might begin all over again. The only difference would be in the identity of the puppet master. And he couldn't let that happen.

Seeing the understanding settle in her eyes, he took hold of her shoulders, pulling her up close. A gentle breeze began to blow, sifting through the silky tangle of her hair. It blew a strand across his lips. And instead of removing it, he moved his lips in a kiss, and in her eyes he saw the reflection of his own desire.

His hands tightened as his glance traveled over her face, his senses—his body—alive to everything about her. Her ivory-smooth skin smelled so sweet that it made his head spin. And the living moistness of her full mouth was a temptation he found hard to resist—*but he had to resist.*

He had to make her understand that she couldn't stay. Now that he had learned what it was to know a close companionship with another, to share thoughts and feelings with that person, to have joined with that person as he had joined with Marina, knowing he would never join with another in that special way, he knew he had to send her home. She was his family. But she had another family with whom she belonged. And he knew there was nothing so bad as the absolute, unremitting loneliness of being without one. He could not let her make a decision she would live to regret.

"You must go," he whispered in a tortured voice. "Your place is with family, not strangers."

"You are not a stranger," Marina reminded him.

Thrusting her from him before he pulled her into his arms, Sammell pretended to study the view, his hands clenched at his sides, working to get these raw emotions he had not yet learned to handle under control. The thought of

nding her away ripped the heart out of him. It was a pain
his gut that far outweighed any pain he'd ever know. But
e had to go—he couldn't accept anything less than know-
g that she was far from this place of battle and strife, safe
the arms of her family.

"I want you to know that I will never forget you." He
uldn't keep the words back. "I will think of you always.
ou have given me something…" He stopped abruptly, the
ords stuck at the back of his throat.

After a moment he cleared his throat and continued.
You have given me something very precious. I can never
ank you enough for that."

"Thanks!" Marina cried, dying inside, feeling helpless
id wanting to strike out at someone. "I don't want your
anks." Placing a hand on his arm, she turned him to face
r. "I love you, Sam. Don't you understand that?"

She stared up into his face, looking for a response she
uld understand. But Sammell tore his gaze from hers and
cused on the distance, his expression impassive.

"I am willing to give up all that I know to follow you,"
arina whispered in a broken voice. "Doesn't that mean
ything to you? *I love you!*" When he made no response,
e struck him lightly on the chest, a futile gesture that did
tle more than reflect her feelings of helplessness.

"I know nothing of love."

"I can teach you!" She stepped closer, wanting nothing
much as she wanted him to put his arms around her and
ll her she could stay. "You're a gentle, caring man—God,
don't know how you got to be that way considering your
ast—but I love you for it. Sam!" She shook his arm.
Don't send me away." A thousand thoughts chased them-
lves around inside her head. What could she say to make
im change his mind?

"I can help your people," she said suddenly. If he
ouldn't respond to her declaration of love, perhaps he
ould respond to an offer of help for his people. "I can
ach the children—I can teach the women womanly things.

Gissel has asked me to stay. *She* thinks I can be of value t
your people. Why don't you?''

Sammell struggled against the desire to give in and tell he
he wanted her to stay—wanted it more than he had eve
wanted anything in all his twenty-nine years, including h
freedom. But he remained silent.

In his lab he had been able to offer her some modicum c
safety. But here—among these mountains—in the midst c
a group of rebels willing to die for the cause, he was help
less to protect her. He was a fugitive now himself. There w:
no safety for either of them.

It would be better to keep the memory of her inside hii
than to keep her with him and take the chance on losing he
forever. But he didn't want her to hate him.

"How can I make you understand?" he asked wretcl
edly, disengaging her hold on his arm. "I do not want yo
here! Your being here was a mistake. I made that mistak:
and now I must put it right."

The pain in her eyes echoed the pain in his heart. He f
cused on her trembling lips and desired to still them with h
own.

"I am sorry," he whispered, his voice barely audib
above the wind, "but you must go."

Before she could make further protest, one of the se
tries strode toward them and suggested that it would be saf
if they moved away from the cliff. They were in plain vie
and would be an easy target in the bright moonlight.

Back at the fireside, Marina lay with her elbow proppir
her up, her eyes on the cold ashes. Sammell had moved b
blankets to the other side of the dead fire.

"What about Larkin?" she asked, knowing she couldn
sleep and needing to keep talking so she wouldn't do som
thing foolish. "Do you really think he has another tin
machine?"

"It is possible."

"What do you think he'll do?"

"I do not know. But if he does have one, we are all in danger. I could chase him through the centuries while he read mischief and never catch up to him. He must be stopped."

"Tomorrow MDAT will be waiting for you."

"Yes," Sammell murmured vaguely—if Larkin had not found it before someone could retrieve it from whatever hiding place had been chosen.

Chapter 4

Chapter 14

Sammell, Marina and the others left early the next mor
ing to ascend the mountain and join Darryn, Gissel and th
group from the north. The trip was slow and tedious b
cause of the steep terrain and Sammell's weakened cond
tion. By nightfall, however, they had reached the summit

"Good day, Sammell." Darryn hurried forward to cla
Sammell's hand on the inside of Sammell's elbow, whi
Sammell clasped Darryn's arm in the same manner. "It
good to see you back on your feet."

"It is good to be here," Sammell replied.

"Good day, Marina," Gissel said from beside Darryn.

"Good day," Marina replied, nodding to them both.

"I am ready to work," Sammell said without preambl
"lead me to MDAT."

Darryn cast Gissel a quick glance from the corner of l
eye. "I am certain you must be tired after your journey. L
Gissel show you to your quarters before we speak on ma
ters of business. Rest and take nourishment, and then
will talk."

Sammell's glance sharpened on the other man's face. But
it of a sense of politeness, and because Darryn was right
thinking he needed rest, Sammell followed Gissel with-
it protest.

Tents had been set up for everyone, and Gissel led them
ist several before coming to one set by itself a little way
om the rest. "This will be yours. I thought you might like
be away from the noise of the children. I hope you will be
ippy here."

Seeing that she was on the point of leaving, Marina
opped her. "I think this will do nicely for Sammell. He
eds peace and quiet for a while. But I love children and
in't mind being around them. So if you have something a
tle closer to the others, I would be glad to take it."

Gissel cast a quick glance at Sammell, then nodded,
iding the way. When they were at the center of the com-
ound, she put a hand on Marina's arm and pointed to a
iall tent to one side and behind a larger one. "Will that
o?"

"Yes. That will do nicely."

They entered the tent and Marina looked around at the
lorful pillows and blankets strewn on the floor. "Uh-oh,
looks as though it's already occupied."

"No," Gissel said, "it is not. It was to be mine, but you
e welcome to it." Stepping to the tent's opening, she
inted to the larger tent nearby. "That is the one Darryn
d I are sharing. I will be close by in case you need any-
ing."

Marina touched her lightly on the shoulder and said,
Thank you."

"Rest now. I will come for you later."

When Gissel had gone, Marina loosened the thin jacket
e wore, made of an unfamiliar synthetic fiber that had
pt her toasty warm, even in the higher elevation where the
nd had sometimes roared at their passing, and removed
She tossed it onto the blankets, then dropped down be-
le it, folding her legs under her, and gazed into space.

Everything she and Sammell had said to each other t night before had played continuously in her head duri their journey up the mountain. Sometimes she wanted cry, thinking about the hopelessness of her situation, a sometimes she wanted to scream at the unfairness of it.

All her life she had searched for someone like Samme and now that she'd found him, she couldn't have hi Pulling off her boots with an angry twist, she threw the across the floor of the tent. Then she unlaced her breech and slipped them down over her hips.

"May I enter?" a soft voice called from outside.

"Just a moment," Marina answered, sitting down a pulling a blanket across her lap.

A young woman Marina didn't recall having seen befo entered the tent carrying a bundle. She wore a color square of cloth tied around her waist, leaving her legs ba to her knees, and a jerkin like the one Marina was weari Her hair was a silver blond, much lighter than any Mari had seen up to now, and it fell in soft waves to her sho ders. Her skin was tanned a light golden peach and her f were bare.

"Gissel sent these to you." She spoke in a soft melodic voice, keeping her glance trained on the floor. "She thou you might like something loose-fitting to sleep in."

"That was thoughtful of her," Marina answered, we dering if the news of her blue eyes had already spre through the group of Northerners now in their mid "Please thank her for me. And thank you for bring them. My name is Marina." She offered her hand.

The other woman looked up as though startled by proffered hand, dropped her gaze, then placed a tentat hand in Marina's. Marina grasped it warmly and shook

"I am called Ameena."

"Well, I am glad to meet you. Are you afraid to look i my eyes, Ameena, because of their color?"

"Oh, no," the young woman said quickly, "that is not it. You are a great woman—you have traveled through time. I lower my eyes out of respect."

"That is very nice, but I would much rather you'd look me in the eye when we talk."

"You would?" Ameena's glance shifted to Marina's face.

"Yes, I would. As a matter of fact, if you have a few minutes to spare, could you sit with me and talk awhile?"

"Me?" Ameena's eyes widened. "You want to talk to me?"

"Yes." Marina smiled. "Please." She indicated a spot beside her. "Sit down and tell me about yourself and where you're from."

Ameena sat down, smoothed the material over her thighs and smiled shyly. "I come from a place over the mountains called Mead."

"What is it like in Mead?"

"We have many lakes. And we have rainy seasons and snow."

"Snow?" Sammell hadn't mentioned snow. It looked like not all of the world's weather was controlled by King Wyndom.

"Do you like it here?"

"I do not know. We have not been here long. Do you like it here?"

Marina grinned. *Touché.* "I don't know. I haven't been here long, either."

Their conversation lasted until a voice outside called for Ameena. The girl explained that she was needed to help with the meal preparations and left after promising to return sometime to talk again.

Marina lay down, folded an arm beneath her head and thought about their conversation. Ameena had been very interested in news of Marina's life and things of the past. The teacher instinct was strong in Marina, and she had done her best to answer all the young woman's questions as thor-

oughly as possible. There was so much she could teach th
people here....

"Marina? We are gathering for a meal. Will you come
Afterward Darryn will speak with you and Sammell."

"Yes, Gissel. Give me a minute to smooth my hair."

She'd slept after her talk with Ameena. Then an olde
woman, introducing herself as Ameena's mother, had com
to show her where she could bathe and take care of pe
sonal needs. Gissel had arrived only moments after Marin
had returned from her bath.

Stepping through the tent's flap, Marina lifted bare arm
and turned slowly. "Well, what do you think? Will I shoc
anyone?" Ameena had sent her a colorful sarong that sh
now wore.

"I think Sammell will think you look lovely," Gissel ar
swered with a knowing smile.

Marina nodded. "Sure he will. And it won't make on
damned bit of difference. He'll still send me home."

"Damned?" Gissel asked curiously.

"Oh, sorry." Cursing was a good thing to teach a ne
generation of people, she thought wryly. "I shouldn't hav
said that. It's not a nice word."

"What does it mean?"

"Well, it means..." Marina searched for a meaning th
woman would understand. "It's a word we use in times c
stress to show anger and frustration."

"Damned." Gissel tried it out and gave a thoughtful noc
"Come now." She turned toward the center of the camp. "
is time to join the others."

Sammell and Darryn were sitting side by side with plate
of food on their laps when Marina and Gissel joined then
Darryn seemed to be enjoying the meal. Sammell had hardl
touched his.

He glanced up as Marina came to stand before the fire
and his expression rapidly changed from one of apathy t
one of desire. The dark eyes smoldered with unleashed pa
sion as his glance moved up over her bare feet and shapel

highs to creamy white shoulders and the swell of full breasts
isible above the sarong knotted between them.

"Good evening, Sammell." Marina smiled, outwardly
alm, while her insides fluttered.

Sammell had learned many things in his short associa-
'on with Marina, but control over his physical reaction to
er nearness was not one of them.

"Good evening, Marina. I hope you rested well."

"Yes, I did," she answered, taking a seat. Nothing he said
r didn't say for the rest of the evening could wipe out that
ne instant of desire she'd seen and recognized in his eyes.

"I would like to know when I may see MDAT." Sammell
urned abruptly to Darryn. Facing the man put Marina out
f his line of vision.

"I am sorry to say that MDAT is not here," Darryn said
luntly.

"Not here?"

"No. Our first day here I sent my most trusted lieutenant
ith two other men to remove the machine from its hiding
lace and bring it here. We have heard nothing from them
ince they left."

"That is not good," Sammell said with a worried frown.
'Are you certain none of Bartell's men were nearby when
ou hid it?"

"As certain as I could be under the circumstances. We
ere surrounded by police and you were unconscious."

"Bartell is very tenacious, he will not give up easily. With
arkin on his side he will be doubly dangerous."

"I fear you are right," Darryn said. "The time machine
s important, but we cannot afford to send more men after
. Bartell sent for reinforcements from sectors three and
even. If my men do not make it out of the city before they
rrive, I am afraid they will be lost and so will your ma-
hine. If that happens, we will have little choice in what we
o next."

"You are planning to do battle," Sammell said flatly.

"What would you do in my place?" Darryn made an expansive gesture toward the press of people around them. "We now have the necessary strength to fight."

"What about weapons?" Sammell asked. "I thought you wanted to use MDAT to secure weaponry for such a fight."

"We have a few. But if we must fight with our bare hands we will. Bartell and his minions must be defeated at all costs. If we can defeat Bartell, then we can defeat Wyndom. We will drive the whole lot of them from the face of the Earth."

Several men sitting around them voiced their hearty agreement.

"Bloodshed—is that want you want?" Sammell asked sadly, shaking his head.

"No," Darryn answered. "We plan to imprison those we capture, not kill them. We want them to know what it is like to suffer enforced captivity—the kind they have made us suffer all our lives."

"You have lost sight of one important fact," Sammell said.

"And what is that?"

"If MDAT is in Bartell's hands, what is to stop him from using it to destroy all of us?"

A taut silence followed Sammell's question.

"You are correct," Darryn said. "I did forget the measure of power one holds when in possession of a time machine."

"It would be better to follow my plan. If I can stop Wyndom in the beginning, the killing of our people would be stopped. Too many have already died."

"Yes," Darryn agreed somberly, "that is true."

"Then wait awhile," Sammell said, pressing his advantage. "Give your men a chance to return with MDAT, before rushing into battle."

Darryn studied Sammell's face in silence. His blood was hot with the need to fight, but he owed this man his life.

"Very well, we will do as you say and give the men a few more days. But if they are not back at the end of the week, e will launch our attack. We cannot afford to wait longer han that. Eventually Bartell's men will find us even if we do othing.''

Food and drink were offered to Marina, who had been an ttentive listener to the men's conversation, and she ac epted it, eating hungrily. Her appetite had returned. She ad new hope. As long as MDAT was not in camp, she ould not be sent home. That meant she had until the end f the week to change Sammell's mind and make him real e that he needed her here with him as much as she needed o stay.

In the next few days Sammell learned something impor nt about himself. He had no patience. And even against is will, he was drawn to Marina.

As for Marina, she was feeling more and more frus rated. It seemed that every time she joined a group that in luded Sammell, he quickly disappeared.

And then he began taking his meals alone in his tent. How ould she get him to admit that he needed her, when he emed perfectly willing to spend what little time they had ft together out of her sight?

She began to lose hope. To fill the time and keep her san y, she decided to do what she did best—teach. Cornering issel, she asked for permission to instruct the younger hildren in the rudiments of reading, writing and arith etic. She also asked to add information about the past— er period of the past—into the curriculum.

Gissel first consulted Darryn before giving her permis ion. Marina needn't have worried about attendance—the hildren were bored and glad to have something to pass the me. Soon they were attending because they were fasci ated by all that she had to tell them.

There were, however, some uncomfortable moments in e growing relationship between Marina and her students. he older children resented the half hour set aside for re xation and play. They saw no reason to waste time partic ating in activities that had no useful purpose.

The younger children didn't agree. Before long, they wen
around the camp singing songs she had taught them an
looking for enough of their number to play tag, hide-and
seek and red rover. Eventually the older children becam
interested in such activities as foot races and baseball.

She thought it was working—her life was going along jus
fine without Sammell—and then she'd catch a glimpse o
him and the longing would start all over again. He had re
moved himself from all but the most elemental contact wit
her, and their paths didn't cross all that frequently. Gisse
did what she could to keep Marina busy when she wasn'
teaching, but nothing could dull the pain caused by Sam
mell's apparent desertion.

As for Sammell, he was weak and he knew it. That's wh
he'd resorted to hiding from Marina. It took every ounce c
determination to keep his longing for her at bay. Each tim
he saw her, it grew harder to resist the urge to speak wit
her—the yearning to touch her.

Marina was very visible around camp and became mor
so with each passing day. She not only taught the childre
but taught the adults, as well. The women were being give
childbirth classes, first-aid instruction and cooking les
sons. Sammell noticed strange-looking hairstyles on som
of the women and decided she must be teaching hair-stylin
too.

Everywhere he looked he saw evidence of her work amon
his people. The things she taught them were good. And a
his people were transformed, Sammell grew to love he
more.

At least he supposed that was what she would have calle
this pulsing knot of feeling twisting his insides day and nig
without any relief. Sometimes he didn't even know what h
was doing. And when she was near, it was worse.

To keep his mind off her, he'd insisted on workin
alongside the other men. And when the call for men fo
guard duty came around, Sammell took his turn and did h

vel best to keep from lingering too long outside Marina's
nt while walking his post.

The last night before the signal for battle arrived, Ma-
na saw Sammell in close conversation with another
oman. That was the last straw. She couldn't wait any
nger.

The loving they had shared was new to Sammell, but he
as a man. And a man who had spent the first twenty-nine
ars of his life without a woman. Human nature being
hat it was—and knowing Sammell's passionate response
her—Marina decided to take matters into her own hands.
heir future happiness was at stake, she told herself to give
rself courage for what she planned.

That night, when Sammell left the bathing pool after
ming off guard duty, Marina was only a few steps behind
he strode to his tent. She was determined to find a way to
ake him change his mind and let her stay. She'd tried
owing him how useful she was to have around, but it
dn't worked. Nothing seemed to work. Most of the time
walked right past her without even acknowledging her
esence. But not tonight! Tonight he was going to see her—
ally see her for the first time in days.

Outside the entrance to his tent, she paused to consider
hat she would say to him. Though she'd been over it in her
ind a thousand times, still she wasn't certain if she was
ing about this in the right way.

Taking a deep breath, she squared her shoulders. Her
outh was open and she was about to call his name when
e tent flap was pushed open and Sammell stood in the en-
ance. An expression of surprise registered in his dark eyes
fore they went blank.

"Marina—what are you doing here?"

"I came to speak with you. Were you leaving?"

"I was going to get a drink of water."

"Shall I wait? What I have to say is important."

She could see the reluctance gathering on his face, but he stepped aside and held back the flap so she could enter. " will go later."

Marina stood inside the entrance, staring at the furnish ings. His were a little more elaborate than hers. He had mattress on which to spread his blankets. There was straight-backed chair and a small table. A battery lamp sa on the table, giving out a bright glow.

"Would you like to sit?" Sammell gestured to the chair "No. I'll stand."

"Is something wrong?" he asked, noting how she twiste her fingers together and stared at the floor.

"I came to tell you—I won't let you send me away. N matter what you say—I'm staying. Everyone in camp, ex cept you, wants me to stay."

Sammell's expression hardened. "We have discussed thi before."

"Yes, we have," she agreed quickly, "but you don't lis ten to what *I* have to say. You *tell* me what I am going t do." Her blue eyes glinted at him defiantly. "I am not child, I have been making my own decisions for a lon time."

Sammell was only half listening to her. He hadn't bee this close to her in days and all he could think about wa how much he wanted to be closer, but at the same time h realized something about her was different.

His eyes roved her face, and suddenly he knew what was. The small brown spots—freckles—had reappeared o her cheeks and across the bridge of her nose. And her ha was hanging loose about her shoulders.

While she worked around the camp, he'd noticed that sh twisted it in a knot that hung down her back. Spread out o her shoulders as it was now, it looked as soft as the silk h had once felt when he'd touched a cape Bartell had worn or day. He longed to push his fingers through the curls and—

"Are you listening to me?" Marina demanded. She coul almost swear he wasn't. He'd had a faraway look in his eye st now and she wondered if he was thinking about the oman she'd seen him with.

Sammell forced his attention on her words. "I am listen-g."

"Then why don't you answer me?"

"I failed to hear your question," he admitted uncom-rtably.

"I asked if you regretted our time together?"

"No!"

"Then what?" she asked unhappily. "Have you discov-ed, now that you are among your own people, that you efer your own kind?" She couldn't meet his eyes.

"My own kind?" he asked with a raised eyebrow. "You e my own kind. We come from different time periods, not fferent planets."

"Well, sometimes it seems like that."

Sammell kept his hands at his sides with difficulty, but his oice softened. "I am trying to protect you," he whis-ered. "Why will you not let me?"

"Protect me from what?" She took a step closer. "I don't ant to be protected. I want . . ."

Sammell saw her bite her lip and glance away. A rush of eling spread through him. As long as he had kept his dis-nce, he'd been able to ignore it, but now . . .

Light sparked off a tear on Marina's cheek and Sam-ell's heart took a nosedive. Memory of the first time he'd en her cry came to mind, and a jolt of desire slammed into is belly. He could almost feel her soft skin beneath his fin-ertips, taste the tear on his tongue.

No! He had to stop this kind of thinking. How could he rotect her from Bartell if he could not protect her from imself?

"It is late," he said.

"And you want me to leave."

No, he wanted her to stay. But he only looked at her, asking his true feelings with blankness.

"I'm sorry," Marina said in a low voice, hanging he
head. *He didn't want her!* "I'm so embarrassed." She trie
to laugh. "I guess I'll go now...."

She was at the door when he touched her. Marina felt i
all the way to her toes. First his hand was on her shoulde
and then he was standing close behind her, his body press
ing into hers.

"Do not go." His breath blew warmly against the side o
her neck.

"But...you said..."

"I want you to stay." His hands spanned her waist
drawing her to him, while his lips blazed a trail of liquid fir
across the smooth skin of her shoulders and neck.

Marina covered his hands with her own and leaned bacl
against his sinewy length for support, her senses spun witl
the strength and feel and scent of him.

"A-are you sure?"

Sammell pressed his lips against the side of her neck jus
below her ear. "Yes...are you?"

In answer Marina turned in his arms and lifted her fac
for his kiss. His mouth moved over hers with exquisite ten
derness and a hot liquid feeling flowed low in her body. He
hands trailed up his arms to his shoulders, and she felt th
muscles tighten and quiver beneath her fingers in response

She pressed against him and felt his impatience in the wa
he thrust his hips against hers. His mouth opened and hi
tongue caressed first the top and then her bottom lip, be
fore gliding past them to taste the sweet dark recesses of he
mouth.

Marina's fingers dug into his shoulders, skimmed up hi
neck and buried themselves in the short hair at the back o
his head. She was on fire for him, an open nerve-ending
filled with a pulsing need.

Sammell's hands were everywhere, in her hair, at the side
of her face, cupping her breasts, sliding down her hips to th
inside of her thighs. He couldn't get enough of touching her
And with every touch the hard knot of desire grew.

Marina's knees turned weak and buckled. Sammell caught er and moved toward the mattress. They went down to- ether, plastered in a close embrace. He couldn't let her go. omething inside was telling him this was wrong, but the ice was short-circuited by the sensations thundering rough him.

Helping each other, they undressed between kisses. As ey kicked aside their clothing, Sammell's hands moved ver Marina with a mastery it seemed impossible for him to ave learned in such a short time. He appeared to have emorized each spot on her body where his touch gave her e most pleasure. And as his hands paid homage to her lken flesh, his need knew no bounds.

Marina felt the surging heat of his maleness against her igh and caressed him. Sammell gave a low moan and uivered. His breathing became labored as he pressed her own against the mattress and blazed a trail of liquid fire the ngth of her body with his lips. The softness of a breast udged the side of his face, and his lips turned toward it gerly.

Marina drew his lips back to hers, and Sammell slipped a g between both of hers and slid over her. Her fingers dug to his back, drawing him closer as he moved between her gs, settling against her with a gentle thrust.

He explored her hungrily, and she opened to him with elight, withholding none of her secrets from him. They ade love with exquisite harmony, each quickly roused to e peak of desire.

Their rhythm increased suddenly, and the world dropped way, leaving them on uncharted ground without a hint of ravity. They soared, they floated, they rushed into noth- gness, found heaven and touched the stars.

Sammell's head dipped as waves of sensation tore through im and fastened his lips onto hers. The kiss lasted until he as forced to release Marina's lips and throw back his head, ischarging a cry of male elation.

They held each other while the shock waves of sensation continued to rock them, their bodies still joined. This night of love would forever be imprinted on their hearts and in their minds.

Exhausted, drained of passion, Sammell reached for the blanket and covered them, closing his mind to everything except how good it felt to have Marina's naked body pressed along the length of his. Tonight she was his—tomorrow could take care of itself.

Marina awoke a few hours later to find Sammell climbing from the bed, wrapping himself in a blanket. She called his name softly, but he wouldn't look at her.

He was ashamed. He'd let the needs of his body put him in a position that required hurting Marina. Keeping his back to her, he moved to the entrance to the tent. There he stopped and half turned without meeting her eyes.

"I am sorry," he said tautly. "This changes nothing."

Clutching the blanket against her nakedness, Marina sat up. "What do you mean?" she asked in a stunned voice.

"I mean that as soon as Darryn's men return with MDAT you go home."

"But... just now... I love you, Sammell. Don't you—'

"I must go." He cut her off and quickly exited the tent.

Marina fell back against the mattress with hot tears burning her eyes. How could he leave her this way, and after what they had just shared?

Gathering her clothes, she dressed hurriedly. She wanted nothing so much as to get out of this tent and away from this bed where she'd offered Sammell her heart and he'd taken it, only to throw it back at her a few hours later.

Maybe he was right when he'd told her he didn't know what love was all about. And maybe she wasn't the woman to teach him.

Chapter 15

By keeping her mind blank, Marina made her way to the bathing pool without breaking down and crying. She'd be all right as long as she didn't think about Sammell's rejection. She would think about it later when she felt stronger.

She expected the pool to be empty at this time of night and it was. Removing her clothing, she stepped into the water, intending to soothe her pain with a long bath.

She was waist-deep in the water when she felt eyes watching her. For an instant she froze, and then the thought that it might have been Sammell coming to tell her that he'd been a fool and he wanted her to stay flashed through her mind. She turned eagerly toward the bank, a smile of welcome on her face.

The smile died the instant she spotted the man standing only a few yards away, watching her.

"Now I see why Sammell was so eager to build a time machine and keep it to himself," Larkin said, devouring her nakedness with his eyes.

Marina covered her breasts with her hands and backe
toward the opposite shore. Darting a swift glance to the lef
and right, she realized she had no place to go where h
couldn't easily catch her. By the time she climbed out of th
water, Larkin would be waiting for her.

Squaring her shoulders, she faced him defiantly. "Wha
do you want? Have you come to join us?"

"*Us?*" Larkin laughed. "I did not realize you were on
of the rebels. If I had, I might have joined before now."

"How did you get here without the guards seeing you?"

Again he laughed. Marina didn't like the sound.

"I have come for you."

"Me?" she asked in surprise.

"Yes. You are the price of my freedom. You and the tim
machine...and Sammell. He's a fugitive with a price on hi
head."

"You're going to turn us over to Bartell?"

"I see Sammell kept nothing from you."

"Why are you doing this? These are your people. If yo
give MDAT to Bartell, you'll be killing them. Don't you fee
any sense of responsibility for what you're doing?"

"I feel a very deep sense of responsibility for myself. If
do not turn you over to *Lord* Bartell, I will be terminated."

"Do you have MDAT?"

Larkin's smile grew. "Come, we are wasting time. /
guard will come along soon. If you do not want anyon
hurt, get out of the water and come with me."

"What if I said no? What if I scream?"

Larkin showed her the maser-weapon he'd kept hidde
behind his back while they talked. "It would be too bad i
you did. Hearing your cries of help would no doubt brin
Sammell to the rescue. And Bartell did not say he had to b
alive when I turn him over to him."

"I'll need my clothes. Please turn your back while I ge
out of the water and dress."

Larkin backed up, allowing her access to her clothing, bu
kept his eyes fastened to her while she dressed.

"You know," she said, securing the sarong between her breasts, "Sammell told me about you. He said you were a good man." Lifting her eyes to his face, she added coldly, "Obviously he was mistaken."

"We have no more time for talk." Moving her away from the water, he motioned for her to precede him. Marina took a step forward and came up against an invisible wall. Wherever she touched it, she became stuck.

The feeling of being sucked into something alive came over her. She recognized it. She was entering a Recep! Larkin had MDAT!

"Sammell," Gissel touched him on the arm. "Marina is gone."

"Gone?" Sammell whirled to face her. "Gone where?"

"No one knows. No one saw her leave camp."

"Has anyone looked for her beyond the perimeters? Maybe she went for a walk."

"We have had men looking everywhere. There is no sign of her."

"Larkin!"

"What?"

"This is Larkin's work. He has Marina, I am sure of it. That means he must have MDAT, too. The only way he could have gotten into camp and taken her without anyone knowing is by using MDAT."

"No." Gissel shook her head. "I am sorry, but you are mistaken."

"What do you mean?"

"The men Darryn sent to recover MDAT have returned. They brought the time machine with them."

"MDAT is here? Quickly, take me to it."

"I am sorry Sammell," Darryn said as he strode into the center of the compound. "We have searched everywhere. I do not know how this has happened—"

"He thinks Larkin has her," Gissel interrupted him.

Darryn looked surprised. "Larkin?"

"Yes. This is his work," Sammell replied. "As I su:
pected, he has a time machine."

"But we destroyed the machine in the lab," Darryn pro
tested.

"Yes, but I suspect that Larkin has another—perhaps on
not even Bartell knows about."

"I do not understand."

"Do you not see? Larkin has taken Marina because h
knows I will go after her. The price of his freedom must b
MDAT, Marina and me.

"I very much doubt that Bartell knows about Larkin'
time machine because Larkin would be a fool to trust Ba
tell, no matter what he has promised him. Knowing the wa
Bartell thinks, I would expect Bartell to take what Larki
brings him and repay him with termination. Larkin .
smart—he must suspect that, too."

"What do you think Larkin plans to do with the secon
time machine?" Gissel asked.

Sammell looked at her. "Fight Wyndom for supremacy
Can you imagine the chaos the two could bring to this plane
by a war waged with such machines?"

Gissel put a hand to her mouth and moved closer to Da
ryn. "What will you do?" she asked fearfully.

"Stop him."

"But how?"

"Outthink him—I hope."

With Darryn and Gissel's help, Sammell set up his ow
machine. Since he didn't know exactly what time Marin
had disappeared, or where she'd been when it had hap
pened, he had to guess.

"I still do not know if I understand what you are plan
ning to do," Darryn said, going over the information San
mell had given him about the settings.

"It is very simple. I will try to travel into the past a shoi
time ahead of Larkin. And I will be waiting for him whe
he arrives."

"Yes, but what will you do then? You refuse to take a weapon. You can be sure Larkin will have one. What if he decides to use it?"

"I will wait and see what happens before I worry about that." Sammell finished assembling the Recep and took his place inside it. "I am ready. Have you locked in the coordinates?"

Darryn checked the monitor and nodded. "Everything is ready when you are."

"Ready," he called and watched Darryn begin to key in the numbered sequence. Since he didn't know where to arrive any more than he knew exactly when to arrive, he'd chosen to arrive outside the camp just after his guard duty had ended. He knew Marina had been in camp at that time.

Focusing his attention on the monitor, he watched the numbers roll across the screen and heard MDAT begin to roar. The whine of the lens opening startled him into looking directly at it, and for a moment he was blinded by the thin beam of bright blue light pouring forth.

The Recep began to glow a deep violet. Sammell looked down at his hands and saw that they were glowing, too. There was a crack of lightning, the world exploded in a burst of blue light and all the air was abruptly sucked out of the Recep.

Falling to his knees, lungs burning, Sammell gasped for air. His senses abruptly began to swim and the world turned black.

He awoke sometime later and looked around. It was dark and he was lying on the ground outside the camp. He could see the campfires in the distance and hear the sounds of people talking and laughing. Laughter was a sound he had not yet gotten used to, but it cheered him.

Getting to his feet, he looked down and realized he was wearing the clothing he'd worn the day before—before he'd gone to bathe after he'd gotten off guard duty. Good, that meant he was at least in the right time frame. Now, if he could only find Larkin.

He moved around the camp on silent feet, keeping in the shadows, watching for the guards. Since he was in the past a warning issued beforehand for them to be on the watch for him had been useless. He was on his own.

He saw Marina leave her tent and wander around the camp, talking to a few people who had not yet retired. A few minutes later, he was shocked to see himself standing near the bathing pool in conversation with one of his people.

It was a strange feeling, watching yourself, knowing there were two of you in the same place and only one knew about the other. He had no explanation for it. This was something he hadn't taken into consideration.

But there wasn't time to concentrate on finding an answer because he had more important things to consider—Marina's safety, for one. He would think about this inexplicable development later when they were both safe from Larkin's treachery.

Sammell moved constantly for the next hour, wandering on the edges of the camp, keeping an eye on Marina. And then he saw her follow him to his own tent and the memory of what had taken place there that night made him feel hot all over. He couldn't help moving to the back of the tent and listening to the conversation taking place inside as though he'd had no part in it.

As Marina and his other self conversed, in his mind Sammell relived the moment when he had touched her—when she had turned in to his arms. And though he couldn't see what the two inside were doing, he tasted Marina's sweetness on his lips. She was so beautiful and he had wanted her so much.

Sounds from inside the tent drifted to his ears. The sounds of their lovemaking blended with his memories and it was as if he lived it all over again. He could feel her soft breasts beneath his fingers, her wet mouth over his, her softness enfolding him and suddenly he was fully aroused, the strength of his arousal a terrible pain in his groin.

Sammell heard Marina moan in ecstasy—a sound he adn't heard at the time of their lovemaking—and he shook ll over with the knowledge that he had been the one to ring such a cry of pleasure from her sweet lips.

He had done that—no, the man inside with her now had one that. He became confused. He was the man inside, yet t this moment he was an onlooker in their play of passion, nd suddenly he felt a black rage at the thought of another aan—even if that other man was himself—making love to Marina.

None of it made any sense, but he wanted to rip the tent shreds with his bare hands and do the same to the man aside it with Marina. He had to keep reminding himself that he man with her was himself.

And then, still feeling that he was listening to two differnt people—and not himself—Sammell heard the man tell Marina their lovemaking just now had changed nothing. hame filled him at the cold brutality of it. He wanted to un away from the pain in her voice when she responded to is words, but his feet would not move.

And then, finally, he was running. His feet took him to he bathing pool, because he knew no one would be there at hat time of night to witness his self-condemnation.

That's where he spotted Larkin. He almost blundered into he man. At first there was no one there, and then suddenly arkin appeared. *He'd been right! Larkin had come for Marina!*

Seeing the weapon in his hands, Sammell quickly took over behind a large rock set back in the trees and waited, oping the other man had not spotted him, too. It wasn't ntil his lungs cried out for air and his mind became fuzzy aat Sammell realized he was holding his breath. Releasing , he gasped, drawing in large drafts of air until his heart ttled down and his breathing became normal.

He chanced a look toward where he'd seen Larkin, and is heart stopped beating altogether. Marina was standing

at the water's edge, and while he watched she dropped her
sarong and stepped naked into the water.

Sammell tore his glance from her lithe figure and searched
for Larkin. The thought of the man seeing her naked was a
bitter taste on his tongue. Almost as painful as the thought
of his kidnapping her.

He had to stop Larkin from carrying out his plan! But
how?

And then he looked back at Marina and saw her grow
rigid an instant before Larkin stepped into view. What was
his plan? Was kidnapping all the man had on his mind,
Sammell wondered as he watched the other man stare at the
woman *he* loved.

At the back of his mind, he heard the conversation taking place between Marina and Larkin, but he was busily
trying to figure out how to save her. Anger flamed through
him when he saw Larkin refuse to turn away while Marina
dressed. Biting his lip to keep silent, he saw Larkin motion
her to go ahead of him. And then he saw Marina stop a
though she'd come up against an invisible wall. She couldn't
seem to get free.

All at once Sammell knew what was happening. A Recep! She was caught in the Recep's force field—and the
same thing would happen to Larkin in a moment! That
would be his chance. Larkin would be vulnerable for a few
moments, and then he would be out of Sammell's reach altogether. He had to stop the man while he was entangled in
the force field if he was going to save Marina.

Larkin stuck the weapon in the waistband of his breeches
and took a deep breath before raising his hands to push his
way through the force field.

"I should warn you to take a deep breath," he called to
Marina. "When the transference begins, travel is at such a
high rate of speed that there is no time to breathe until you
land."

Marina looked at him sourly. "I'll be sure and remember
that for the next time."

Larkin laughed and began to ease his way into the Recep. ammell waited a beat longer. Then, when Larkin was ompletely helpless, he made his move.

Darting from behind the rocks and through the trees, his ands spread out in front of him, he rushed toward Larkin. le had to get hold of him before he passed into the Recep.

Sammell didn't have time to look at Marina, who had ootted him the instant his figure had emerged from the ees. And then his fingers touched Larkin's jerkin and he as using all his strength to pull the man free.

For a man who did not like violence, Sammell was quick ith his fists. The instant he was free, Larkin went for the eapon at his waist. Sammell was there first, jerking the eapon free with one hand and shoving Larkin away with e other.

Leveling the weapon at the man, Sammell forced a hand trough the Recep's force field and offered it to Marina. She ld on tight with both hands while he pulled her through. a a moment she was standing at his side.

For an instant Sammell's attention was off Larkin and ocused on the woman. Larkin took advantage of it. Grabing a handful of dirt, he threw it into Sammell's face and, hile he was blinded, reached for the weapon.

But Sammell didn't give it up easily. The two men struged for the weapon with Marina an anxious spectator. They ipped each other and rolled on the ground, Sammell takg several blows from Larkin's fists before returning them kind.

They rolled across the ground and into the water. Larkin nk below the surface. Sammell had the advantage. He ld Larkin down until he felt the man relax his hold on his ms, then he was pulling him to the surface. Bending him cedown over a rock, he forced the water from the man's ngs.

Larkin lay on the ground panting, looking up at Samell, anger in his dark eyes. "What are you going to do w?"

"Where is your time machine?" Sammell asked.

Larkin grinned. "I do not think it is in my best interest to tell you."

Sammell took the weapon from Marina, who had picked it up from the ground where they had dropped it during their struggle. He pointed it at Larkin's forehead.

"You and I both know, thanks to your lord and master Bartell, what this can do to a man."

"But you will not use it," Larkin replied confidently. "You forget that I know you, Sammell. You do not believe in violence."

"You are right. I do not." Sammell backed up until he was standing beside Marina. Keeping the weapon trained on the other man, he reached out and took one of Marina's hands and closed it around the handle of the weapon.

"You have met Marina," he said. "She is a visitor from our rough and violent past. The use of weapons is quite common in her time.

"Do you know how to fire a weapon?" he asked Marina, keeping his eyes trained on Larkin's uneasy expression.

"Yes," she answered. "My brothers taught me when I was about eight years old."

"The use of this one is not difficult. You simply put the red light on the spot you wish to hit and depress this button."

"I can do that," Marina said clearly.

Larkin looked from Marina to Sammell. "You are trying to fool me," he said. "You will not terminate me. You want my machine—"

"Correct me if I am wrong," Sammell said across his protest. "Bartell knows nothing about a second time machine—other than mine. That means yours is well hidden. And as long as no one knows where it is—as long as Bartell does not know where it is—I am satisfied. Shoot him."

Marina gave Sammell a quick glance, lifted the weapon and pointed it at Larkin's forehead. "Now?"

"Now—"

"No! I will tell you! I will tell you where the machine is ⸢h⸣den!" Larkin threw his hands up before his face and ⸢co⸣wered away from them.

"Keep the weapon on him," Sammell told Marina. ⸢W⸣here is the machine?" he asked Larkin.

"Not far from here. I will take you there."

⸢S⸣ammell gazed at the chronometer around his neck. He ⸢ha⸣d one hour before his own time frame came to an end and ⸢th⸣e force field of his own machine would close and leave him ⸢str⸣anded here. They would have to be quick.

"How long before your time frame ends?"

"A few more minutes at the most," Larkin responded.

Hauling him to his feet, Sammell shoved him toward the ⸢inv⸣isible wall of the Recep. "We will go in this. It will be ⸢qu⸣icker."

"Wait!" Marina called urgently. "Why didn't you just do ⸢thi⸣s in the first place? You could have simply stepped inside ⸢the⸣ Recep and traveled to wherever it is hidden."

"Because I do not trust Larkin not to have set a trap for ⸢me⸣," Sammell replied.

⸢O⸣nce he and the other man were inside the Recep, Sam⸢me⸣ll instructed Marina to find Darryn. "Tell him all that has ⸢ha⸣ppened here. I will see you tomorrow."

"Tomorrow?" Marina took a step toward them in ⸢pro⸣test. "Are you sure you're safe with him? Take the ⸢we⸣apon."

"No. I will be fine. Go quickly and find Darryn."

⸢B⸣efore she could make any further protests, the men be⸢ga⸣n to waver before her eyes. Sammell yelled something, but ⸢she⸣ couldn't make it out. It sounded as though he were ⸢spe⸣aking down the end of a long hollow tube. And then they ⸢we⸣re gone.

"What are you planning to do with me?" Larkin asked ⸢as⸣ they stood before the time machine he'd duplicated from

Sammell's blueprints. As Sammell had guessed, the ma chine had been wired with a vapor bomb.

"I plan to place you where you will do no one, includir yourself, any harm," Sammell replied.

"And where is that?"

"You wanted to go into the past for Bartell. How woul you like to take a trip there now?"

"You are going to send me into the past?"

Sammell noted that he didn't seem at all worried at th prospect. "Yes. I think that is where you belong."

"I look forward to it," Larkin replied. "Rest assured, yc have not seen the last of me.

"You cannot wipe my thoughts from my mind and e erything I have ever seen, heard, or read, I remember. I w. build another machine and return. Then I will rule th world."

Sammell half believed him. But if he set the time f enough into the past, where the elements needed to bui MDAT were not readily available, there was little chance his building such a machine in his lifetime.

He decided to send Larkin to a country where the la guage spoken was not English. In their world, all languag except English were dead by King Wyndom's decree.

Sammell knew it wouldn't take Larkin long to learn an other language, but it was another of the things that wou slow him down. He chose France. The year he chose at ra dom, the numbers being a one, a five, a zero and a three.

He set the coordinates, keyed in the formula and MDA began to power up. Larkin stood watching him, laughin "You are a fool! Do you think you can get rid of me so ea ily?

"Think of me, Sammell, think of me often when you a with your woman of the past, because I will be thinking you. You have not heard the last of me! History has n heard the last of me!"

The lens on the time machine began to open, drownir out some of what Larkin said, but he lifted his voice abo he noise and continued his tirade. "I will follow you into he future—mark my words, Sammell! The whole world hall hear of me—my name shall be on everyone's lips. You annot stop me! *I will live forever!*"

"Goodbye, Larkin," Sammell said softly. "I wish you the est."

There was a flash of blue light. Sammell covered his eyes, nd when he looked back Larkin was gone. He felt sadness or the man's passing from this time to a place where he new nothing about the life lived there, but reflected that Marina had been a time traveler forced to adapt to another ime and she had done well.

He took heart in the knowledge that he'd accomplished he man's silence without violence. Larkin would now live lsewhere—*but he would live out his life.*

Now all Sammell had to do was to destroy the machine. Ie glanced down at the chronometer and saw that he had ess than twenty minutes left before he lost his own time rame. He had to get back. There was already one Sammell n this period of time, there wouldn't be room for two. He lidn't know what would happen to him if he got trapped ere, but a vision of his suddenly disappearing flashed hrough his mind and he worked quickly.

It took only a few moments to reset the vapor bomb and hen he was on his way, running through the trees to the spot vhere his own Recep awaited him. As a sudden draft of resh wind swept over him and the surrounding country-ide, bending the tops of the tall trees almost to the ground, e stopped to look back over his shoulder. Larkin's ma-hine was gone.

He made the Recep with five minutes to spare. Soon he vould be reunited with Marina.

She was waiting for him at the bathing pool. He stood vatching her as she sat on the bank dangling her feet in the vater. Forever would not be nearly long enough to have her t his side.

She was as he had first thought her...a woman like no other.

"You're back," Marina observed without turning.

"Yes."

"Larkin?"

"Somewhere in a place you call France in the sixteenth century."

"So you have your time machine, the bad guys have all been taken care of and it's time for everyone to head home."

"No."

"No?"

"Bartell has not been stopped, only contained for a little while. And there is much here yet to do. In these mountains we will build a new world, where peace and freedom—and love—can grow."

"Love?" Marina laughed, but it was a laugh without humor. "Aren't you the same man who told me the other day that you knew nothing about love?"

"I know that it makes my knees go weak, my hands to shake and causes my insides to feel as though they are on fire. It turns me cold and hot all at the same time, it addles my brain...and makes me say imprudent things."

Marina closed her eyes. What was he saying? Did he mean what she thought—prayed—he meant?

"Have I hurt you so badly?"

There were no more than a few feet separating them, but he felt as though a distance greater than the amount of time through which she had traveled to reach him stood between them.

He wanted to touch her, hold her against his chest and feel her heart pound in rhythm with his. He wanted to taste her sweet lips and know the fulfillment of making love with her. And he knew he might never know any of these things ever again...after the way he had treated her, she might now want to leave and return home.

"I am sorry," he said huskily. "My heart aches for you.
would rip it from my chest and lay it bleeding at your feet,
that would erase the pain I have caused you."

Marina made no response. He had spoken words of love
o her before. How could she know if he meant them this
me?

A bitter, cold despair welled up inside Sammell. He had
st her. This new life he had spoken of now held little
eaning for him. When she left this place for her own time,
ith her would go his desire to go on living.

"I would go with you to your own world," he said
uickly, "if that would make you happy."

Marina caught her breath and held it. He would go with
er? What about his world and all the work there was yet to
e done? He was needed here.

"When you are ready," Sammell said bleakly, "come to
ue and I will send you home."

He was in the trees, headed for camp, when she finally
poke. "Just like that? Come and you will send me home?"

Sammell halted abruptly. That is not what he wanted.
Vhy was he giving up so easily?

"No!" he thundered, turning toward her. "I will *not* send
ou home. Come and I will love you with everything that is
a me, until the day I die ... and beyond. But if you beg me
very day for the rest of your life—I will never let you go!"

Marina rose and faced him. "You won't?"

"No. I love you."

Marina smiled. He held out his arms and she ran to him.
winging her up against him, he whirled around, his lips
aking hers in a kiss that sent her stomach all the way to her
oes.

Drawing back, he asked eagerly, "You will stay?"

"I will stay."

"And you will join with me—no, that is not right." He
nought a moment, searching quickly among the things she
ad told him for the right words. "Marry—you will *marry*
ith me?"

"Oh, Sammell, I love you so much." She hugged and kissed him. "Yes, I will marry with you, just as soon as you like."

"I like now."

Still held in his arms with her feet off the ground, she threw her head back and laughed gaily. "So do I."

"And babies?" he asked gravely. "You will have babies with me?"

"Just try to stop me. I want lots of babies—lots and lots of babies. And I want to teach them—I want to teach the baby Gissel is going to have and those Ameena will have, and all the others," she added excitedly.

"But first we must stop Wyndom and Bartell," Sammell said, sobering. "We must make this a world safe for our children."

The joy was instantly wiped from her face. "Oh, Sammell, for a moment I had forgotten about all that."

"We must not forget. Not until they are no longer a threat to our world. Then we will forget them and live in peace."

"Yes."

Setting her on her feet, he took her hand and they walked toward the encampment. "Let us find Darryn."

"Yes." Marina nodded, a bubble of joy rising in her heart.

Darryn and Gissel were not hard to find. A group of people all talking at once were gathered around them.

"What has happened?" Sammell asked, after greetings were exchanged and he had been congratulated on finding Marina and putting an end to Larkin's mischief.

"Our spies report that an army far greater than our own is amassing in the city below," Darryn said gravely.

Sammell and Marina looked at each other. This might be their last night together.

"We would like to be married," Sammell announced suddenly.

"Married?" Gissel asked.

"Yes," Marina said. "In my time, people go through a remony when they love someone and want to live with em and have children. Sammell and I want to do that."

"You are staying!" Gissel said with a smile, forgetting for moment the threat to their survival gathering in the city low. "I knew it!"

"Darryn," Marina said, "since you are the leader, would u marry us?"

"I would be honored," he replied, "if you will tell me hat to do."

That night, beneath the stars, with an army bent on their struction only a few miles away, Marina and Sammell ere married. They spent their wedding night preparing ammell for his trip through time, never knowing if this ight be their last night on Earth.

Epilogue

"Good morning, Marina. How are you feeling?"

"Never better, Gissel. And you?"

"Fat and tired," the other woman replied, sitting dow[n]
on the riverbank beside her friend and dipping her tired fee[t]
in the cool water.

"Yes, well, the last few weeks of pregnancy are th[e]
worst." And she wouldn't change a moment of it, sh[e]
thought with a smile.

"You ought to know," Gissel said, nodding towar[d]
Marina's swollen belly.

"Hey, you two, aren't you joining us?" Sammell calle[d]
from beneath a large oak tree. He patted the place besid[e]
him. "Come, wife, and join me in this picnic you put t[o]
gether."

Marina shook her head. "You come wading with me. I'[m]
the pregnant one here. I prepared the food, so now it's you[r]
turn to do something to please me."

Sammell got to his feet slowly and strolled toward he[r]
He'd thought her beautiful the first time he'd seen her l[y]

ng on the floor of the Recep, but in the past few months her
eauty had grown until he could hardly look at her without
is throat closing up. She and the child she carried were his
whole life. And life had never been better.

Bending down so she was the only one who could hear his
words, he whispered in her ear. "And do I please you? I
ought so last night."

Marina blushed and pushed him away. "Hush, she'll hear
ou."

"I don't think so. She's too busy at the moment."

Marina turned to see Darryn lift his pregnant wife in his
rms and carry her into the trees. Sammell sat down to re-
ove his shoes and Marina watched him lovingly.

Life in these mountains was wonderful, just as Sammell
ad told her it would be. In fact, life on planet Earth was
ood all over, now that Sammell had freed it from Wyn-
om's evil domination.

Sammell had gone back into the twentieth century and
revented Wyndom from developing his mind-control drug.
ut that did not prevent the man from becoming president
f the United States. Nor did it prevent him from attempt-
ng world domination through the means of force.

But all that was finished before Sammell and Marina were
orn. The Methuselah drug Wyndom had invented to pro-
ong his own life had failed to last beyond a century. He died
n old, old man in a mental institution.

Other men had come to power since then, chosen by the
eople, and they had united the world in peace. And though
was taking time, they were making progress toward re-
oving the evil Wyndom had done during his reign of ter-
or.

The hole in the ozone layer was repaired and they learned
o control the weather and live at peace with their neigh-
ors. But they could do nothing about the history books
Vyndom had burned, forever destroying their link with the
ast.

Still, the Earth flourished as never before, and life wa good.

Sammell built his time machine, hoping to recover som of what Wyndom had taken from his people, and Marin got caught up in it just as before. They fell in love and Ma rina decided to stay with him and help him build a new fu ture.

They were married and on their wedding night Samme destroyed MDAT and burned the blueprints.

Marina began to teach and write books on the history of the Earth and its people. She became quite a celebrit Sammell loved and supported his wife in whatever manne she needed.

He was working hard on a new project—a machine tha would count the stars and determine which planets wer most likely to support life.

He never regretted his construction—or the destruc tion—of MDAT. In creating it, he had brought Marina int his life and helped to make their world a better place to live And in destroying it, he had helped preserve that life.

The Earth had become a paradise for him and Marina and he wanted no part in unwittingly admitting a serper into their Garden of Eden.

*   *   *   *   *

Take 4 bestselling love stories FREE

Plus get a FREE surprise gift!

HE'S A LOVER...
A FIGHTER...
AND A REAL HEARTBREAKER.

Silhouette Intimate Moments is proud to introduce a new lineup of sensational heroes called **HEARTBREAKERS**—real heavyweights in matters of the heart. They're headstrong, hot-blooded and true heartthrobs. Starting in April 1995, we'll be presenting one HEARTBREAKER each month from some of our hottest authors:

> Nora Roberts
> Dallas Schulze
> Linda Turner—and many more....

So prepare yourselves for these heart-pounding HEARTBREAKERS, coming your way in April 1995—
  only in

Now what's going on in

CONARD COUNTY ?

Guilty! That was what everyone thought of Sandy Keller's client, including Texas Ranger—and American Hero—Garrett Hancock. But as he worked with her to determine the truth, loner Garrett found he was changing his mind about a lot of things—especially falling in love.

Rachel Lee's Conard County series continues in January 1995 with A QUESTION OF JUSTICE, IM #613.

Return to the classic plot lines you love, with

ROMANTIC
TRADITIONS

January 1995 rings in a new year of the ROMANTIC
TRADITIONS you've come to cherish. And we've
resolved to bring you more unforgettable stories
by some of your favorite authors, beginning with
Beverly Barton's THE OUTCAST, IM #614, featuring
one very breathtaking bad boy!

Convict Reese Landry was running from the law—
and the demons that tortured his soul. Psychic
Elizabeth Mallory knew he was innocent...and in desperate need of the right woman's love.

ROMANTIC TRADITIONS continues in April 1995
with Patricia Coughlin's LOVE IN THE FIRST DEGREE, a
must-read innovation on the "wrongly convicted"
plot line. So start your new year off the romantic
way with ROMANTIC TRADITIONS—only in

INTIMATE MOMENTS®
Silhouette®

Maura Seger's
BELLE HAVEN

Four books. Four generations. Four indomitable females.

You met the Belle Haven women who started it all in Harlequin Historicals.
Now meet descendant Nora Delaney in the emotional contemporary conclusion to the Belle Haven saga:

THE SURRENDER OF NORA

When Nora's inheritance brings her home to Belle Haven, she finds more than she bargained for. Deadly accidents prove someone wants her out of town—fast. But the real problem is the prime suspect—handsome Hamilton Fletcher. His quiet smile awakens the passion all Belle Haven women are famous for. But does he want her heart...or her life?

Don't miss THE SURRENDER OF NORA
Silhouette Intimate Moments #617
Available in January!
